Th...

Disgrace is their middle name!

Left destitute by their philandering parents, the three Summerfield sisters— Tess, Lorene and Genna—and their half-brother, Edmund, are the talk of the *ton*… for all the wrong reasons!

They are at the mercy of the marriage mart to transport their family from the fringes of society to the dizzy heights of respectability.

But with no dowries, and a damaged reputation, only some very special matches can survive the scandalous Summerfields!

Read where it all started with tempestuous Tess's story
Bound by Duty

Read Edmund's story in
Bound by One Scandalous Night

Read Genna's story in
Bound by a Scandalous Secret

Read Lorene's story in
Bound by Their Secret Passion

All available now!

Author Note

Bound by Their Secret Passion is Book Four in The Scandalous Summerfields series—the last of a series that has been a delight to write.

As I said in my **Author Note** for *Bound by Duty* (Book One), the Summerfields are very loosely based on my mother, her two sisters and her brother. This book will be about the oldest Summerfield sister, Lorene, who represents my Aunt Loraine.

My Aunt Loraine was the oldest sister as well. When their parents died, Geraldine—the youngest—was only sixteen, and my mother and Loraine were barely in their twenties. Aunt Loraine took custody of Gerry, helping her to finish high school and go to nursing school.

The three sisters lived together and were extremely close. In fact when my parents were married my father moved in with them. Aunt Gerry married eventually, and for many years while we kids were being born the two families lived in a duplex. When my father went back into the army Loraine moved in with us, living with us until I was in high school. She was a career woman—a secretary who still took notes in shorthand even in her eighties.

Loraine never had her happily-ever-after—at least not in the romantic sense. She almost married once, but the man who proposed to her wanted to go into politics and wanted her to give up her religion, which in those days would have been an impediment to his success. She refused.

Will my fictional Lorene find that happily-ever-after—or will it escape her like it did my aunt? I hope you enjoy reading *Bound by Their Secret Passion* to find out.

BOUND BY THEIR
SECRET PASSION

Diane Gaston

MILLS
BOON

HarperCollins
PUBLISHERS
Since 1817

Published in Great Britain 2017
by Mills & Boon, an imprint of HarperCollins*Publishers*
1 London Bridge Street, London, SE1 9GF

© 2017 Diane Perkins

ISBN: 978-0-263-92571-5

Diane Gaston's dream job was always to write romance novels. One day she dared to pursue that dream, and has never looked back. Her books have won Romance's highest honours: the RITA® Award, the National Readers' Choice Award, Holt Medallion, Golden Quill and Golden Heart®. She lives in Virginia with her husband and three very ordinary house cats. Diane loves to hear from readers and friends. Visit her website at: dianegaston.com.

Books by Diane Gaston

Mills & Boon Historical Romance

The Scandalous Summerfields

Bound by Duty
Bound by One Scandalous Night
Bound by a Scandalous Secret
Bound by Their Secret Passion

The Masquerade Club

A Reputation for Notoriety
A Marriage of Notoriety
A Lady of Notoriety

Three Soldiers

Gallant Officer, Forbidden Lady
Chivalrous Captain, Rebel Mistress
Valiant Soldier, Beautiful Enemy

Linked by Character

Regency Summer Scandals
'Justine and the Noble Viscount'
A Not So Respectable Gentleman?

Mills & Boon Historical *Undone!* eBooks

The Unlacing of Miss Leigh
The Liberation of Miss Finch

Visit the Author Profile page
at millsandboon.co.uk for more titles.

To the memory of my Aunt Loraine,
who taught me to dance the Charleston
and the Jitterbug and to be undaunted.

Chapter One

Lorene leaned back against the soft leather seat of the carriage. Outside snowflakes fluttered down from a sky almost milky white from the light of the moon. The snow on the fields glowed and the sounds of the horses' hooves and the carriage wheels were as muffled as if passing over down pillows. It was the perfect end to a perfect day, a day-long visit with her two sisters, their husbands and the man she adored.

Thank goodness her husband had refused to come with her.

Her husband, the Earl of Tinmore, a man in his seventies and at least fifty years her senior, had forbidden her to spend Christmas Day with her sisters at their childhood home, Summerfield House. Lorene had defied her husband's dictate. She'd walked the five miles to Summerfield House that morning. Snow had been falling then, too, but the cold merely filled her with vigour and made her feel more alive.

How different it was at Tinmore Hall where she had to kill every emotion merely to make it through the day.

'Will you be all right?' the man seated next to her asked.

She turned to him and her heart quickened as it always did when looking at him, Dell Summerfield, the Earl of Penford, the man who had inherited her childhood home. His blue eyes shone even in the dim light of the carriage. His well-formed lips pursed in worry.

She could not help but stare at those lips. 'I suspect he will be asleep. He retires early, you know.' She did not have to explain that she spoke of her husband.

'What of tomorrow?'

She loved his voice, so deep, like the lowest notes on the pianoforte, felt as well as heard.

How silly to have a schoolgirl's infatuation at the advanced age of twenty-four, especially since she was a married lady and he'd merely been civil.

No, he'd always been more than civil.

He'd been kind.

The last thing she wanted was for him to worry

about her. Or to think of her. He must never know how much she thought of him. Or how much his kindness towards her meant to her.

She smiled. 'The worst I will endure is a tongue lashing, but I might earn one of those for choosing the wrong dish for breakfast, so I am very used to it.'

Dell frowned and glanced away.

'It is equally as likely he will say nothing,' she added quickly. 'One never knows.'

Dell had insisted upon returning her to Tinmore Hall in his carriage and insisted on accompanying her. Lorene treasured these rare moments alone with him when she could pretend they were the only two people in the world and that she had not been forced to choose marriage to Tinmore.

Although no one had forced her. She had approached Tinmore and offered herself to him. She'd done so because her father had left his children penniless and Lorene could think of no other way to help her sisters and half-brother. She'd promised to marry Tinmore and to devote herself to his comfort for the rest of his life. In exchange he agreed to provide generous dowries for her sisters and enough money for her brother to purchase a captaincy.

Nothing turned out as she'd thought, though. Her sisters and brother found happiness, but who could say it was not in spite of Tinmore, instead of because of him?

Their happiness was a sufficient prize for Lorene, though, even if the cost had been her own happiness.

'I did have the most lovely day,' she said to Dell.

She'd felt close to her sisters again. She'd basked in the joy they shared with their husbands.

And in being near Dell.

He turned back to her, his gaze meeting hers and warming her all over. 'I am pleased.'

Once when she'd been a child caught in a thunderstorm, lightning struck a tree near her, so close she'd felt the crackle of the bolt around and through her. Sometimes it felt like that lightning bolt crackling when she was with Dell.

How silly was that?

The carriage reached the iron gates of Tinmore Hall and their gazes broke away. The cupolas of the huge country house came into view, like wagging fingers chastising her.

She'd done nothing wrong, though, except to defy her husband who had no good reason to keep her from Summerfield House. It certainly had not been wrong of her to want to spend Christmas Day with her sisters at their childhood home. Her infatuation with Dell had nothing to do with it.

Besides, being enamoured of Dell was her secret and no one would ever know of it.

Especially not Dell.

When the carriage pulled to a stop in front at the entrance, the butler opened the door. Dell climbed out and turned to Lorene. She clasped his hand, so warm and strong, as he helped her descend the carriage steps.

He walked her up the stone steps to the massive mahogany door where the butler waited.

'Thank you, Dell,' she murmured, not daring to look at him.

He stepped back and she crossed the threshold into the hall, where her husband stood leaning on his cane and shooting daggers from his eyes.

Dell watched Lorene disappear through the doorway. He hated to relinquish her to that old man who was her husband and who neglected or scolded her in turn. Life could be cruelly fleeting. One should cherish those nearest and dearest while one could.

Tinmore's raspy voice rose as the door closed. 'A visit with your sisters, eh? A tryst with your lover, more like! I'll show you—!'

The door closed.

Dell froze.

Lover?

Ridiculous! She'd gone to see her sisters, nothing more, and Tinmore very well knew that.

Dell called to the coachman, 'I'll only be a moment.'

Without bothering to knock, he opened the door.

The butler jumped back and Tinmore's eyes bugged in surprise. 'How dare you, sir!'

Tinmore stood at the bottom of the grand staircase. Lorene was halfway to the first landing.

'Lord Tinmore, you are mistaken—' Dell began.

Lorene interrupted him. 'There is no need to explain. Please, Dell.' But her panicked voice did not reassure him.

Tinmore pounded his cane on the marble floor and waved her away. 'Go to your room.' He pointed his cane at Dell. 'I will speak with you.'

Tinmore led him to a small drawing room, not the opulent one Dell had visited before when calling at the house to do his neighbourly duty to Tinmore, but one reserved for lesser callers and tradesmen.

'Sir, you misunderstand.' Dell started to speak as soon as he entered the room.

'I completely comprehend, Penford. You have been carrying on with my wife since last Season and then you have the gall to invite her to your house—' His words were slurred, as if he'd imbibed too many spirits.

'So she could be with her sisters at Christmas,' Dell broke in. 'And the invitation included you.'

'Hmmph!' Tinmore lifted his nose. 'That was merely a ruse. You knew I would not come.'

'I knew no such thing.' Although Dell had not been sorry Tinmore refused to come. The man put a pall on everything.

Tinmore's hairy eyebrows rose. 'Do not take me for a fool. You were constantly attending her in town, at every social event to which we were invited.'

Of course Dell had approached her. Was he not obligated as a gentleman of her acquaintance? Because of some distant ancestor, he'd inherited her father's estate. Surely that was reason enough to do her a kindness. 'You left her alone, sir.'

Tinmore's face turned red and his voice rose to a shout. 'You dare to criticise me when you are the one carrying on!'

Was Tinmore demented? Did he not know how difficult it had been for his wife at those balls and routs? The scandals of her parents and of her marriage to Tinmore caused most of society to shun her. Tinmore could have eased those times for her with the strength of his status.

If he'd have remained at her side.

'There has been no carrying on!' Dell's voice rose above Tinmore's. 'Your wife has done nothing but visit with her sisters. As you would have seen had you come with her.'

'Humph!' Tinmore lifted his nose. 'Her sisters are as scandalous as their parents. That is why I forbade her to go; that and to forbid her to be in your company.'

Dell met Tinmore's glare. 'You forbade her to go? I received an acceptance of the invitation with your signature.'

Tinmore's gaze faltered. 'I changed my mind.'

'At the last minute.' To be as cruel as possible, Dell suspected.

Tinmore knew Lorene was devoted to her sisters. She'd married Tinmore so her sisters and brother would have advantages denied them when their father left them penniless. Tinmore knew she would want to share Christmas Day with them.

God knew Dell would have done anything to share another Christmas with his family. Nothing would have kept him apart from them.

Nothing except death.

Tinmore sputtered. Dell had forgotten him for a moment.

'You seek to evade the truth, Penford,' Tinmore accused. 'That you are making love to my wife behind my back!'

Dell leaned down to glare into Tinmore's rheumy eyes. 'This is nonsense, sir, and you well know it. I'll hear no more.'

Dell turned away and strode to the door. He made it to the hall before hearing Tinmore's cane tapping after him. 'Do not walk away without my leave! I have more to say to you—'

Dell glanced to the stairway and saw Lorene still standing there. How much had she heard? He hurried on to the door which was opened by the butler.

'Wait!' shouted Tinmore, advancing on him.

Dell walked outside on to the stone steps. Tinmore still came after him.

'You stay away from my wife!' Tinmore swung his cane at Dell.

Dell caught it before it struck him in the head.

Tinmore released his grip on the cane and clapped his hands against his head. He uttered a high-pitched cry as he stumbled backwards. Dell reached out to catch him, but Tinmore slipped on the snow-slick surface and tumbled down the steps. He hit the cobbled ground, his head smacking against the stones.

And he was still.

Chapter Two

Dell leapt down the steps to the stricken man.

'My lord!' The butler dashed out of house right behind him.

'What happened?' Lorene appeared in the doorway.

Dell turned to her. 'He fell.'

'Fell?' the butler cried. 'I think not! You pushed him.'

One of Dell's coachmen jumped down from the carriage's box. 'Lord Penford did nothing! I saw the man fall.'

'You'd lie if he told you to,' the butler shot back.

Dell's heart pounded as he pressed his fingers against Tinmore's neck, but he already knew he'd feel no pulse. As a British army captain in the Peninsular War Dell had seen enough death to recognise it instantly. He opened one of Tinmore's eyes. It was blank and dilated. There was nothing he could do.

He glanced up at Lorene. 'He's dead.'

She covered her mouth with her hand.

'Dead?' The butler kneeled at Tinmore's side and took his hand. 'Dead?' He glared at Dell. 'I am sending for the magistrate!'

This would not be easy. 'Send for the coroner, too. And a physician. The coroner will want to know the physician's opinion as to the cause of his death.'

'There can be no dispute.' The butler sounded near tears. 'You pushed him!'

Lorene came down the steps and stood at Dell's side.

'I did not push him,' he said to her. Would she believe him? Would any of them? 'He tried to strike me with his cane. I grabbed it. He clutched at his head and fell.'

She knelt down next to Tinmore's body and tentatively touched his hair. 'He was so angry.'

By this time two footmen stood at the door.

Dell gestured to them. 'Come. Carry him inside.'

The two men did not move.

The butler swung round to the footmen. 'Do not move him! The coroner will wish to see his lordship where he lay.'

'We cannot leave him here!' Lorene cried.

Dell spoke to the butler in a commanding tone. 'It is already late and it is Christmas night. The coroner is not going to come. We will not leave Lord Tinmore out in the cold all night. He deserves some dignity.'

Lorene faced the butler. 'We will move him, Dixon.'

The butler's face was red with anger. 'Then you must stay, sir. I'll not have you escaping to the Continent!'

'Enough, Dixon!' Lorene's eyes flashed. 'Do not speak to Lord Penford in that manner!'

The butler clamped his mouth shut, but his expression was unrepentant.

'He is right,' Dell addressed Lorene. 'I should stay. It will simplify matters when the coroner arrives.' He stepped over to his coachman. 'Jones, return to Summerfield House and leave word of what happened. Lady Tinmore will need her sisters here in the morning. Make sure they know that. And I expect the coroner will want to speak to you and Samuel, so you both bring Lady Tinmore's sisters in the carriage.' Samuel, the other coachman, held the horses, but nodded his agreement.

Jones gestured for Dell to step away from the others. Dell walked him back to the carriage.

The coachman frowned. 'I did not actually

see what happened, my lord. I saw the man fall, though.'

Dell could not think about that now. 'Very well, Jones. When the time comes just tell the coroner precisely what you did see.'

'As you say, m'lord.' He climbed back on to the carriage.

Lorene twisted around to face the footmen. 'Why do you stand there? Carry Lord Tinmore to his bedchamber and lay him on his bed.'

The butler, still thin-lipped, nodded to the footmen who scrambled down the steps to pick up Tinmore's lifeless form.

Dell helped Lorene stand.

He walked with her behind the body. As they entered the house, another servant, almost as ancient as Lord Tinmore—his valet, perhaps—stood on the landing and screeched at the sight of his master. 'My lord! My lord!'

Lorene ran to the man and held him back as the footmen passed him with Lord Tinmore's body. 'Wicky, his lordship had a terrible fall. It has killed him.'

The valet burst into loud sobs and Lorene's chin trembled, but she made him look at her. 'Calm yourself, Wicky. Your lordship needs you. One last time. Make him presentable.'

The old man nodded and followed the footmen up the stairs.

Other servants emerged, looking alarmed. Lorene turned back to the butler. 'Tell them, Dixon. Make certain all the servants are informed. And kept calm.'

Another old man dressed in nightclothes and a robe came from the floors above. 'Ma'am?' he said to Lorene.

She put a hand on his arm. 'He is gone, Mr Filkins. He fell on the steps outside.'

The man's face twisted, but he quickly composed himself. 'May I be of service to you?'

She stared blankly for a moment, then said, 'Ask Dixon if he might need you. And, if you would be so kind, find Mrs Boon and have some tea brought to us in the yellow sitting room.'

'I will do so, post-haste,' the man said.

She turned to Dell. 'Come. We can sit in here.'

He followed her to a comfortable sitting room on the first floor, its walls decorated with a cheerful yellow wallpaper with birds and flowers abounding. The bright setting could not be in greater contrast to Dell's feelings inside. Lord Tinmore was dead and, though he'd done nothing to cause the man's fall, it never would have happened if he had not entered the house.

'Please sit, Dell.'

He placed his hat on a nearby table and removed his gloves and topcoat. She lowered herself on to a sofa upholstered in gold brocade. He sat near in a matching chair.

'That was Mr Filkins, Lord Tinmore's secretary,' she explained. 'It was kind of him to do as I asked. He is not a servant.'

No, a secretary would be one of those unfortunate souls who fell somewhere between servant and family. Like governesses and tutors.

Lorene averted her gaze. 'He is the only one who likes me a little.'

Her words broke through his own worries. 'The only one?'

She gave a wan smile. 'The servants are very attached to Lord Tinmore—' She caught herself. '*Were* attached to him. He was not warm to them, of course, but he paid them well and most have been with him longer than you and I have been alive. They considered me…an outsider, I suppose.'

He'd heard members of the *ton* describe her as a fortune hunter. Unfair when her marriage was more properly a selfless act. Besides, she'd paid a high price. Her husband neglected and belittled her by turns. And the servants resented her?

What a lonely situation to be in.

She wrung her hands. 'I—I am not certain what I should be doing. I feel I should be *doing* something.'

'If you need to leave, do not hesitate. You do

not need to stay with me,' he assured her. 'This room is comfortable enough.'

'No.' She pressed her fingers against her temples. 'I should have ordered a bedchamber made ready for you. I had not thought of it.'

'No need. I do not want you burdened with me.' He paused. 'Especially because what—what—happened was because of me.'

Her face turned paler. 'No. Because of me. Because I defied him.'

His anger at Tinmore flared once more. '*He* refused you a visit with your sisters on Christmas Day. That was very poorly done of him.'

'Still…' Her voice trailed off.

What would happen to her now? Had Tinmore provided for her? Or did Tinmore neglect to do so, the way he neglected her in other ways?

Tinmore's accusations would not help. No doubt she'd become the victim of more gossip because of the way Tinmore died. God knew she did not deserve that. Would anyone truly believe he and Lorene were lovers? Or, worse, that he'd caused Tinmore's death?

They would not be entirely wrong. He'd certainly been the catalyst for it.

She rose from the sofa and began to pace. Dell stood, as well.

'I wonder…should I have stayed with him?'

Her voice rose, but fell again. 'I do not know what is expected of me.'

'What do you wish to do?' he asked. 'If you wish to be with him, do not let my presence stop you.'

She glanced at him with pained eyes, but looked away and paced to the marble mantelpiece, intricately carved with leaves and flowers.

It was agony to see her so distressed. He ought to comfort her somehow, ease her pain, but how could he do so?

When he'd caused it.

'I am sorry this happened, Lorene,' he murmured. 'I cannot tell you how sorry I am.'

She glanced at him again with those eyes so filled with torment. 'Sorry? You are sorry?'

He stepped closer to her and wanted to reach out to her, but did not dare.

Death arrived when least expected.

Tinmore's death had been quick, but death had not been as kind to Dell's family. His father, mother, brother and sister, as well as several servants, perished in a fire in their London town house in April of 1815. Think of the terror and pain of such a death.

He shook himself. If he thought of that, he would descend into depression and this time not come out. 'I never anticipated this would happen,' he forced himself to say.

She leaned her forehead against the white marble. 'Nor did I,' she whispered. 'I never dreamed he would think—'

That they were lovers? Who *could* think such a thing? He had been nothing but polite to her.

With a cry of pain she flung herself on to the sofa again and buried her head in her hands.

He sat next to her, his arm around her. 'I know what it is to grieve,' he said. 'Cry all you wish.'

She turned to him, her voice shrill. 'Grieve? Grieve? How little you understand! I am the most wretched of creatures! I do not feel grief! I feel relief.'

She collapsed against his chest and he held her close, murmuring words of comfort.

The door opened and she pulled away from him, wiping her eyes with her fingers.

'Your tea and brandy, ma'am,' a footman announced in a tone of disapproval.

'Put it on the table,' she managed in a cracked voice. 'And please tell Mrs Boon to make a room ready for Lord Penford.'

The footman put the tray on the table next to the sofa and bowed, leaving without another word.

'Brandy?' she offered, lifting the carafe with a shaking hand.

He took it from her. 'I'll pour. Perhaps you would like some brandy, as well. To steady yourself.'

She nodded and another tear rolled down her lovely cheek.

He handed her the glass and she downed the liquid quickly, handing it back to him for more. He poured another for her and one for himself, which he was tempted to gulp down as she had done.

He sipped it instead.

She blinked away more tears and took a deep breath. 'You must think me a dreadful person.'

'Not at all.' The dreadful person had been her husband. 'Perhaps you have endured more than you allow others to know.'

She shook her head and took another big sip. 'He—he was not so awful a husband, really. He merely liked for people to do as he desired. All the time.'

Tinmore had been autocratic, neglectful and, at times, extremely cruel, from Dell's observation, no more so than this day when he sought to deprive her of her family on Christmas Day. His accusation that they were lovers was unjust and unfair. Tinmore should have known his wife was much too honourable to be unfaithful.

She swallowed the rest of the brandy in her glass. 'So it is terrible of me to feel relief, is it not?' Her chin trembled and tears filled her eyes again.

Dell felt as helpless as when he'd watched Tinmore tumble down the steps. 'You are merely numb. It is not unusual to feel numb after such a tragedy.' Dell had felt numb when he'd been told the news about his family. It took time for the wrenching grief to consume him.

He finished his brandy and poured another for himself, offering her a third glass.

She refused. 'Perhaps I should go to him. Perhaps that is what is expected of me.'

He hated for her to leave. Not because he needed her company, but because he felt she needed him in this house with no allies. But, thanks to Tinmore, the false rumour of them being lovers had been heard by the servants and one footman had witnessed what must have seemed like an embrace between them. He must distance himself from her.

For her sake.

And his.

Lorene rose from the sofa and reached for Dell's hand. She held it between her own. 'I will go to him now. Thank you for sitting with me.'

He covered her hands with his. 'You mustn't thank me. But do not concern yourself with me. Take care of yourself.'

His hands were warm and strong and she relished the feel of them against her skin. And instantly felt guilty for even noticing.

She pulled away. 'Someone should come to show you to your room. At least I hope they do...' Tinmore's servants were so loyal to him. But not to her. Never to her.

He looked at her with such an expression of sympathy it almost hurt. 'I will see you in the morning. You must get some rest.'

The day would not be easy, would it? A magistrate. The coroner. Things she must do but, what? She could not think. 'I'll bid you goodnight then.' She curtsied.

He bowed.

She turned and fled from the room.

Lorene forced herself to make her way to Lord Tinmore's rooms on the same hallway as her own, but thankfully not too close. She knocked before opening his bedchamber door.

Wicky was seated in a chair next to the bed. The bed curtains blocked a view of the bed. She was glad. She had a sudden horror of seeing the body again.

'How are you faring, Wicky?' she asked from the doorway.

He turned his head slowly to face her. 'I would like to stay here if I may, my lady.'

Her heart went out to the old man. Wicky had loved her husband. Wicky, Dixon and Mr Filkins were especially devoted to Tinmore. Goodness. They'd served him for decades.

'Of course you may stay,' she said, backing out of the room and shutting the door.

She walked down the hall to her own bedchamber where her lady's maid, grim-faced, helped her prepare for bed, speaking only when it was absolutely necessary. Finally the woman left and Lorene burrowed under the bedcovers.

Her heart pounded rapidly as if she'd run a great distance and she realised she'd felt that way since seeing Tinmore at the bottom of the steps. How could she calm herself? She tried to sort through the emotions twisting inside her. Uncertainty about the following day. Would there be trouble with the magistrate or the coroner? Would they question what Dell told them? Would they believe she and Dell had been lovers?

Why had Tinmore thought such a thing? Her infatuation with Dell had always been her private delight. She'd never talked about Dell. She'd always schooled her features when around him. Tinmore could not have guessed. No one could.

Tinmore had never cared a fig when she was thrown into Dell's company. At social events Tinmore always left her as soon as it was expedient. He'd never shown any interest in whose company she kept while he played cards or conversed with his cronies. He'd shown little interest in Dell, a mere earl, much preferring Dell's friend, her sister Genna's husband, the Marquess of Rossdale, a duke's heir. Or the Duke himself. What had worked its way into Tinmore's mind for him to make that outrageous accusation?

When Tinmore told her to go to her room, she'd known that would not be the end of it. At least now she didn't have to listen to him rail at her.

She suddenly felt as if a huge weight had been lifted off her shoulders. She was free! She would wake in the morning with no one to answer to but herself. No worries about being accused of having a lover, or of saying the wrong thing, acting the wrong way. No more pushing down her feelings. No more biting her tongue. She was free to dream again.

If she were ever able to get to sleep.

She tossed and turned in the bed and finally threw off the covers and walked barefoot to her window. She curled up on the window seat and gazed out at the snow-covered park. How bright it looked even at this late hour, so white and clean. It was a new landscape, changed from before the snow.

And now she would have a new life.

She thought over the almost two years she had been married to Tinmore.

He'd done what she wanted most. To provide for her sisters and brother. He'd also given her a home, beautiful clothes, jewels, a comfortable life in so many ways. She'd been grateful to him for that. She never complained about him for that reason. Except maybe that little bit in the carriage when she'd spoken to Dell. That had not been complaining, really. How awful it would be to complain about Tinmore when he'd been the rescue of her family.

After a fashion.

She could say with absolute sincerity that had she not married Tinmore, her sisters and half-brother would not have found their spouses.

What's more, they'd found love.

Lorene asked very little for herself, only that Tinmore provide her with the means to live in simple comfort after he was gone. She had no idea if he had done so.

Even if not, the jewellery he'd given her would be worth something, she figured. Tomorrow she would make certain she had it safely in her possession. Filkins would help her. Who knew what the servants might do, with their loyalty to Tinmore and resentment of her.

She did not know where she would go or how she would live, but, even so, wretched woman that she was, she would be glad to leave this place.

She left the window seat, found a shawl to wrap over her shoulders and slippers for her feet. Carrying a candle, she made her way to the formal drawing room Tinmore called the Mount Olympus room, because of the murals of Greek gods and goddesses painted by Verrio and commissioned by some earlier Earl of Tinmore.

Placing the candle on the opulent gold gilt pianoforte Tinmore bought for her, she pulled out her favourite music, Mozart's Quintets in G Minor, and began to play.

Someone had sent her the music after a musicale last Season. She did not know who. Not her husband, though. He'd fallen asleep during music so wonderful, Lorene felt its indelible stamp on her soul.

She played at a slow tempo, appropriately mournful, but the chords she thought of as sword thrusts, piercing what otherwise would have been a typical minuet, perfectly reflected the pangs of anger she felt towards Tinmore for accusing her of infidelity, for involving Dell in his death, for all the times Tinmore had been thoughtless and hurtful.

The music filled the room and it seemed as if the murals of Greek gods and goddesses were watching her and absorbing the music. If her playing could be heard outside the room, she did not care.

She needed the solace only music could bring her.

Chapter Three

Lorene played the pianoforte for at least two hours before returning to her bedchamber. She slept fitfully and awoke before dawn. By then it was no use trying to go back to sleep. She sat on the window seat and waited until it was a decent time to ring for her maid, who was even more grim than usual. Lorene could not tell if it was because the woman was grieving or because she'd been roused earlier than usual.

After Lorene finished dressing and was making her way down the stairs, she heard voices in the hall. Several voices.

If this was the magistrate, surely it was too early an hour for him to call! She rushed to the landing and leaned over the bannister for a view of the hall.

Her sisters had come! Tess and Genna were here with their husbands.

She quickened her step.

Her sister Genna saw her first and ran up the stairs to give her a hug. Tess soon caught up.

'Oh, Lorene!' Genna cried.

Tess put her arms around both of them. 'How do you fare, Lorene? Are you all right?'

'Yes. Yes,' Lorene replied, her tears flowing again at the sight of them. 'But you shouldn't have come, Tess. Shouldn't you be resting?'

'I'm not ill,' Tess countered. 'I am merely going to have a baby.'

Tess's Christmas present to all of them was this happy announcement, but now it seemed long ago that Tess told them this news, even though it had only been the previous day.

The sisters descended the rest of the staircase, arm in arm.

'Lorene,' Genna's husband, the Marquess of Rossdale, strode over to her and kissed her on the cheek. 'We are at your beck and call. Whatever you need, you must tell us.'

Just for them to be here was more than enough.

Tess's husband, Marc Glenville, also approached her. 'Our condolences, Lorene.'

Condolences was not the right word, though.

'Where is Dell?' Rossdale asked. He and Dell had been close friends since they were boys.

Lorene shook her head. 'I do not know.' She turned to Dixon. 'Where is the Earl, Dixon?'

'In the east wing.' The butler's words were clipped.

The lesser guest rooms.

'Send for him, man,' Rossdale ordered. 'Tell him we are here.'

'Where shall you await the Earl?' Dixon asked haughtily.

Lorene answered him. 'In the morning room.' She turned to her sisters. 'Did you eat?'

'Eat?' cried Genna. 'As if we could eat after hearing what happened.'

Lorene turned back to Dixon. 'Alert Cook, then, Dixon. We have guests for breakfast.'

Dixon bowed.

'Tell us what happened,' Tess said as they walked to the morning room.

'I did not see,' Lorene answered. 'Tinmore fell down the stone steps there where you came in.'

'On those steps?' Genna broke in. 'What was he doing outside?'

'He was angry.' Lorene's head was pounding with the memory. 'Dell tried to speak to him, but there was no reasoning with him.'

'I'll bet he was angry that you came to see us yesterday,' Genna said. 'I can just see him in high dudgeon over that. His wife defied him. Imagine that.'

'He *was* angry over that,' Lorene snapped. 'My defiance possibly killed him, if you must know.'

Genna touched her arm. 'Forgive me, Lorene. My tongue ran away with me again.'

They entered the morning room, brightly lit with the morning sun. The many windows of the room revealed clear blue skies dotted with puffy white clouds. The bright sun glistened on the snow-covered ground.

Lorene spoke to the footman attending the room. 'We have more guests for breakfast, Travers. Would you please bring us tea and coffee?'

The footman bowed and left the room. Rossdale and Glenville pulled up additional chairs and helped the ladies to sit.

When they were settled, Rossdale asked, 'Dell's coachman told us the magistrate would be sent for. For what reason?'

'Dixon—the butler who was in the hall—believes Dell pushed Tinmore, but Dell didn't.' Dell was too honourable to do such a thing, Lorene was certain.

Rossdale frowned and exchanged a look with Glenville. 'It is good we came.'

What could they do, though, if the magistrate believed Dixon and not Dell?

'What's more, we are not leaving you alone here,' Genna added.

During Lorene's marriage, Genna had been with her the longest and knew best what it was like to live at Tinmore Hall, where they were always treated as intruders.

Lorene's gaze travelled from one to the other and her eyes stung with tears. She'd not realised how alone she felt here. 'I—I know I must do something, but I do not know what to do.'

Tess leaned over and touched her hand. 'We will help you figure it out.'

Rossdale spoke. 'Tinmore's solicitors must be informed and the will read. And, of course, someone must notify Tinmore's heir. Do you know who that is?'

Lorene shook her head. 'Some grand-nephew, I believe. Mr Filkins probably knows.'

'Mr Filkins?' Glenville asked.

'Lord Tinmore's secretary,' Genna answered. 'He sometimes comes for breakfast.'

The footman returned with coffee and tea and enough cups to serve them all. Lorene hoped they knew to guard their tongues around the servants.

'Where is Dell?' Rossdale asked. 'How long should it take to inform him we are here?'

'You would be surprised,' Genna responded sarcastically.

Lorene turned to the footman again. 'Travers, please ask Dixon if he sent for Lord Penford. If not, make certain someone finds Lord Penford and shows him to the morning room.'

The footman bowed and started to leave.

Lorene stopped him. 'Tell me first if Mr Filkins will breakfast here today.'

'He has already done so,' the footman responded and exited the room.

Dell finally found his way to the hall. He'd been wandering up and down corridors and stairs for a good quarter of an hour before reaching the hall and glimpsing his first servant.

Unfortunate that it was the butler, Dixon, who glared at him with undisguised displeasure.

He'd faced more fearsome men on the battlefield. One grieving butler would not daunt him. He actually felt sorry for the elderly man.

'Good morning, Dixon,' he said in a mild voice. 'Will you direct me to the breakfast room?'

Dixon worked his mouth, as if trying to decide whether or not to answer.

At that same moment a footman reached the hall. 'Oh!' he exclaimed as if surprised to find Dell there. The footman spoke to Dixon, though, not to Dell. 'Lady Tinmore requests Lord Penford's presence in the morning room.'

Dell didn't give Dixon a chance to respond. 'Show me where it is,' He nodded politely to the butler, though, before following the footman.

When he entered the room, it was his turn to be surprised. Her sisters and their husbands had come from Summerfield House as he'd known they would. He'd merely not expected them so early.

'Dell!' Ross rose from his chair and crossed the room to shake his hand. 'How are you faring?'

Dell shrugged. 'Well enough.' He directed his gaze to Lorene. 'The room was comfortable. I thank you.'

She looked pale, but lovely in a plain black dress. The lack of colour did not favour her. 'I fear the housekeeper chose one in the far recesses of the house. I apologise for that.'

He managed a half-smile. 'It only took me a quarter of an hour to find my way to the hall. No harm done.'

'I had your valet pack a clean shirt and neck-cloth. And your razor.' Ross gestured to his face.

Dell rubbed the stubble on his chin. 'Forgive my appearance, ladies. I will retire and make myself more presentable.' He turned to Ross. 'Where are my things?'

'We left them with the butler,' Glenville said. 'Did you not see him in the hall?'

'I did, but he was not inclined to be helpful.'

'I am so sorry!' Lorene exclaimed. 'Dixon is behaving very badly.'

'He blames me.' Dell turned back to the door. 'I'll be back directly.'

Lorene rose from her chair and hurried across

the room to him. 'Please stay, Dell. Your appearance is of no consequence. Have something to eat.'

Two other servants were placing dishes of food on the side board.

He shook his head. 'I'd best clean myself up. We do not know when the magistrate will arrive and I would prefer to look presentable.'

He returned to the hall and confronted Dixon. 'Where is the change of clothing the Marquess brought me?' His tone was no longer mild.

Dixon disappeared behind a door for a moment and emerged with a valise, handing it to Dell without a word.

Dell found his way back to the room where he'd slept. Thank goodness the maids who made up the room had provided soap and towels. He shed his coat, waistcoat and shirt, and lathered his face. Shaving was a task his valet usually performed, but he'd had plenty of practice on the Peninsula during the war where he'd preferred to dress and groom himself.

After shaving, he changed his shirt and tied his own neckcloth. When he donned his waistcoat and coat, he felt he at least looked the part of a gentleman. Nothing with which a magistrate could find offence.

Dell had been correct about the magistrate's arrival. He had barely finished breakfast when it was announced that the magistrate had arrived and wished to see both Lorene and him.

'Do you wish us to come with you?' Ross asked, ever the steadfast friend.

'I think it best I see the magistrate alone.'

Ross's brows rose. 'And not show him what support you possess?'

'I have done nothing deserving reproach.' Except perhaps thinking he could dissuade Tinmore of his erroneous beliefs. 'I refuse to give the appearance of needing the support of the future Duke of Kessington.'

Ross turned to Lorene. 'And you, ma'am. Do you wish one or all of us to come with you?'

'I want to be with you,' Genna piped up.

Lorene darted a glance towards Dell. 'I will see him alone, as well. We will join you afterwards.'

Genna looked about to protest, but her husband put a calming hand on her arm. 'I *will* see the man before he leaves, Dell.'

Dell knew better than to resist when Ross used such a tone. 'As you wish.'

With luck it would all be settled before then.

After Dell and Lorene left the morning room, he said, 'I would offer my arm, but I fear the politeness would be misconstrued if seen by one of the servants.'

She nodded.

It was his first opportunity to see her alone. 'How do you fare, Lorene?'

'I am well.' She averted her gaze. 'I do not know if I am well. I suppose I am numb. I really feel very little of anything.'

That was better than suffering, he knew.

'I am dreading this interview, though,' she murmured.

Of course she was. Telling of it would bring it all back.

'Speak with complete candour,' he said. 'That is the only way.'

Dixon attended the door. He gave them a smug look that set Dell's teeth on edge, but acted the proper butler, opening the door and stepping ahead to announce them.

The room Dixon had chosen was not the opulent drawing room with murals of gods and goddesses where he and Ross had once been received in this house. This was another lesser drawing room tucked away in one of the corridors on the first floor. Once they entered the room, Dell knew exactly why the butler had chosen this place. Every available space on the wainscoting walls was filled with family portraits, reminding those entering that generations of Tinmores would be watching.

Lorene's step faltered.

Two men were present in the room. One, a

pleasant-looking, somewhat corpulent man in his fifties, sat behind a desk, paper, pen and ink in front of him. The other man, taller, thinner with dark assessing eyes, stood at his side.

'Lady Tinmore and Lord Penford,' Dixon announced in a voice tinged with disdain.

The gentleman behind the desk stood and walked around to greet them. 'Come in. Come in.' He spoke as if inviting them for tea.

Lorene walked up to him. 'Squire Hedges. Do you remember me? I was Miss Lorene Summerfield, now Lady Tinmore. You were frequently a guest in my father's house.'

'Ah, yes, indeed I remember you,' he replied with an engaging smile. 'But you were in a pinafore last I saw you. Your father and I were indeed fast friends...for many years until he...but never mind that. I was sorry to lose him.' The Squire seemed to collect himself and his expression sobered. 'May I express my condolences? For the loss of your husband, I mean. Not your father.'

'I do understand, sir.' She made a nervous glance to the other man.

Dell had heard of Squire Hedges, a local landowner. Was he the magistrate? He would have known Tinmore, perhaps for decades. Who, then, was the other man?

Lorene turned to Dell. 'Lord Penford, may I present Squire Hedges. The magistrate here.' She again addressed herself to the Squire. 'Lord Penford inherited Summerfield House.'

Dell bowed. 'Squire.'

The man bowed in return. 'I intended to call upon you, sir. Forgive the omission. Busy, you know. Time gets away from a person.'

'Yes, it does.' Dell pointedly looked at the other man.

'Oh.' The Squire stepped over to the stranger. 'Allow me to present Mr Walsh. He is the coroner.'

'The coroner?' Lorene's brows rose, but she collected herself. 'Oh, yes. Lord Penford said there would be a coroner.'

'Must call in the coroner, my lady,' Squire Hedges explained. 'Not a natural death and all that.'

The coroner bowed. 'My lady. Lord Penford.'

'Sir,' Lorene responded.

The Squire smiled at her, sobered again, cleared his throat and clapped his hands together. 'Well! I suppose we should proceed, should we not?' He walked back to the chair behind the desk.

'Lady Tinmore.' Mr Walsh spoke up in a deep voice with little modulation. 'Perhaps you would be good enough to leave the room while we speak to Lord Penford?'

Squire Hedges smiled again. 'We will call you forthwith.'

A worry line formed between her eyes before she curtsied and left the room.

The Squire gestured with his finger. 'Please sit, sir.'

Dell took a step closer to the desk. 'I would prefer to stand. I have no objection to you sitting, though.' His years in the army taught him it was better to stand when facing a man who might have power over him.

The Squire lifted his shoulders and sat, folding his hands in front of him on the desk. Mr Walsh remained standing.

Dell waited for one of them to speak.

The Squire cleared his throat again. 'Uh…suppose you tell us what happened?'

Dell glanced from one man to the other. 'First tell me what you have heard already.'

Had Dixon already spoken to them? he meant.

Squire Hedges picked up the pen and rolled it in his fingers.

'We interviewed Dixon, the butler,' Mr Walsh answered, which told Dell very little.

Dell straightened and gave each man a steely glance. 'You spoke to the *butler* before me?' To speak to a servant before a member of the aristocracy was a breach of proper conduct.

Squire Hedges tapped the feather pen on the desk. 'Well, he greeted us in the hall, you see. Expedient to talk to him first.'

By Dixon's design, Dell was certain. Dell stared at the Squire, until he squirmed in his seat.

Still holding his gaze steady, Dell spoke. 'What did the butler tell you?'

Hedges looked even more uncomfortable.

'He believes you pushed Lord Tinmore to his death,' Walsh said.

Dell turned to Walsh and spoke in a firm, no-nonsense tone. 'You have placed me at a disadvantage by speaking to Dixon first, but I assure you I did not push Lord Tinmore to his death.'

Walsh shrugged. 'Then tell what did happen.'

Dell answered, 'Lord Tinmore attempted to strike me with his cane. I seized it to fend off the attack. He abruptly let go, put his hands to his head and staggered backwards. He lost his footing on the steps. I attempted to catch him, but he fell down the steps to the paving stones below.'

'You did not push him?' Walsh asked.

'No. I merely seized his cane.'

Walsh's brows rose. 'And why did he try to strike you with a cane?'

Of course the man would ask this question. 'He quarrelled with me. I was attempting to leave when he came after me, following me out of the house. That is when he tried to strike me.'

'What was the quarrel about?'

Dell anticipated this question, much as he detested having to answer it. This coroner, though, would notice any hesitation in responding.

Dell met the man's gaze. 'Lord Tinmore believed Lady Tinmore and I to be engaging in an affair. It was not true. I attempted to convince him of that fact. When he would not listen to reason, I tried to leave. That is why he was outside with me without a topcoat, trying to strike me with his cane.'

'Without a topcoat.' Squire Hedges dipped the pen in some ink and made a note. He looked up again. 'It was not true? The affair, I mean?'

Dell bristled. He'd already said it was not true. 'Not true. I merely escorted Lady Tinmore home from Summerfield House. She and the Earl were invited for Christmas Day. He declined at the last minute, but Lady Tinmore came to spend the day with her sisters, who, with their husbands, were my guests. They are at Tinmore Hall now,' he added. 'Lord and Lady Rossdale. Mr and Mrs Glenville.'

'I will speak to them,' Walsh declared.

Would he believe them, though, when they told him there was no affair?

Walsh looked askance. 'Why did Tinmore decline the invitation?'

'I do not know why.' How could Dell speak for Tinmore?

'Why did he believe you and Lady Tinmore

were…' he paused and his voice dipped even deeper '…having an affair?'

'I do not know. There was no reason for him to believe it.' Lorene would never be so dishonourable and Dell—Dell did not form attachments. Not any more. 'Lady Tinmore and I met on social occasions. And I sometimes did my duty by her and her sister as their father's heir, but nothing more.'

Walsh's brows rose. 'Nothing more? Tinmore was an old man and you are not—'

'To suggest that is to insult Lady Tinmore.' Dell snapped. 'She is an honourable lady.'

'But you invited her to this house party. Why have a house party at what must be a minor property of the Earl of Penford, instead of at Penford?' Walsh asked.

'Do you not know my history, sir? Surely you heard that my mother, father, sister and brother—my whole family—died in a fire not two years ago. I am not yet comfortable in the country house I once shared with them. The Marquess of Rossdale, though, is a friend and he is married to Lady Tinmore's sister. To please my friend's wife, I offered to open Summerfield House to her and her sisters for Christmas.'

Of course, Dell did not mention that when he'd invited Lorene and Genna to Summerfield House a year ago, both he and Ross had met them for the first time. He did not speak of pocketing the miniature Genna had painted of Lorene, the one Tinmore tossed aside at Christmas a year ago. Nor did he mention he had sent sheet music to Lorene as a gift last spring, even though he sent it anonymously.

He certainly would not be able to explain his motivation to do those things, because he did not understand why himself.

'You don't know why Tinmore thought there was an affair?' the Squire asked.

'I do not know why he thought what he did. I do not know why he would not listen to reason when I told him his fears were unfounded,' Dell continued in a firm voice. 'I grabbed his cane to keep him from striking me, but that is all. When he let go of the cane, his feet were firmly on the stone outside the door. Something else made him stagger backwards. Something made him press his hands on to his head.'

'Yes. Well.' Squire Hedges tapped his fingers on the desk.

Dell turned to the coroner. 'You will call in Lord Tinmore's physician, will you not? Tinmore looked as if he was seized with some sort of fit. Something caused him to stagger and fall. Perhaps his physician will know what it might have been.'

Walsh glanced at the Squire, who dipped his

pen in the inkwell and wrote a note. 'Yes, indeed. Speak to Tinmore's physician.'

Walsh turned back to Dell. 'Thank you, Lord Penford,' he said. 'You may go now.'

That was it?

Dell nodded to each of them and turned to go.

'But do not leave town until after the inquest,' Walsh added.

As if he would return to London before all this was settled.

Dell nodded. 'You have my word.'

'If you would be so good as to send in Lady Tinmore,' Walsh said.

Dell left the room only to encounter Dixon attending the door.

'Where is Lady Tinmore?' he asked the butler.

Dixon avoided looking at him. 'Returned to her guests.'

Dell made his way back to the morning room and the Summerfield sisters and their husbands all looked at him expectantly when he entered.

'Nothing is resolved,' He turned to Lorene. 'They wish to speak to you.'

She nodded and stood.

He escorted her back to the magistrate and the coroner, although there was really no reason for him to do so.

'What did they ask you?' she asked as soon as they were out of the morning room.

'They asked me to tell them what happened,' he responded. 'Then they asked about Lord Tinmore's accusation.' He did not need to explain what accusation he meant.

Her eyes widened. 'But that was all nonsense!'

'Then you have nothing to worry about.' He put his hand on her arm. 'Tell the truth and all will be well.'

'Sometimes men do not listen to reason,' she said.

She was speaking of Tinmore, of course. Certainly he had not listened to reason.

'You can only control what you say and how you say it,' he responded. 'You cannot control what they will think.'

'That is why I am afraid,' she murmured.

They fell silent when nearing the room, its door still guarded by Dixon. When the butler saw them, he opened the door to announce her, just as he ought.

Dell gave her a reassuring look and watched her disappear behind the door.

Chapter Four

Dell turned and encountered Dixon's scathing glare.

Dell met the butler's gaze. 'I regret what happened, Dixon, but, I assure you, I did not push Lord Tinmore.' He turned to leave.

Dell was willing to accept his part in the sequence of events that led to Tinmore's death. He should have returned to his carriage instead of confronting Tinmore. But his intentions were honourable. He wanted to defend Lorene and prevent her husband from believing ill of her. But he had not killed Tinmore. Killing was what one did in battle. The images of those soldiers he killed could never be erased from his mind.

Dixon spoke. 'You killed him, sure enough. You and Lady Tinmore.'

Dell whirled on him. 'Enough of this talk. Lady Tinmore has done nothing.'

'That is not what his lordship said,' Dixon persisted.

'Tinmore was wrong. His wife's attachment is to her sisters, not to me. I am merely a friend of her sister's husband.'

What was the use? This butler was as thick-headed as Tinmore had been. Not listening to reason. Nothing good would come of trying to convince a man who was determined to think otherwise.

Dell turned to leave again.

'I could be quiet about it,' Dixon called after him.

Dell looked over his shoulder, not certain he'd heard correctly.

Dixon smirked. 'You have money, Lord Penford. You wouldn't miss a few quid. You'd see how easily I could change my mind. Tell them I was mistaken and no harm done.'

Enough sympathy for this man. Dell had thought him motivated by grief, which Dell could well understand, not greed. 'You want me to pay you to keep quiet?'

'If you like.' Dixon sounded all innocence suddenly. 'I could say I misspoke—out of shock at losing my lord. I could say I didn't see you push him.'

'You did not see it. It did not happen.' Dell's voice deepened. 'Perhaps you would like me to tell those gentlemen behind the door that you attempted to extort money from me?'

Dixon continued to look smug. 'My word against yours, is it not? Who has the most to lose if it comes to that?'

The word of a servant against a peer of the realm. A lying servant at that. Dell would like to believe there would not be much contest.

Unless a jury were willing to believe a young wife of an old man would engage in an affair with a younger man who seized upon an opportunity to hasten her becoming a wealthy widow, assuming Tinmore made a generous settlement on her. That made for a good story. Especially if the young wife was one of the Scandalous Summerfield sisters.

'Your lie against my truth,' Dell countered. 'I'll bank on the truth and I suggest you do the same.'

He strode away.

Curse Dixon. Grief Dell could accept, even understand, but he'd be damned if he'd pay Dixon to keep the man from lying.

He headed back to the morning room, but Ross intercepted him on the way.

'You look like thunder,' Ross said.

'I feel like thunder.' He still reeled from the exchange with Dixon. 'Do you know what that butler said to me?'

'What?'

'He asked for money. If I paid him money, he would not lie about what he saw.' Dell shook his head. 'Can you believe the man?'

Ross's brows knitted. 'He could cause you a great deal of trouble, Dell.'

'I know that, but I'll be damned if I pay the man.'

'I'm not suggesting you pay him,' Ross countered.

'This death was not my doing and I'll not be intimidated by some butler who thinks he can make it appear so.'

'I want to talk to the coroner, Dell.' Ross tried to pass him. 'I'll make him listen to me.'

Dell held him back. 'You will have your chance. They wish to speak with all of you.'

'Good.' Ross nodded. 'They need to know who you are and who your friends are.'

'They know who I am. The Earl of Penford.' He released Ross. 'But all that is irrelevant. You being my friend is irrelevant. All that matters is what really happened. And I have nothing with which to reproach myself.'

They started back to the morning room.

'Damned Tinmore,' Ross said. 'If anyone is to blame, it is he. Fitting end, I say. He tried to manipulate everyone. Tess and Glenville told me what he did to them.'

'What did he do to them?'

'Forced them to marry. They did not even know each other. They were caught in a storm together and Tinmore used that as an excuse to marry her off without paying her dowry. He put pressure on Genna to marry, too.'

Dell knew about Tinmore's pressure on Genna. That was partly why Ross came up with his scheme to pretend to be betrothed to her.

'Lorene should never have married him. She and her sisters deserved better than his treatment of them,' Dell said.

Of course, it was really Dell's father who put Lorene in a position to agree to marry the elderly, autocratic Tinmore. When Lorene's father died, Dell's father inherited the Summerfield estate. It was Dell's father who turned out the Summerfield sisters. His father might have been generous to them instead. Allowed them to stay at Summerfield House; provided them dowries. He might have done so, but Dell's father assumed the sisters were as morally loose as their parents.

What possessed his father to be so heartless?

A pang of guilt hit Dell.

How could he reproach a father he so tragically lost a few months after his father made that decision?

Ross went on. 'I am going to tell the coroner and the magistrate just what I think. I would be remiss if I did not.'

'Do not bully them, Ross,' Dell insisted. 'It will not work with this Walsh fellow.'

'I can at least let them know I expect them to proceed properly,' Ross insisted. 'And that I expect them to protect Lorene's reputation.'

For Lorene's sake, Dell would not further argue with his friend. Her reputation must be protected above all else. After all, the Summerfield sisters had suffered enough damage to their reputations, most of it due to their parents, not themselves.

Lorene, though, had often been the object of gossip, accused of tricking the ancient, but wealthy, Lord Tinmore into marrying her. Yes, she had married Tinmore for his money, but not for herself. For her sisters and her half-brother.

She deserved their esteem, not more gossip.

Lorene's knees shook as she stood before Squire Hedges and the coroner. There was no reason for her to be fearful, but she could not help it. She glanced around the room, but it did nothing to still her unease. Rather, the portraits on the wall seemed to be glaring at her, blaming her for what happened.

If she had not defied him, they seemed to say, *he would be alive today.*

Would the Squire and the coroner see her guilt?

Or did they already believe Dell had pushed Tinmore?

Dell would never have done such a thing. Never. Surely they would have believed him and not a grieving butler too upset to realise who he accused.

Squire Hedges gestured to a chair near the desk. 'Would you care to sit, Lady Tinmore?'

Sitting would make her feel too small, somehow. She was Lady Tinmore, she must remember. Here was one rare occasion that she must assert her rank.

She straightened her spine. 'I will stand, thank you.' She pointed to the pen and paper on the desk. 'But you must sit so you may write.'

The Squire inclined his head and lowered himself into his chair. Mr Walsh, the coroner, stood with his arms folded across his chest. He was the one who made her insides tremble.

Squire Hedges smiled. 'Tell us what happened, my lady. What you saw. What you heard.'

She decided to begin with her return from Summerfield House. 'I spent the day with my sisters at Summerfield House and when the day was over, Lord Penford offered his carriage and his escort to return me to Tinmore Hall—'

Mr Walsh interrupted. 'You did not have a carriage at your disposal?'

She faced him. 'No.'

'Then how did you travel to Summerfield House?' he asked.

'I walked.'

His dark brows rose. 'You walked?'

'Lord Tinmore was supposed to have come with me to spend Christmas with my family. At the last minute he declared that we would not be going. He gave no reason for declining the invitation right before we were expected to arrive.' It had been a deliberate cruelty, which had surprised her. Tinmore's cruelty was more commonly thoughtless. 'He knew how much I desired to see my sisters. I had not seen my youngest sister since her wedding to Lord Rossdale. I decided to go without him even though he refused me the carriage. So I walked.'

'You defied him,' Walsh stated.

'Yes.' No use denying it.

Walsh nodded. 'Go on.'

She wished she could tell what the man was thinking. 'When Lord Penford's carriage reached Tinmore Hall, Lord Penford walked me to the door. I entered the house and encountered Lord Tinmore in the hall, waiting for me. He immediately started to accuse me of—of things that were not true. I started up the stairs when Lord Penford opened the door and tried to speak with Tinmore, to tell him he was mistaken—he must have heard Lord Tinmore shouting at me through the door. Tinmore took him to one of the drawing rooms to talk, but only for a minute or two, then Lord Penford returned to the hall and walked out. Lord Tinmore followed him.'

'Followed him?' Walsh repeated.

'Yes.' Was she telling Walsh too much? 'Tinmore was angry. First angry at me, then at Lord Penford, but without reason. I never saw him so angry.'

Walsh's face remained expressionless. 'Then what?'

She took a breath. 'Lord Penford left, but Tinmore followed him outside.' She swallowed. 'I heard a cry and I ran outside, too. Lord Tinmore was—was on the pavement.'

'You did not see him fall?' Walsh asked, somewhat ominously.

'I did not.'

He glanced away. 'And in what position did you find him when you came outside?'

She was confused. 'I—I—he was at the bottom of the steps.'

Squire Hedges spoke, his voice kinder than the other man's. 'This is a delicate question, we do realise, my lady. Mr Walsh means for you to describe the position of your husband's body. Describe how he looked.'

She closed her eyes, but it only made her see it all again. 'He—he was on his back, his head to one side in—in a pool of blood.'

'Where were his arms and hands?' Walsh asked.

'Up.' She raised her arms to demonstrate. 'Up above his head.'

Walsh nodded. 'Tell us, ma'am, was your husband ill?'

'Not that I knew of,' she responded.

But he had been acting strangely that day. Had he been ill? If so, she never should have left him. Although he always refused to allow her to tend to him when he was ill, so what good would her presence have done?

'He was acting very unlike himself, though. Very irrational,' she added.

Walsh's brows rose. 'Are you referring to your husband's suspicion that you and Lord Penford were having an affair?'

She felt her cheeks grow hot. 'Yes. That. There was no reason for him to think such a thing.'

Tinmore could not have known of her infatuation.

'Come now, Lady Tinmore,' Walsh began, in a smooth tone that did not ring true. 'Lord Tinmore was a very old man and Penford…' he paused significantly '…is not. Why would your husband not believe you engaged in a little dalliance?'

Her face turned hot with anger this time. 'I promised fidelity to my husband and I kept that promise. Lord Penford has always acted as a gentleman ought. He thought he could explain to my husband that my husband was wrong, but Tinmore would not listen. It was as though Tinmore was crazed.'

Walsh's brows rose. 'Crazed? But would not a man who suspected his wife of infidelity act crazed?'

She lifted her chin. 'I do not know. How would I know of such things?' Except, perhaps, from the loud arguments between her mother and father before her mother ran off with a lover. 'I do know I never saw my husband behave that irrationally before.'

Of course, she had never so blatantly defied him before. Why had she done so? She could admit to being weary of his dictates and it was true she wanted to see her sisters, to share Christmas with them.

But was it also true she wanted most to see Dell?

Walsh made an incomprehensible sound.

Did he believe her about Dell? Or not?

'Do you know for certain that your husband did not scuffle with Lord Penford?' he asked.

Her jaw stiffened when she tried to answer. 'I did not see what happened.'

Walsh glanced at Squire Hedges, who stood. 'Thank you very much, Lady Tinmore. That will be all for now. We will be questioning your servants, as well.'

The servants!

She had completely forgotten. This was Boxing Day. The servants would expect the day off. And their boxes. She was supposed to distribute their boxes. She'd scoured the attics and closets and old linens and had found enough cloth and old clothing to make a box for each family. Tinmore was to have given them money and she was to have stood at his side, handing them each a box.

'Please do not delay in speaking to them,' she requested. 'They expect to have the day off.'

Squire Hedges walked around the desk to escort her to the door. 'We will move as quickly as possible. Dixon will organise them for us.'

Certainly. Dixon would be pleased to do so, Lorene was sure. He would probably be pleased to tell them what to say, as well.

Squire Hedges opened the door for her and she stepped into the corridor where Dixon still stood on guard, but the area soon filled with other voices. Her sisters and their husbands. And Dell, who looked absorbed in his own thoughts.

'Tess. Genna. I forgot it was Boxing Day. I do not know where Tinmore put the purses for the servants and tenants.'

'Filkins will know,' Genna said. 'I'll find him.'

She dashed off, but her husband, the Marquis of Rossdale, heir to the Duke of Kessington, marched right past Dixon, entering the room with the Squire and the coroner.

'What is he doing?' Lorene asked, alarmed that Rossdale just barged in on the men.

Glenville, Tess's husband, answered, 'He wants to be certain they handle this properly. And as quietly as possible.'

She supposed a future duke would have some influence. It was a good thing to have someone even more important than Earl Tinmore to advocate for her.

And for Dell.

'Surely they will decide that it was merely a horrible accident,' she said.

'Dell tells us there will be an inquest,' Glenville explained. 'The coroner will have to find jurors and swear them in. They will have to see where the death occurred and view the body, so you cannot bury your husband until that takes place.'

It all sounded dreadful. She hated thinking of his body lying on his bed for as long as it took to find the jurors. Between Christmastide and winter weather, it could take more than a week.

She glanced at Dell, who leaned against the wall, a scowl on his face. He glanced up at her and his expression changed to something more tender, something like regret in his eyes.

She held his gaze for a moment before glancing away.

* * *

The afternoon was exhausting. Not only the sheer numbers of gifts to distribute, but over and over to hear and accept condolences, to answer questions about what had happened, to attempt to reassure the servants and tenants that Tinmore's heir, whoever he was, would do right by them.

She really had no idea what would happen to any of them, including herself. She had signed a marriage contract with him, but it stipulated that her sisters receive a handsome dowry, that her half-brother receive funds to purchase an advance in rank, and that she receive a modest living upon his death. As it turned out, neither of her sisters received the dowry, nor did her brother keep the money Tinmore bestowed on him. Would she fare any better?

She also did not know the heir to Tinmore's title, lands and fortune. A great-nephew, he'd said, but never named the man. Was he among the important people Tinmore invited to house parties and whom he called upon in London? She did not know. She hoped her reassurances to the servants and tenants would be true. Any decent man would see to it.

Lorene had insisted Tess leave to rest while she finished up and Genna had hurried away to see what Cook had provided them all to eat and to see to making tea immediately. Lorene was alone with her thoughts in this drawing room, the same room to which Tinmore had taken Dell the night before.

There was a light rap on the door.

Lorene rubbed her face and straightened in her chair. 'Come in.'

Dell appeared in the doorway. God help her, her body flushed with awareness just looking upon him, even though his expression was dark.

'May I disturb you for a moment?' he asked.

She stood. 'Yes. Come in. You do not disturb me.'

He crossed the room to her. 'I came to bid you goodbye.'

'Goodbye?' She had not thought of him leaving. The idea of it made her insides twist.

He nodded, still looking grim. 'My coachmen need their holiday and—' his impossibly blue eyes captured her gaze '—there is no reason to stay.'

'No reason?' Goodness. Could she do nothing but repeat his words?

'The Squire and Mr Walsh left.'

Had that been why he'd stayed this long? 'But surely you will stay for dinner.' If Cook left them anything to eat.

He shook his head. 'Ross and Glenville will stay. And your sisters. They will…' He paused. 'Look out for you.'

She'd have no friends here if they did not stay,

except perhaps for Mr Filkins, but he had no power or status.

'Still…' she murmured. Still, she wanted him to stay.

Again his eyes met hers, piercing into her as only his eyes could. 'It is better I leave. And better I stay away, lest my mere presence makes it seem as though—as though there was truth to Lord Tinmore's accusations.'

She could not deny the sense to that.

'So—' He bowed rather formally. 'Goodbye, Lady Tinmore.'

Her arm reached out to touch his. 'Dell,' she rasped. 'I am so sorry. I have caused you a great deal of trouble and I am so worried sick over what could happen—'

He took her hand in his warm, strong one. 'You have caused nothing.'

But she had! If she had not defied her husband, if she had not formed this schoolgirl worship of hers, none of this would have happened. Instead of standing here with him, feeling the heat of his palm against her fingers, she would be taking tea with Tinmore, hearing all his praise of his generosity and his complaints of those less than deserving. He'd correct something about how she gave away the boxes and instruct her on how a lady ought to have done it.

She lowered her gaze and he dropped her hand,

but she still did not wish to let him go. 'What of this inquest? Will you be accused of killing him?'

He could lose his life.

His face hardened. 'I did not kill him.'

She blushed. 'I know, but Dixon will have said—'

'He did not see what happened.'

She did not want to obsess about who the coroner and Squire Hedges would believe, not any more than she had already done.

She absently straightened the items left over on the table where she'd piled the boxes. 'Things change so rapidly.' She glanced back up at him. 'Yesterday was such a lovely day. A lovely Christmas. That was your doing, I know. You came to Summerfield House so we could all be together.'

His eyes darkened. 'Not only for you. I did not want to be alone.'

Her heart lurched for him. He'd lost his whole family. She reached out for him once more, placing her hand on his arm. 'But you also came here for us. I am so grateful to you.'

He glanced away. 'To go from such a happy day to such a horrific one—I am so sorry for it.'

She squeezed his arm. 'You must never apologise, not for what happened.'

His gaze pierced her again. 'It will get better, Lorene. I promise you.'

It must, but if he were held responsible for this dreadful event, she would never forgive herself.

She remained captured by his eyes. It seemed as though she would stay there for ever, but he abruptly broke contact and stepped back.

'I must leave.'

'When will I see you next?' It was the question of a lover, not the sort she should be asking, but it burst from her lips.

'At the inquest.'

He bowed again, turned and left.

Chapter Five

⦿⦿⦿⦿⦿⦿

The next several days for Lorene went by as if in a dream.

At least she had not been alone. Tess and Glenville stayed with her at Tinmore Hall and Genna and Rossdale called almost every day. Their presence further disgruntled the servants, but Lorene had long ago given up being accepted by them. Most were old retainers who had served Tinmore most of their lives. She knew nothing of the history of their service to him, but they'd perceived her as an interloper. When Tinmore had been alive, they'd barely been civil, but now their animosity was palpable. Only Filkins, Tinmore's secretary, exerted himself to be helpful to her, writing to the solicitors who were executors of Tinmore's will, notifying Tinmore's heir. The secretary even made tentative arrangements for Tinmore's burial, although the funeral had to meet the executor's approval. More than that, the funeral had to be delayed until all the jurors had paraded through the house to examine Tinmore's body and the place he fell. The jurors were good and lawful men recruited from neighbouring properties and, though they must not have been pleased to have their Christmastide so interrupted, they all seemed to take their task seriously.

By New Year's Eve, all jurors had seen what was required of them. The inquest was scheduled for January the thirteenth, a week after Twelfth Night, so as not to interfere with any of the festivities of those involved. There were no festivities at Tinmore Hall.

On January the eighth, Lord Tinmore's solicitors arrived from London and gathered all interested parties to a drawing room to read the will.

Lorene's sisters and their husbands accompanied her.

Rossdale muttered under his breath as they walked into room, 'He had better have done well by you.'

'I do not expect much,' Lorene cautioned. 'Contrary to what everyone believes, I did not marry him to make myself a wealthy widow.'

All she wanted was enough to purchase a little

cottage somewhere and to live quietly. A place where scandal would never touch her again. That had been all she asked of Tinmore. Enough for her to live comfortably in some quiet village somewhere and never, ever, be under the thumb of a husband again.

'Well, I think Tinmore owes you a great deal,' Genna huffed.

'He already gave us a great deal,' she responded.

They'd had beautiful places to live, plenty of food, social connections and the prettiest gowns money could buy, but now she needed no more than a little cottage where she could plant flowers in a garden and not be waited on hand and foot by a brigade of servants. One or two maids to help in the house and a man to do the heavy things would be lovely, but, even so, she could do with less.

They took their seats. This drawing room was the same room where the coroner and Squire Hedges had interviewed her and Dell. There were two men, the solicitor and his partner, both attended by Mr Filkins, who'd made certain the proper people had been invited. The room was filled with the servants who had been in Tinmore's employ the longest, Dixon, Wicky, the housekeeper, Lorene's lady's maid, and a smattering of others, including the estate manager and others important to the running of the estate. Lord

Tinmore's heir was not present, having declined to make the trip.

'Shall we begin,' the solicitor intoned, unfurling the document.

The room fell silent and he began to read.

Lorene fancied she could hear Tinmore's voice in the words and it disturbed her mostly because she had no feelings about it. She could not say she missed him. She could not even say she'd been fond of him.

The most she could say was she was glad she no longer had to listen to his voice.

She glanced around the room at the portraits of his ancestors on the walls. In them, though, she saw Tinmore's features. His brow here. A nose there. His eyes. His disapproving mouth.

She forced her gaze to the window. The snow had melted and the landscape bore the bleakness of winter and none of its beauty.

The solicitor's voice broke through. '… And to my widow, née Lorene Summerfield, the town house on Brook Street in Mayfair and an income of twelve thousand pounds a year…'

Genna gasped.

Lorene shook her head. Surely she had misheard.

The solicitor went on to specify certain carriages and horses that were to be hers, as well as some pieces of furniture and the gilt pianoforte that had been one of Tinmore's more extravagant gifts.

She murmured, 'It cannot be so.'

She'd not even known he owned a town house on Brook Street. While in London they'd stayed at the town house on Curzon Street, which she knew to be entailed.

The solicitor continued with a long list of other bequests to persons present and others who would need to be informed. When all the bequests had been spoken, he rolled up the will again and indicated that they were free to leave.

The servants and others milled around briefly talking among themselves. They seemed pleased, as well they should, because Tinmore had generously provided for them.

Finally they filed out of the room and Lorene walked up to the solicitor. 'Did I hear you correctly?'

He unrolled the will and reread the words pertaining to her.

She still could not believe it. 'How much income?'

'Twelve thousand.' The man rolled up the document again. 'Quite the generous man, was he not?'

Lorene nodded and turned away.

She'd wanted to be comfortable, but now she would not be comfortable after all.

She'd be wealthy.

Rossdale and Glenville also approached the solicitors and she withdrew to let them gather all the petty details of how and when she was to receive this fortune and the deed to the town house she did not want.

Tess took her arm and sat her back down on the sofa between Genna and herself.

'This is marvellous.' Genna took her hand. 'You will want for nothing!'

Tess looked at her with concern. 'Why are you so shocked? Surely you expected a decent inheritance?'

'I—I did not,' she said.

'Humph!' Genna made a face. 'He probably did it so the *beau monde* would call him generous.'

Tess shot Genna a quelling glance. 'No matter the reason, he *was* very generous.' Tess looked thoughtful. 'Although I suppose it is less than if he'd given you dower.'

Dower would have given her a third of the value of Tinmore's property for her lifetime, but she'd signed away her rights to dower when she married Tinmore in exchange for his providing for her siblings.

'I did not expect this.' Lorene pressed her fingers to her temple.

Tess took her other hand and squeezed it. 'Now you can come to town and live in a lovely town house and always be near me.' Tess and her husband spent most of the year in London.

But living in Mayfair was an appalling thought for Lorene. To be in town, among the *beau monde*, as Genna called them, the very people who whispered behind her back and remarked how she was just like her mother, who was scandal personified. She could hear them now, boasting how they knew all along she was after Tinmore's fortune.

Genna hugged her. 'This must be a huge relief to you. Now you will have no worries at all. You may do as you please. Everyone knows that widows are the most fortunate of women. You can make your own decisions. Control your own money. No husband will dictate to you.'

Tess gave her younger sister a horrified look. 'Genna! How can you say such a thing when you are so newly married?'

Genna laughed. 'I was not talking of me. Goodness knows, Ross is the best husband a woman could desire.' A dreamy look crossed her face, but fled again, replaced by a pragmatic one. 'I was speaking of other men.'

'Not Marc,' protested Tess.

'Of course not!' Genna appeared affronted. 'Your husband is nearly as wonderful as mine.'

Tess smiled and absently touched her abdomen. 'Yes, Marc is wonderful.'

Lorene regarded them and her heart swelled

with fondness. That deep core of contentment inside her would never leave her. Her sisters and brother had found what she had most wanted for them and what she once dreamed of for herself.

Love and marriage.

And Lorene was convinced that her decision to marry Tinmore had led to their happy outcomes, even if none of it had happened as she'd thought. She gazed from Tess to Genna and was glad she'd made the sacrifice to give up her own dreams of such happiness.

Dell's handsome face flashed through her mind, though she scolded herself for it. These feelings for him were simply ones she'd used to counter Tinmore's nagging displeasure or thoughtless disregard of her. Dell was the antithesis of her husband, the perfect gentleman, always doing what was right and good. But their connection was not a romantic one.

She must stop mooning over him. What if she'd somehow shown her secret regard for Dell and that was why Tinmore had accused them of being lovers?

She'd not seen Dell since the day after Tinmore died. How was he faring? She knew he stayed away deliberately lest people think they really had been lovers and, worse, lest they think he pushed Tinmore to his death because of it. Look how coming to her aid had hurt him.

'Lady Tinmore.' The solicitor was gesturing for her to approach.

She rose and walked over to where Rossdale and Glenville were still standing with him.

'Mr Filkins tells us the funeral and burial can take place as soon as two days hence,' the solicitor told her. 'That is, if you approve of such a simple ceremony. We could, of course, plan to wait until we can plan something grander.'

Wait? She could not bear to wait.

'No, let us proceed with a simple funeral in two days,' she said. 'I am certain that is what he would wish.' Not precisely. Tinmore would probably relish a great deal of pomp and fuss.

'As you desire.' The solicitor inclined his head. 'You will, of course, not be expected to attend.'

Wives and other female mourners were not welcome at funerals and burials. They might break down in tears, which would be most unseemly. Lorene, though, feared her lack of tears would be what offended.

She turned to Mr Filkins. 'Thank you for arranging this.'

He nodded solemnly.

She seemed to remember the will had provided well for him. 'Will you retire, then, Mr Filkins?'

'Who would hire me?' He attempted a smile. 'I have a cousin in Yorkshire. Mayhap I will settle there.'

She put a hand on his arm. 'You must let me know if you do. I will write to you.'

He looked embarrassed and pleased at the same time.

She released him. 'Do not think I am insensible to your assistance and—and your support, Mr Filkins. I will always cherish it.'

Now his face did turn red. She smiled and let him escape.

Tess walked up to her. 'Do you have need of me, Lorene? Because I am suddenly quite fatigued.'

'No. No need of you.' Tess's health and that of her baby were of utmost importance. 'Rest for as long as you like.'

Glenville peered worriedly at his wife. 'Are you unwell?'

Tess smiled and touched her abdomen. '*We* are quite well. But I am in great need of a nap.'

He gestured to the solicitor. 'I was going to accompany Mr Filkins and the solicitors to call upon the vicar, to make final arrangements for the funeral.'

'Go,' said Tess. 'I assure you I simply need a nap.'

Rossdale stood nearly at Lorene's elbow, listening to this exchange.

She turned to him. 'You and Genna need not stay, either, Rossdale. I am grateful that you were here for the reading of the will, but I suspect nothing more will require your presence today.'

Rossdale gave her a direct look. 'Are you certain?'

She nodded. 'I will relish some quiet time.'

He continued to peer into her face. 'Because we will stay if you need company.'

'No, at the moment I desire solitude more than company.'

She thanked the solicitors and walked with the entire entourage to the hall, saying goodbye to Genna and Rossdale, and letting the others know she would see them all at dinner. Glenville, Filkins and the solicitors called for their topcoats and hats. The vicarage was only a short distance away and, after some discussion, they decided to walk there rather than order the carriage.

Lorene walked up the stairs with Tess and saw her to her bedchamber. 'Are you certain you are all right?' she asked.

Tess took her hand. 'Very certain. You could do with a rest, too, you know. We have some more days to get through.'

Tess meant the funeral. And the inquest.

Lorene gave her sister a kiss on the cheek. 'Perhaps I will.'

But when Tess disappeared into her room, Lorene wrapped her arms around herself for a moment and leaned against the wall. The thought of retiring to her bedchamber or to her sitting room or to any room in this house was unbearable. Left alone with her thoughts? It was the last thing she wanted.

But she also did not want company. She loved that her sisters and their husbands were so attentive, but, to a certain extent she had to hide her emotions from them. The only one who knew how she felt inside about Tinmore's death was Dell. The others might guess or even presume, but they did not hear it from her lips. She'd told Dell, though. She'd told him that her overwhelming feeling about her husband's tragic death was... relief.

Thinking of it now filled her with shame. What sort of wife felt like this? Not even sad for him?

These were precisely the thoughts she sought to escape.

She glanced at the walls surrounding her and suddenly wished they would disappear. Even the air in the house felt oppressive. She wanted to breathe fresh air. She wanted to be free of walls. She wanted to feel the way she had walking to Summerfield House on Christmas Day.

She hurried to her bedchamber and pulled out her warmest cloak, the one she'd worn that day. She kicked off her slippers, put on her half-boots, gloves and a warm hat and she was ready to escape.

Lorene hurried down a back stairway and slipped out a side door rarely used by anyone. She crossed the park in front of the house in the opposite direction from the way Glenville, Filkins and the solicitors went to the vicarage. She had no destination in mind except to walk far enough to be off Tinmore's land where she still felt his spirit scolding and belittling her. When she'd walked to Summerfield House on Christmas Day, she'd been free of him. She walked in that direction now.

The day was grey and dismal, like her spirits, and her mind spun into knots of confusion. How could Tinmore have given her such wealth when she could not even bring herself to mourn him? What should she do with that money? With that Mayfair town house? She did not want to think of such things!

The further she walked, the more her mind cleared itself. She was left with only the sensation of inhaling cold air into her lungs and feeling the wind sting her cheeks. The earth beneath her was frozen hard and that cold seeped through her boots. The wind whistled in her ears and rustled the bushes and trees.

It felt glorious!

She quickened her step and wished she could be like the deer that bounded across the fields. She wished she had the courage to run so free.

Why not?

She gathered her skirts in her hands and took flight, dashing across the field with nothing and no one to stop her.

* * *

Dell had been restless the whole day, knowing from Ross that Tinmore's will would be read this day. Would Tinmore have done well by her?

If not, she needn't want for anything. He'd help her himself if it came to that. Most likely, though, he need not concern himself over it. Ross or Glenville would step in for Lorene if it were necessary.

Any help he gave would arouse suspicions. Make it seem there was a connection between them, when there was not. True, he was related to the Summerfields, but the connection was through a distant ancestor. Possibly he was no blood relation at all. It was said the Summerfield sisters were not fathered by Sir Hollis, but by their mother's different lovers.

Their appearance certainly fuelled that rumour. The three ladies were about as unlike as sisters could be. Genna was tall and blonde. Tess, shorter and chestnut-haired. Lorene's hair was the shade of fine mahogany, although it glistened with auburns and golds when the sun hit it just right. She was the shortest of the three even though the oldest. Their eye colours were different as well. Only Lorene had those dark brown eyes that seemed perpetually warm and inviting.

He liked Lorene. He could admit that much, could he not? But that did not matter, did it? He did not want to feel any connection with her. He did not want anyone to matter to him. His family had mattered and their loss was too painful to bear.

Grief threatened to engulf him once again.

He strode out of the house and down to the stables. A good ride would set him to rights.

Within a few minutes his horse was saddled and he was galloping over fields and up the hills that made the undulating Lincolnshire landscape so pleasing to the eye. He gave his mare a rest at the crest of a hill. Both he and the animal sucked in the brisk winter air and savoured it.

Out of the corner of his eye he spied a figure in the distance. He turned and knew immediately it was Lorene, even though he was atop the hill and she below, running as if the devil himself was chasing her. What a lovely sight. The hood of her cloak had fallen back and her hat was held on to her neck only by its ribbons. Her hair had come loose of its pins and flew wild and free behind her.

He shook himself. *Why* was she running? Was she in trouble?

He signalled his horse to action and they galloped down the hill as fast as they were able. No matter his promise to avoid her—if she needed him, he would be there for her.

He reached the valley ahead of her, still a distance away. She stopped immediately when he came into her view and waited while he slowed his horse.

He rode to her and dismounted. 'Lorene' was all he could manage.

'Dell.' Her voice was equally as hushed.

'How—how do you fare? Are you in need of assistance? You were running.' What was this unease he felt being near her? She—no one—could matter that much.

Her lovely smooth cheeks turned a deeper shade of pink. 'I—I *was* running. Silly of me. I simply—wanted to run.' She sounded out of breath.

His shoulders relaxed. 'I saw you and thought something was wrong.'

'Nothing…bad.' But she remained unsmiling. 'I just needed to run. Hoydenish of me, I realise, but I did not expect to be seen.'

He felt the rebuke. 'Forgive me. Perhaps I should not have—'

She interrupted him. 'Oh, no. I did not mean any criticism of you. I simply realised how I must look to you.'

He had never seen her lovelier. 'May I ask the reason you—?'

She cut him off again. 'Why I was running? I—I felt so closed in all of a sudden. Penned in, you know. I just wanted to escape. For a little bit. I will return, of course, and preside as hostess for dinner.'

They began to walk, a leisurely aimless pace that his horse was content to follow.

He spoke first. 'Ross told me the solicitors had arrived to read the will.'

She made an anguished sound. 'Indeed. They read it today.'

'Did they?' he asked.

She nodded, but the expression on her face was doleful.

'What happened? Did Tinmore not provide for you?' The miserable miser.

She gave a dry laugh. 'On the contrary, I—I inherited a fortune. And a town house. And carriages and such.'

His brow knitted. 'That is good news, is it not?'

She would be a wealthy widow, but she would also be prey to every impoverished, fortune-seeking gentleman in town. That was not good news.

She smiled wanly. 'I am churlish to be distressed by it, I know.' Her gaze was earnest. 'But, Dell, I did not want a fortune. I did not expect it. I am not even sure I deserve it, the way I am feeling about his death.' She rolled her eyes. 'Or not feeling. I cannot seem to feel much of anything. That is so very bad of me, I know.'

He wanted to remind her that Tinmore did often treat her very shabbily, especially that last night.

'It is honest,' he said instead.

She sighed. 'That is another thing. I am *not*

honest. I am hiding how I feel. You are the only one I have told.'

It warmed him that he would be the person in whom she confided. He was a confidant to his sister when they were growing up, but he had not been there for his sister at the end.

'There is no reason to speak aloud what might rain criticism upon your head.' Or what might fuel Tinmore's accusation about the two of them.

Her shoulders relaxed. 'I am so glad you think so.'

They walked a few more steps in silence.

'I must decide what to do with this fortune,' she said, as if musing to herself. 'At one moment I decide to give it all away; at another, I think I must keep it and live in a manner that does not please me.'

'What would please you?' he asked.

She sighed again. 'I just want to hide in a little cottage somewhere.'

That surprised him.

'You do not have to decide now, you know,' he said. 'You have your year of mourning. Plenty of time to figure it out then.'

'My year of mourning…' she repeated, her voice trailing off. 'Where can I go for that year?' She spoke firmly. 'I will not stay at Tinmore Hall or in its dower house—or, at least, I do not want to.'

'I am certain Ross and Genna would welcome

you.' He knew his friend well enough to be certain of that. 'Or Tess and Glenville.'

She frowned. 'Tess and Glenville live with his parents. And the baby is coming. I should be in the way.'

'Ross and Genna, then.'

'Theirs is such a visible, high-society life,' she said with feeling. 'It would not suit me at all.'

The sun fell lower and the sky turned greyer. The temperature dropped and Lorene wrapped her cloak more tightly around her.

After a while he said, 'Then stay at Summerfield House.' What could be better for her than to be among people she knew since childhood, people who cared about her?

She stopped and averted her gaze so he could not see her face. 'Summerfield House?' Her voice sounded anguished.

He suddenly felt discomfited. 'I would not be there, of course. Nothing to fuel gossip, I assure you. I merely thought you might be most comfortable where you grew up.'

She whirled towards him and flung her arms around him. 'Dell.' Her voice still sounded strained. 'I could not desire anything more.'

He held her against him, glad to give her some comfort. Well he knew how necessary comfort could be. 'It is done, then. We will accomplish it somehow without causing talk. Say you are leasing the place or something.'

He released her, but she took his hands in hers. 'I should be able to breathe in Summerfield House.' She seemed to collect herself then, letting go and avoiding his eyes. 'I thank you.'

'It is the least I can do,' he said.

It was a pragmatic idea. He did not need the house and she did. It meant nothing more.

He glanced at the sky. 'I think you should turn back now, though, before it gets too late.'

She nodded. 'Walk with me a little?'

'Of course.'

When they reached the spot where he'd met her, they said their goodbyes.

'I will see you again, will I not, Dell?' she asked.

'At the inquest,' he said. After that he would return to London.

Her face fell. 'Of course. At the inquest.'

Chapter Six

Four days after Tinmore's burial, Dell, Ross and Genna rode in Dell's carriage to a village inn near Tinmore's estate where the inquest was to take place.

As they entered the town there was little to indicate that anything noteworthy would occur there that day. A few more carriages, more people on the street, perhaps. Dell's coachman pulled up in front of the inn and the three passengers stepped out to the pavement below.

Dell took a steadying breath. He'd attended courts-martial while in the army, but an inquest was something new to him. A court-martial determined guilt or innocence, an inquest merely whether a crime had been committed.

And if it was ruled that a crime had been committed, he would be accused of it.

He followed Ross and Genna through the inn

to the room where the inquest would be held. As soon as they entered the room heads turned and murmurs erupted from those already present. What did they expect? To see an earl accused of cuckoldry and murder?

Ross led the way to seats at the front of the room, assuming, as the heir to the Duke of Kessington always did, that they would be provided for him. As they reached that row, Dell saw Ross was indeed correct—and that Lorene, Tess and Glenville were already seated there. Dell took the last seat, as far away as possible from Lorene and, he hoped, from the chance someone would make something of him sitting with her family. Tess and Glenville included him in their greetings to Ross and Genna. Lorene acknowledged him with a slight incline of her head. He returned it in a like manner.

Two gentlemen in London garb sat in the row behind them. Tinmore's solicitors, perhaps? Others he recognised as servants from Tinmore Hall. Dixon was among them. Dell's coachmen would be there soon, no doubt, after the horses were stabled. Who the other people were, Dell did not know. Curious villagers, perhaps.

Closer to London an inquest into the death of the Earl of Tinmore might have caught the interest of various newspaper reporters. Thank God they were this distance away and that the Christmas and Twelfth Night festivities had occupied most peoples' minds.

Dell's chair faced a table behind which the magistrate and coroner would sit. In front of it was a dais where Dell presumed those who were testifying would stand. To the left of the table were twelve chairs for the jury, the people who would ultimately determine his fate.

On the Peninsula, he'd faced sabres and cannon and muskets and battle-crazed enemy soldiers in the throes of blood lust. These he knew how to fight. With what weapons did one fight lies and distortions?

Truth? His word?

He girded himself. He'd done nothing criminal. He'd done nothing but come to Lorene's defence. Tinmore had set his own fate in motion when he'd unjustly accused her of infidelity.

That fact would be of little consolation if this inquest believed Dixon.

Ross leaned towards him and whispered near his ear, 'They had better do the right thing.'

Or what? Dell wanted to say. What could Ross do if the jury decided Tinmore had been murdered?

The minutes ticked by and finally Squire Hedges and Mr Walsh entered the room and took their seats. Twelve men followed them and noisily settled in their chairs. All wore what appeared to be their Sunday best. Some had coats of fine cloth, others were more simply attired. Some were nearly as old at Tinmore himself; others looked barely out of schoolroom.

The formalities were attended to and the first witness was called.

'The Earl of Penford.'

Dell started. He'd expected Dixon to be the first one questioned.

Walsh gestured to the dais facing the table.

Dell stood, walked to the dais and faced the magistrate and coroner.

The coroner questioned him much as he had at Tinmore Hall. Dell answered as he had that day. He kept his voice strong and unwavering, telling of escorting Lorene back from the Christmas dinner, of hearing Tinmore's accusation, of coming to her defence, of what happened on the steps of Tinmore Hall.

Would the jury believe him? When he finished he glanced at their faces, but it was impossible to tell if he had convinced them or if they thought he was trying to get away with murder.

'That is all, Lord Penford,' the coroner said. 'But I may have more questions, so please remain available.'

Dell took his seat.

Walsh glanced at a piece of paper before looking up and saying, 'Mr John Jones.'

Dell's coachman was called next, though whether his presence was to support the truth or dispute it he couldn't fathom.

Jones came forward, was sworn in, and testified that he did not see Tinmore fall. The man would have lied if Dell had asked him to. Should he have done so?

No. The truth must be told, nothing else.

Walsh asked Jones, 'Did you have any reason to believe that Lord Penford had a dalliance with Lady Tinmore?'

Dell's insides clenched. Would the jury believe that he and Lorene had not been lovers?

Jones looked surprised at Walsh's question. 'Me? I never heard of it.'

Lord Tinmore's physician was called next and testified that it was entirely possible that Tinmore had experienced an attack of apoplexy.

Dell's hopes rose. An attack of apoplexy made perfect sense.

Although a conspiracy between two lovers to murder made a much better story.

'Thank you, Doctor.' Walsh inclined his head. 'That will be all.'

The coroner turned to Lorene next. 'Lady Tinmore, would you be so kind?' He gestured to the dais.

She stood and walked to the dais with her head held high. Her courage in the face of what could be humiliating questioning was indeed something to admire. She answered the questions without hesitation, keeping her composure throughout, but it disturbed Dell that she must endure this questioning in front of all these people.

Dell wished he could tell what the jury members were thinking as she talked. All he could tell was that they seemed to be listening intently.

The next person called to testify was Ross.

'Tell us, my lord,' Walsh asked deferentially, 'of your acquaintance with Lord Penford.'

Ross's voice practically boomed. 'We have been friends since our school days. He is closer than a brother to me.'

'Do you have any reason to suspect an…attachment between your friend and Lady Tinmore?'

'None,' Ross responded. 'And I have had occasion to witness them through their whole acquaintance.'

Except Ross had not been present the few times when Dell and Lorene had been alone. Like a few days ago when he'd seen her running across the fields like a young deer, so if Dell and Lorene had engaged in an affair, Ross would not have known. Would the jury realise this? Would they believe Ross or think him trying to cover for his friend?

Walsh finally called Dixon to the dais.

Dell clenched a fist and tried to control his

anger as Dixon spun his tale of infidelity and con-spiracy and murder as dramatically as Dell feared he would.

But Dixon also admitted he had not seen Tin-more fall and had never seen evidence of an af-fair. Unfortunately, one of the footman testified to seeing Dell embrace Lorene. It had been that one moment of comforting her after Tinmore's death.

Could that one brief moment get him hung for murder?

Walsh excused the footman and asked the crowd if there was anyone present who witnessed Lord Tinmore's fall. No one came forward.

Squire Hedges instructed the jury to deliber-ate on their decision and the twelve men filed out to do so.

Ross turned to Lorene, Tess and Glenville. 'I arranged a private dining room for us with some refreshment.'

Dell remained seated while the group gathered themselves to retire to this private dining room.

Ross leaned down to him. 'You, too, Dell.'

Lorene caught glimpses of Dell from across the private dining room while the others discussed how the proceedings had gone. He sat at a slight distance from the rest of them and appeared to be caught in his own thoughts.

'What do you think, Ross?' Glenville said.

'The physician made a good case for an attack of apoplexy.'

'He did,' said Rossdale frowning. 'It all depends on who the jury believe, Dell or Dixon.'

Lorene sipped a cup of tea, not too reassured of the outcome, even though the inquest had not been as horrible as she'd feared. She'd feared the infidelities of her parents would be brought up.

Who knew what the jurors would think? They surely knew of her parents. Who had not heard all the stories? They might presume she was just like her mother and, therefore, capable of colluding in a murder. It had not occurred to her to fear what her fate might be if the jury determined Tinmore's death was murder. She was more concerned about Dell. What if, because of her scandalous family, he was accused of murder? How could she bear that, when he'd merely been attempting to come to her defence?

She glanced over at Dell and found him looking at her. Their eyes held for a moment and she experienced that schoolgirl thrill she feared had led them into all this trouble and that was so terribly out of place at this time, in this situation.

She glanced away again and lifted the teacup to her mouth.

She felt penned in by these walls, by the inquest itself. How often had she felt that same sensation when at Tinmore Hall, when in the pres-

ence of her husband? If Glenville and Rossdale
were correct and Tinmore's death would be declared accidental, perhaps then she could feel free.

She was afraid to hope.

Tess sat down next to her. 'This will be over
soon. The solicitors will be gone. All will be settled. Have you decided yet whether to come to
town with Genna or with me?'

'I would not impose on Lord and Lady Northdon.' Lord and Lady Northdon were Glenville's
parents with whom Tess lived.

'Nonsense!' Tess exclaimed. 'They would be
delighted to have you stay with us. And it would
be so nice to have you with me when the baby
is born.'

'We will all be with you when the baby is
born!' Genna cried. She slid into the seat on the
other side of Lorene. 'You must come with Ross
and me, Lorene. We have plenty of room and you
will be close by Tess. We can see her every day,
if you like. You can't stay at Tinmore Hall, that
horrid place!'

'I won't stay at Tinmore Hall,' Lorene said.
'But I do not want to stay in town. If I did, apparently I have a house of my own to live in.'

'Do you plan to stay at that horrid dower
house?' Genna made a face.

Lorene glanced away. 'Not the dower house. I
prefer no connection at all to Tinmore Hall.'

Genna threw up her hands. 'Where then?'

Lorene took a breath. 'Summerfield House.'

'Summerfield House!' Genna and Tess cried in unison.

'Dell offered it to me.' Even talking about it made it feel like a refuge. 'To stay there through my year of mourning.'

Genna jumped up and rushed over to Dell. She gave him a kiss on the cheek. 'How very kind of you, Dell. Lorene will be among people who love her.'

Instead of servants who resented her.

Tess spoke up. 'But will that not cause talk? I mean, there is the matter of Tinmore's accusation.'

'Pfft!' exclaimed Genna. 'What does that matter? She will be home!'

'Marc.' Tess turned to her husband who had been conversing with Rossdale. 'What do you think?'

He smiled at her. 'About what, my love?'

'About Lorene staying at Summerfield House during her year of mourning.'

Glenville looked taken aback. 'It is Penford who must say.'

Dell's gaze rose. 'There should be no talk, Tess. I will not be there.' His glance swept all of them. 'But you must visit any time you wish. Lorene may treat it as her house.'

Rossdale turned to him. 'Very decent of you, Dell.'

He shrugged. 'It is at no great cost to me.'

But it meant everything to Lorene.

There was a knock at the door.

The innkeeper poked his head in. 'Squire Hedges said to fetch you. The jury has made its decision.'

'Already?' Genna cried.

Was that a good omen or a bad one?

Lorene's gaze met Dell's once again. Her hands trembled as she set down her teacup.

They left the private dining room and made their way back to the room where the inquest had been held. The jurors were seated, but the spectators were scrambling for their seats. Finally Squire Hedges silenced them all and asked the jury for their conclusions.

Lorene gripped the ribbons of her reticule.

'We find Lord Tinmore's death to be accidental,' the jury foreman announced.

Dell would have been glad to merely slip away after the inquest, but Ross offered to pay for drinks all around. The innkeeper led everyone to the public room and the taps flowed with a spirit of celebration Dell thought inappropriate.

Almost everyone who'd been present for the inquest stayed for the free drinks. Not Dixon, though, Dell noticed right away. Some local gentry took this opportunity to make Dell's acquaintance.

'Bad business, sir,' one man said, lifting a large tankard to his mouth. 'Came out all right in the end, eh?'

Dell nodded, not knowing how else to respond.

Some members of the jury came up to him, eager to explain why they determined Tinmore's death to be accidental.

'It all fit,' one gentleman said. 'What you said. What the physician said. We weighed the facts and did not give credence to suspicions and assumptions.'

'I am grateful you listened to the truth,' Dell said. 'I am only sorry that this interrupted your holiday celebrations.'

'Nothing to apologise for, m'lord,' another juror said. 'Seems to me Lord Tinmore caused all the trouble.'

'All that nonsense about Lady Tinmore,' another added. 'We've never heard a word of gossip about her and gossip travels, y'know.'

As the group turned louder and more jovial, Dell looked for a quiet place where he might sit and wait until Ross and Genna were ready to leave. He found Lorene seated alone at a table in a dark corner of the room.

As he approached, she said, 'I am hiding.'

He could not help but smile. 'May I hide with

you? I fear the gaiety does not suit me at the moment.'

She gestured to the chair next to her. 'It does not suit me either. I am glad without measure that the jury decided as they did, but none of it seems cause for celebration.' He sat and she continued. 'I am so sorry for what this has put you through, Dell. You did not deserve it.'

'It is over. We can put it behind us.' He resisted an impulse to take her hand.

Her lovely brow furrowed. 'I do hope you will not be plagued with gossip about this in town.'

'Do not worry over me.' Having someone be concerned about him was too close to him caring about them in return and he did not want that. 'Tend to yourself. Do as you like at Summerfield House.'

She sighed. 'Do as I like? I wonder if I know how?'

'You will have your year of mourning to learn.'

She smiled. 'I will, won't I? And thanks to you I will spend my year back home. I cannot tell you how grateful I am for that.'

Her sincerity warmed him.

'Do not stay long at Tinmore Hall,' he cautioned. 'You are welcome to move in tomorrow, if you like. I am leaving Summerfield in the morning.'

Her smile fled. 'So soon.'

He needed to put some distance between them, not only to forestall gossip, but also to keep from thinking of her so much.

'I will miss you, Dell,' she said.

As Dell suggested, the very next day Lorene moved to Summerfield House. By week's end her sisters and their husbands left as well. It took time, though, to feel at home.

Both she and the Summerfield servants kept a reserve between them that had not been there when she'd been at home. It took time for her to shed the veneer of Lady Tinmore—and for the servants to accept her again as plain Lorene Summerfield. But, slowly she accepted their coddling and their pampering, as if she were still a small girl with a stubborn case of fever, and generously they provided it.

At first she dressed in black, although she did not mourn Lord Tinmore. He'd been generous to her in some ways, in the fortune he left her, in the gifts he'd given her, even in his willingness to help her siblings. She had given to him, too, though, she realised. He'd been a recluse before their marriage, but afterwards he'd rejoined the world, returning to London and the House of Lords, becoming alive again after years of withdrawal.

Unfortunately, becoming alive meant becoming tyrannical.

She'd done her best, though, to acquiesce to his demands; that is, until her one defiance on Christmas Day.

After a week or so, she put her black dresses away, donning them only if someone called and people rarely did. Instead she wore the old clothes she'd worn before her marriage. She needed to impress no one with her finery. She could be comfortable. She could be herself.

She played her old pianoforte every day, sometimes for hours if her spirits turned low. She'd left the gilt pianoforte at Tinmore Hall. She never wanted to see it again.

When the weather turned fair she took long walks—often breaking into a run and reminding herself of Dell discovering her that day he offered her this respite here.

One day coming from a long run, she returned to the house and walked through the rooms, noticing chips in the plasterwork, frayed upholstery on the furniture and walls in need of fresh paint.

She hurried off to find the estate manager who was in his office in the far west wing.

'Mr Barry, I have a request for you.' Mr Barry had been the estate manager for as long as Lorene could remember. Though of an age with her late father, he was strong and vital, built like a firmly planted tree one could safely lean upon and be sheltered by its leaves.

'Indeed, my lady,' he said. 'How may I be of service?'

'I would like for you to write to Lord Penford and ask if I might oversee refurbishment of the house. I should like to restore it to its former beauty.'

He nodded. 'I will do so, if you ask it, but could you not write to him yourself?'

'I could,' she admitted. A widow could write to a single man. 'But I do believe he will be more honest in his answer if you make the request.'

Before a fortnight had passed, Dell's letter to Mr Barry arrived, giving her permission and asking Barry to charge the costs to his accounts. That Lorene would not allow, though she convinced Mr Barry to keep it secret. She was, after all, wealthy enough to pay for every bit of it.

Lorene threw herself into working room by room, project by project. Soon the house shone with the beauty she remembered when her mother had still lived there and visitors came often. As the beauty was restored, so were her spirits. She felt useful, a part of something bigger than herself, and happy again, as she'd been in her childhood days. She also became stronger in body and will.

* * *

Ross and Genna visited briefly at the beginning of summer and marvelled at what she had done. Tess gave birth to a baby boy, second in line to become Viscount Northdon. Edmund wrote of his and Amelie's son thriving.

They were settled, safe and happy—Tess, Genna and Edmund.

One day on a walk to the hill looking down on Summerfield House, Lorene let go of them. No longer did she need to take care of them, protect them, see to their happiness. It was her turn now and she knew precisely what she wanted.

A house and property of her own. Nothing grand, just a place where she could be left in peace, as she'd been this whole year, a place where no man could tell her what she could do and not do. From now on she would take care of herself and do whatever she pleased.

First she would dispose of her Mayfair town house, then her carriages and horses. She'd find an agent to search for the perfect property for her, but she would have to go to town to accomplish both. She felt strong enough to face London, strong enough to refuse to care about London society.

Who certainly did not care about her.

Chapter Seven

March 1818

Dell made an impulsive decision to leave London after the passing of the Indemnity Bill. Over a year had passed and he knew from Ross and Genna that Lorene, her year of mourning over, planned to leave Summerfield House. By the time he reached there, she would be gone. He needed the respite of a few days in Lincolnshire and Summerfield had become a home without the memories and ghosts of Penford, his family's estate.

He'd been opposed to the Indemnity Bill. It seemed to him that the rights of citizens were being taken away instead of respected. Last year the government suspended Habeas Corpus and now this year it absolved any official of wrongdoing even if they'd abused their powers. Where was the protection of the citizens in this?

He chose to ride his horse to Lincolnshire, to take his time, and forgo the services of his valet. He wanted to be alone.

In London Dell had felt a profound need to carry on the work of his father, a zealous Whig reformer. Dell believed in much of what the Whigs stood for, but not all of it. For one, the Whigs had been opposed to the war with Napoleon, but Dell fought in that war. Napoleon had been a dangerous tyrant bent on conquering the world. Dell would have given his life to vanquish him.

He wished he'd been a part of that last great battle, Waterloo, when Napoleon was defeated. But it had been shortly before the battle when he'd been in Brussels awaiting the call to arms that Ross showed up, informing him of the fire that destroyed his family.

He must try to live for all of them, his father, brother, mother and sister. To champion the Whig cause like his father and brother. To heed the needs of the poor like his mother. To enjoy balls and routs and musicales like his sister. His family were the voices in his head. And in his ear was Ross's father, the Duke of Kessington, urging him to marry and beget an heir to carry on the family line. The Duke's wife was pushing Lord Brackton's daughter, Lady Alice, the young woman she and the Duke wished Ross would have married instead of Genna.

Dell had no objections to Lady Alice, a young woman of good temper and excellent reputation, but he didn't want such an attachment. He did not want to care about anyone when losing them could send him into despair.

Ross was the sole person with whom Dell felt close. They were friends, not family, but if anything happened to Ross, Dell would have no one. Even so, he tried not to depend on Ross, although Ross continued to reach out to him in friendship. At times Ross's friendship had been all that stood between him and the abyss.

When Ross became involved with Genna, it threw Dell into company with the Summerfield sisters. With Lorene. Because of Ross he'd invited them all to Summerfield House that Christmas. Last summer, when Tess went into labour, Dell had a terror of her dying. Women died in childbirth. Princess Charlotte died in childbirth last November.

That convinced him. He kept his distance after that. He was at too great a risk of having all of them matter too much to him.

On the other hand, Lady Alice did not inspire those same feelings of connection.

He needed some time at Summerfield House. He needed time to think. He'd missed that house in Lincolnshire. And if he were completely honest, he'd also missed Lorene.

He'd thought about her much too often. Whenever he glimpsed a woman on the street who resembled her. Whenever he heard someone play a pianoforte.

After his second full day on the road, Dell rode into Wansford village, to the Haycock Inn. He'd stayed at the inn on previous trips and the innkeeper, Mr Percival, greeted him by name.

'Lord Penford, how good to see you back.' The innkeeper bowed.

Dell extended his hand. 'Good to see you, too, Percival.'

'You will be wanting a room, will you not, m'lord,' Percival went on. 'I just now gave away my best room to a lady traveling with her maid.'

'Any room will do,' Dell said. 'I merely need to clean off the dust from the road and taste one of your meat-and-potato pasties.'

Percival glanced beyond him. 'Is your valet with you?'

Dell lifted his bag. 'I rode alone this trip.'

'Come with me, then.' Mr Percival led him up the stairway past the room the innkeeper had called his best.

The room he showed Dell was perfectly adequate.

'Shall I send a man up to assist you?' the innkeeper asked.

Dell shook his head. 'I will manage.'

After the innkeeper left, Dell brushed the dirt from his clothing and washed his face and hands. He thought he might skip shaving. This was dinner at an inn, after all.

He opened the door and entered the hallway. Ahead of him the lady who had been given the best room stepped out as well.

Something about the way she moved.

But that was too fanciful. She would be in London by now.

Keeping a comfortable distance, he followed the lady to the stairway and down the stairs.

When she reached the hall, Mr Percival strode over to her. 'My lady, your dining room awaits you.'

'Thank you, sir,' Dell heard her say.

She turned then, perhaps to see who followed her.

Her eyes widened.

Dell froze on a step, feeling as though the air had been knocked from his lungs. 'Lorene.'

It took her a moment to react. 'Dell. What a surprise.'

Mr Percival grinned. 'You are acquainted?' He laughed. 'Of course you are. Lords and ladies are always acquainted.'

Dell collected himself and descended the rest of the stairs. He bowed to her. 'I hope you are well.'

'I am in very good health, thank you.' She smiled nervously. 'I—I was on my way to dinner.'

'Were you?' Why were his insides squeezed tight? 'I highly recommend the meat-and-potato pasty.'

'You have stayed here before?' she asked, her voice rising.

He found it difficult to breathe. 'Yes. More than once.'

Mr Percival spoke. 'Lord Penford usually stays in the room I gave to you, my lady. As I said, it is the best in the house.'

'Oh?' She turned to Dell with a worried look on her face. 'Did I take your room? I am so sorry.'

'Not at all,' he responded, his words coming too fast. He took a breath and slowed them. 'I am quite comfortable.'

'Yes. Well.' She lowered her gaze, then glanced towards the innkeeper. 'I must not keep Mr Percival waiting.'

'Come, then, my lady.' Percival gestured for her to follow. 'I will show you to your dining room.'

They walked to the entrance to the public rooms, but as Mr Percival opened the door, Lorene turned back to Dell.

'Would—would you care to join me?' Her brows knitted. 'That is, if you are not engaged.'

'I am quite alone.' He should refuse, but instead he said, 'I would be honoured to join you.'

'Excellent idea!' exclaimed the innkeeper. He opened the door and waited for them to pass.

Dell crossed the hall to Lorene and offered his arm. The touch of her hand felt so familiar, so pleasant that for a moment it felt as if he were about to enter a sun-filled garden instead of a dimly lit room filled with the scent of hops, roasted meat and the buzz of travellers' discourse.

The innkeeper led them to a door and into a small private dining room with a window that let in the waning light of the day. Outside the window was a view of the park and the River Nene.

Mr Percival held a chair for Lorene facing the beautiful view. 'So shall I tell you what our fare is for this day?'

'I am content with the pasties, if Lord Penford recommends them,' Lorene said.

'I do,' Dell responded. 'For me, as well, and some ale.'

Lorene glanced up at the innkeeper. 'Do you have wine? Some claret, perhaps?'

'Indeed, my lady. Your food will arrive shortly.' He bowed and left.

Dell felt too restless to sit right away. He walked to the window. 'Pleasant view.'

'It is lovely,' she agreed.

He turned to her. 'Do you travel alone?' He suddenly thought it was not a good thing for her to travel alone.

She stood again and joined him at the window. 'My maid travels with me. But she was ill from the ride so I sent her to bed and ordered soup to be brought to the room.'

'Kind of you,' he murmured.

She slanted him a glance. 'She was one of the maids at Summerfield House. She had a great desire to see London, so I offered her the chance to come with me. I hope you do not mind.'

'Why should I mind?' She and her sisters had grown up at Summerfield House. 'The servants always felt more yours than mine.'

A serving girl entered the room with a pitcher of ale for Dell and a bottle of wine for Lorene. She curtsied and quickly left again.

Dell poured Lorene's wine and handed her the glass. He filled his tankard with ale and took a long sip.

Lorene watched him, which made him self-conscious. 'Forgive me. I developed a great thirst on the road.'

'Do you come from London?' she asked.

'Yes. I needed a few days away, I'm afraid. I decided to travel to Summerfield House to see what you have done with it.' He paused. 'Ross and Genna told me you were to have left the house a week ago.'

'I was a little delayed.' She smiled. 'Who could imagine we would meet on the road?'

'I certainly did not think it a possibility.' He'd planned this trip thinking she would be gone by the time he arrived. He'd never guessed they might arrive at the same inn on the same day. 'I assume my man of business took care of the expenses you incurred. For the refurbishment and repairs.' Why was it so difficult to talk to her?

She glanced down at her wine. 'It was all settled.' She returned to her chair and lifted the glass to her lips. 'I do hope what I've done will meet with your approval.'

He had no doubt it would.

He sat opposite her. 'I did not mean for you to work, Lorene. I meant for you to have leisure.'

Her lovely face filled with pleasure. 'Oh, but I adored it! I loved being useful and it was a joy to see the house restored to its former beauty.'

He liked seeing her happy. 'Then I am glad for it.'

The serving girl returned with their pasties, along with a loaf of bread warm from the oven and a large wedge of cheese.

'Thank you,' Lorene said to the girl. 'This looks delicious.'

The girl curtsied and left.

They cut into the pastry and steam rose from the inside. Lorene took a bite. 'Mmm… You were correct. This is delicious.'

He beamed inside. 'Simple fare, but I would take this over many a meal I've eaten in Mayfair.'

'Simple fare is often such a comfort.' She cut another piece. 'I made certain Cook did not fuss for me at Summerfield House. We ate very plainly and, I must say, it agreed with me.'

He had to agree. She looked vibrant and… beautiful.

'Tell me more about your work on the house,' he said, searching for a safe topic. 'What will I find when I arrive there?'

She talked about paint and plaster and upholstery with an enthusiasm that captivated him more than it ought. He asked questions and, as they talked, he realised his interest in the changes and improvements was greater than he would have guessed. He was impressed by her management of various craftsmen hired to do the work. Her changes were strategic and thoughtfully done, and he certainly could not have done better himself.

By the end of the meal Dell had relaxed and simply enjoyed their conversation and her company.

When she finished telling all she'd done in the house, she asked him, 'You said you needed a few days away from London. Why?'

He poured another tankard of ale for himself. 'Sometimes…sometimes I need to escape.' He'd not meant to be so honest.

Her warm brown eyes filled with concern. 'Escape?'

He placed his tankard on the table and leaned towards her. 'The politics—I attend the House of Lords. I know some do not, but I feel I must.' For his father's sake. 'But I am in the minority party and it is difficult to see voting go against what I believe is right.'

Her eyes narrowed. 'What was it that went against you?'

He could not answer right away.

She persisted. 'It was something you did not believe was right?'

He found himself pouring out the story of the whole Habeas Corpus situation, how citizens' protections against unjust arrest and seizure had been summarily swept away the year before and now how those who abused the act and jailed innocent persons could not be held accountable.

She reached across the table and he thought for a moment she would place her hand on his arm. She withdrew again. 'I am sorry.'

He took a breath. 'I must stay away only briefly, though. There is always another battle to fight.'

'That is why I prefer the country,' she said. 'I will not stay in London. It is all politics.'

And social events at which she was liable to be cut or whispered about. He remembered how it was for her. He might now have mentioned his ambivalence about courtship and marriage—and about Lady Alice—but something stopped him.

'Where will you go?' he asked instead.

'I do not know.' But her face filled with excitement again. 'I would like to find a cottage that needs refurbishing on a small farm. I want to redo it all from top to bottom in every way I like.' She faced him and smiled. 'I really did so enjoy redoing Summerfield House.'

'That is my good fortune, I am sure.' He frowned. 'Is your trip to London merely for a visit, then, and not for the Season?' Would he see her there, he meant.

'Only long enough to sell the town house I inherited and find another place to live. And to see Genna and Tess, and the baby, of course.'

They talked until the serving girl brought tea and dessert.

Dell felt more content than he had in a long time—certainly since…his life had changed. They talked until the sky sparkled with stars around the soft glow of a full moon.

Lorene glanced towards the window. 'It is late. We should retire.'

He did not want to part from her. 'As you wish.'

He stood and held her chair for her. She took his arm as they left the dining room and walked through the public rooms, still noisy with a motley crew of travellers.

When they entered the hall she hesitated. 'Would you do something for me, Dell?'

'Of course.' He would do anything for her.

'Would you step outside with me? Just for a little while? I cannot go by myself and I would love a bit of fresh air.'

'It will be cold for you,' he said.

She wrapped her shawl around her shoulders. 'I have my shawl to keep me warm and we will not stay for more than a little while.'

He gestured towards the door. 'Then we shall go.'

The door led to the yard where ostlers were still tending to horses and carriages.

She looked up at the sky. 'It is so clear out tonight. I think I am able to see every star.' She glanced back at him. 'Might we walk around the inn to the river?'

He nodded.

They passed through an archway that led to the back of the inn and the small park they'd seen from their dining-room window. The moonlight and light shining from the inn's windows made it bright enough to see where they were walking. The air was crisp and clean. They walked to the water's edge.

'Isn't it lovely?' she said. 'I can almost forget we are in a village and that there are other people about.'

A sudden breeze chilled them.

Dell put his arm around her to keep her warm. 'Is that what you want, Lorene, for there to be no people about?'

She turned to face him, tilting her head back to gaze into his face. 'I don't want anyone around me who would talk about me. Or who would tell me what I must do or must not do.'

He held her still, almost in an embrace.

She turned her gaze away. 'I've had too much of it. I merely want peace. Like right now.'

Like right now? Yes, it was peaceful holding her under the stars.

At the moment it was all he wanted as well.

His arm felt wonderful across her shoulders. The heat of his body warmed her more than her heaviest cloak.

She turned to face him again and he held her with both arms. 'We—we should go in.'

She did not move and neither did he.

'It is cold out,' he said.

Another breeze blew as if proving his words. His arms tightened around her. She let him hold her close, savouring the warmth of his body, the scent that was only his. How wonderful it was to be with him again. How easy she felt in his company. They had talked for hours, so comfortably, she'd not even thought once about when they'd last been together.

At her husband's inquest.

It seemed a decade ago, even if it was only just over a year. She trembled with the memory.

'We should go in,' he said, thinking she was having a chill, no doubt.

'Yes, it is becoming a bit cold,' she agreed.

He released her, and they walked back in the inn and up the stairs to the first floor, stopping in front of her door.

'Goodnight, Dell,' she murmured. 'It was quite the loveliest dinner.'

He merely stared down at her, his face illuminated by the sconce by the stairway. His blue eyes seemed to glow in the dim light, not looking as sad as they usually did. Now, though, she was filled with the overwhelming sense of how much she cared for him and how grateful she was for all his kindnesses to her.

She reached up and touched his face, her fingers scraping against his day's growth of beard. 'Goodnight.'

He leaned closer, close enough that it seemed their lips might touch, but he quickly straightened.

'Goodnight, Lorene.'

* * *

Good God! What was he about?

Dell returned to his room and paced the floor. Had he almost kissed her?

Very shabby of him to take advantage of her that way, especially when he was contemplating a courtship with another lady. He could not turn romantic on her, not after all that happened a year ago. Tinmore accusing them of having an affair. Tinmore going into a rage. Falling to his death.

No. He could not start something with Lorene. She could too easily become very important to him.

He must remain firm on his plan. Live for the family he lost. Continue his father's legacy. Carry on the family name.

And do all of it without engaging his emotions.

The next morning Lorene rose early. She and her maid ate a hurried breakfast and walked into the yard at the time she'd arranged her hired coach to be ready. As she and her maid waited for their portmanteaux to be loaded on to the coach, she spied a horse and rider leaving the stable.

It was Dell, riding comfortably in the saddle of a chestnut Arabian, his hat tall, his topcoat billowing behind him.

Her breath caught.

How handsome he looked!

She remembered her first glimpse of him the night before, on the stairway behind her. He'd looked rakish with his beard shadowing his face and his brown hair tousled as if he'd just come in from a windy day. She had steeled herself to see him in London—how could she not see him when he was the close friend of Genna's husband?—but she'd been totally unprepared to run into him at this inn in Cambridgeshire.

It had been quite the loveliest dinner she'd ever had, spending so much time with him. Every now and then during the dinner it would strike her that she was with Dell and without a care. They would never have another chance like that one. Walking in the moonlight with him had been magical, almost like her youthful romantic dreams, the ones she used to have before she married.

Her romantic notions must have been running amok, because afterward she even fancied he'd been about to kiss her. Now she was certain she'd been imagining things.

He rode away without having made any effort to say goodbye.

The snub pained her.

Chapter Eight

Lorene's first days back in London kept her so busy that she had little time to think about Dell and the lovely interlude they'd shared at the inn in Cambridgeshire. She'd spent two Seasons in London in the past, but those had been under the thumb of her husband. She knew very little of how to conduct business in town. Goodness, Tinmore would hardly allow her to even hear the word business. No lady involved herself in such matters.

She asked for assistance from Genna's husband. Lord Rossdale helped her find a man of business to act on her behalf. Mr Jeremy Walters, son of Ross's father's man of business, was eager to do whatever she needed. He helped her hire more servants to put the house in order and engaged a property agent to facilitate the sale of the house. With any luck she would be out of London in a month.

* * *

This morning her sisters had convinced her to go with them to the modiste to order new dresses. New gowns were a must because Easter, having come early this year, was past and now society's entertainments would begin in earnest.

Not that Lorene had any intention of attending society events. Her old clothes would have done well enough, but the modiste was Tess's former lady's maid and Lorene wanted to see her more for a visit than for new dresses.

While there Tess and Genna had convinced her to order a few gowns and to stop at other shops for new hats, gloves, and shoes.

After their shopping expedition the three sisters returned to Lorene's town house.

Mr Walters met them in the hall as the footman was collecting their packages, hats and wraps. 'Oh, my lady! I did not expect you to return so soon. I hope it is not too inconvenient, but the property agent is at this very moment showing the house to a potential buyer! I did not think you would mind.'

Lorene handed her shawl to the footman. 'Of course I do not mind! I am delighted. We will retire to the drawing room for tea and be out of the way.'

But from the top of the stairs they heard a woman's voice. 'It is a bit small, but it will do nicely, I think.'

A man's accented voice responded, 'I am still unsure why you wish to buy.'

The three sisters turned in the direction of the stairs as an elegant lady in her middle years, blonde hair fading but still lovely, descended the steps, a greying gentleman behind her.

Tess reached for Lorene's hand. 'Mama.'

Lorene and Genna gaped at her, then turned to the woman.

'Tess?' The lady broke into a smile and rushed down the stairs. 'Tess! My darling girl! I never dreamed I would see you so soon.' She embraced Tess and kissed both her cheeks.

Tess pulled away. Genna moved behind Lorene.

Lorene stared. Was this their mother?

Tess was the only one who would recognise her, the only one who had seen her since they were children. Tess had been reunited with their mother in Brussels during the days of Waterloo.

Their mother looked remarkably like Genna, Lorene thought. She could see in her mind's eye an image of her mother the night she left them. Yes, this woman. Older. But…her mother, indeed.

'Mother,' Tess said in a tense voice. 'This is Lorene and Genna.'

Her mother's face lit up again. 'No! Lorene!' She put her hands on Lorene's cheeks. 'And Genna. My baby!' Genna stepped out of reach.

'How beautiful my daughters are!' Her mother turned to the gentleman. 'Ossie, look at how beautiful my daughters are!'

The gentleman had reached the bottom of the stairs. 'Indeed. Quite beautiful.' He bowed. 'I can see that emotions are too high for introductions. I am Count von Osten.'

The lover with whom their mother ran away.

Lorene shook herself. 'Yes. Well. Perhaps you should come into the drawing room. Some tea?'

Another man walked down the stairs. The property agent, she supposed.

Mr Walters strode up to him. 'Ah, sir. Perhaps it is best if you return to your office. Your purchasers will not be talking of buying at quite this moment.'

The man frowned. 'If any deal is made behind my back, I will hear of it! I expect my commission.'

Mr Walters guided the man towards the door. 'If any deal is made you will certainly receive your commission.'

The footman was ready with the man's hat and topcoat.

'Come into the drawing room,' Lorene repeated to her mother and von Osten.

'I will see to your tea,' Mr Walters said.

Genna mumbled under her breath, 'I am going home.'

Lorene took her by the arm. 'No, you are not. We all should be together.'

Their mother wrapped her arm through Tess's and walked to the drawing room. 'It is such a treasure to see all of my daughters at once!'

'What—what are you doing here, Mother?' Tess asked.

Their mother and Count von Osten sat together on the sofa. Genna took the chair furthest from them and Tess and Lorene sat facing them.

'We are here to see you, of course!' their mother replied, smiling as charmingly as Lorene remembered. 'And I missed England. London, especially. We are staying at Mivart's Hotel on Brook Street, but, you know, I fancied a house of our own and I was told this one was for sale.' She laughed. 'I never dreamed you would be in residence, dear Lorene! Who could have guessed I would look for a house and find my daughters?' She reached over and squeezed Lorene's hand. 'Edmund sent me word of your husband's death, my darling. How very fortunate you are!'

'Edmund might as well be a town crier,' mumbled Genna.

'And, Tess, my love!' their elegant mother cried. 'You have made me a grandmother! I cannot wait to hold that little one in my arms. Of course, I quite consider Edmund's son my own grandchild, but he is not really, is he?'

'Why did you not write and tell us you were coming?' Tess asked.

'Yes, why?' Genna echoed.

'I told you to write them,' the Count said. 'That we should not come unannounced.'

'Nonsense!' she said. 'Of course, I meant to tell all that I was here in London. After I was settled. I do detest a hotel room.'

The Count broke in. 'Mivart's is quite agreeable.'

Their mother ignored him. 'Lorene, dear. Are you truly selling this lovely house?'

'Yes, Mother,' she said.

Her mother swept her hand across the room. 'Whatever for? It is a fine house.'

'I do not intend to live in town.' Lorene's head was spinning. Surely this was not truly happening. This was not her mother returned to England and acting as if she had never left.

'But you must stay for the Season! Now that you are free!'

'Never mind that,' Tess persisted. 'Why are you in London, Mother?'

Von Osten leaned forward. 'We are here to be married. Now that your father has been gone a respectable amount of time, we can finally be married.'

Their mother's smile turned stiff. 'Now, Ossie, we agreed we *might* marry. I am not so eager as you in that regard.' Her gaze swept over Lorene and her sisters. 'We are here, though, to enjoy the London Season. To attend the theatre, to shop, to attend balls and routs. And to see my beautiful daughters.'

'As an afterthought,' Genna whispered just loud enough for Lorene to hear.

The footman brought in the tea, which Lorene poured and served to everyone. Genna and Tess placed their teacups on the table untouched. Lorene needed the hot liquid warming her throat and chest to reassure herself she was not dreaming this.

Her mother began to rattle on about Mivart's Hotel and its accommodations and food when Genna slapped her hand on the table next to her. 'How can you go on about a silly hotel? Do you not know how hard this is for us?'

'What is hard, my darling baby girl?' her mother responded.

'What is hard?' Genna stood. 'You. Being here. Without a word to warn us. Acting as if you were only gone a few days? Do you not have anything to say about why you left us?'

Lorene thought she should stop Genna, but her mouth would not form the words.

Genna went on. 'I think you owe us an explanation.'

Her mother carefully placed her cup on the

table and looked up at her youngest daughter. 'First of all, I did not plan to see you this way. I am also taken aback. And you know why I left.' She cast a loving glance towards von Osten.

Genna's eyes flashed. 'You left your children. I was only six. And Lorene was nine. Did you know she took over the care of us after that? At nine years old? And she had to marry that detestable old man for us. Did you know she did that for us, because our father left us without a penny?'

'Genna, please—' Lorene begged. It was over.

'I am sorry for all that,' her mother said, 'but had I been here, would I have been able to stop any of it from happening? I would not. Besides, it has worked out well for you, has it not? You will be a duchess some day.'

As if that mattered to Genna.

Lorene lifted her hands. 'Let us not quarrel. We must get used to each other.' She turned to von Osten, because, unlike the rest of them, he seemed to have his wits together. 'Maybe we just need a little time.'

Von Osten nodded. 'Wise idea, my dear.' He stood. 'Hetty, let us take our leave and allow your beautiful daughters time to become used to the idea of having their mother back.'

Having her back? Tess and Genna and Edmund had needed their mother when they were little, not now.

They all stood and their mother dashed over to each of them to give them huge hugs. 'Oh, my darlings!' she exclaimed. 'I am so happy to see you. So very happy!'

Von Osten took her by the elbow. 'Come, love.'

Lorene escorted them into the hall and waited with them while the footman retrieved their things.

'Please have the agent contact my man of business if you decide you want the house.'

'Oh, no.' Her mother smiled. 'I cannot take this house from you!'

'I do not want it, I assure you,' Lorene told her.

She patted Lorene's hand. 'Do not be hasty, my darling daughter.'

The footman brought her cloak and put it over her shoulders.

Lorene spoke suddenly. 'Oh. I did not think. Do you need my carriage? I can send someone for it, if you do.'

'Kind of you, my dear,' von Osten said. 'But we have hired a carriage. He will be circling the streets.'

The footman opened the door.

Lorene's mother dashed back to her and hugged her again. 'I am so very happy to see you!'

They were out the door and gone.

Lorene stared at the door for a moment before returning to her sisters.

* * *

The next day Lorene's butler came to her while she was writing a letter to Edmund. 'Lady Summerfield and Count von Osten to see you, m'lady.'

The blood drained from her face. Not so soon!

But perhaps they had decided to purchase the town house. She would have to ask them to wait, though, until Mr Walters returned the next day.

'Thank you, Trask. I'll be right down. Show them to the drawing room.'

She capped her bottle of ink and wiped her pen and steeled herself for another bout with her mother while she was still reeling from the one the day before.

When Lorene entered the drawing room, her mother ran up to her, hugged her and kissed her on the cheek. 'I am so glad to see you again. I believe you look even prettier than yesterday!'

'Thank you, Mother,' Lorene said reflexively. 'To what do I owe the honour of your visit?'

'We are intruding,' Count von Osten said with an apologetic smile.

Her mother took her hand and led her to the sofa. 'Well, after yesterday, I was thinking of you all alone in this big house.'

Yesterday she had called the house a bit small.

'And I wanted so very much to be reacquainted so I convinced myself—and Ossie—that the best thing to do was for us to become your guests.'

'My guests?'

'Your guests.' Her mother smiled her charming smile. 'I am certain you would have invited us if you'd had any time to think of it.'

'Invited you?' She was still not certain what her mother meant.

'We have come to stay!' Her mother clapped her hands. 'Will that not be delightful? Say yes, my darling daughter, and we will have the coachman unload our luggage.'

They'd brought their luggage?

No! They could not stay!

But if it became known Lorene had turned them away—and she could just hear her mother telling her friends that her daughter turned them out into the street—there would be talk. And Lorene detested this sort of gossip.

No one would expect Tess and Glenville to invite them to stay. Tess and Glenville lived with his parents. Genna would throw them out with her bare hands and damn the consequences, which her mother must have guessed.

'You may stay,' she said finally. 'But only until you find a house of your own.' She stood. 'I'll have the main bedrooms readied for you.' She'd chosen to stay in one of the smaller bedrooms, thinking it would make a better impression on potential buyers to have those main bedrooms untouched.

'That will be lovely, my darling. We will need rooms for Marie and Fabron as well.'

'Marie and Fabron?' Lorene asked.

'My maid and Ossie's valet.'

Soon four trunks and assorted other baggage were brought into the house, as well as her mother's lady's maid and the Count's valet.

'And another lovely thing,' her mother said as they were served tea in the drawing room. 'We are invited to a ball tonight.'

'How very nice for you.' And very surprising. Lorene had been convinced that her mother would have been cut from everyone's guest list.

'The Duchess of Archester included *you*, my darling.'

Lorene remembered the Duchess. The older lady had been kind to Lorene the last time Lorene had been in town and had said she'd been a friend of Lorene's mother.

'I cannot attend,' Lorene said.

'You must attend! Your sisters will attend. You must attend, as well.'

'I did not pack any ball gowns.' Her mother would understand that reason for not going. She remembered that much about her mother.

'No ball gowns!' Her mother seized her hand. 'Come quick. You will wear one of mine. Marie can alter it after she unpacks the trunks.'

Lorene held back. 'Really, Mother, I did not

come to London to go to balls. I am only here to sell this house and be about finding a property in the country.'

'Nonsense!' Her mother halted on the stairs and took Lorene's face in her hands. 'You cannot hide that lovely face in the country! You are a widow! A widow is in the best position to enjoy herself.'

Lorene was swept along to the bedchamber she'd given her mother. A pretty woman was in the room, unpacking one of three trunks.

Nellie, Lorene's lady's maid, was assisting her. 'Oh, m'lady. I knew you would not mind if I helped. So many trunks to unpack! Besides, I thought it would be a way to help Marie feel more at home here.'

Now even Nellie seemed caught up in the whirlwind that was Lorene's mother. 'That was kind of you, Nellie.'

'We need to find ball gowns for tonight,' Lorene's mother told the maids. 'One for Lady Tinmore and one for me.'

It was three against one. The maids embraced the project with as much enthusiasm as her mother. Four ball gowns were pulled out of one of the trunks, each more beautiful than the next.

'The colours are all wrong!' her mother lamented. 'With that beautiful fair skin and dark hair, you will look so much better in dark, rich colours. Not these pale things.' She picked up the skirt of one of the gowns and tossed it down again.

She picked up one dress and held it to Lorene's body. 'This will do.'

The dress had a white silk underdress with three layers of net in a golden yellow. The net overdress was embroidered with flowers in gold thread along the hem and bodice. It was a lovely gown, but nothing like Lorene would pick for herself.

'Here, girls, alter this to fit her.' Lorene's mother handed the dress to the maids. 'We need it by tonight.'

So against Lorene's wishes, her mother and her mother's lover were staying in her house and with them she would attend a ball given by the Duchess of Archester. No doubt the presence of her mother and Count von Osten would cast much attention on the Summerfield sisters as well as their mother.

She did not look forward to this ball.

Chapter Nine

Dell stood with Ross's father, the Duke of Kessington, when the butler announced, 'Count von Osten, Lady Summerfield, Lady Tinmore.'

A collective gasp went over the guests in the ballroom and all heads turned to see the notorious Lady Summerfield, tall and blonde, and von Osten, dark and foreign.

'Good God,' exclaimed the Duke. 'I read the announcement in the *Morning Post* that they were in town, but I never expected to encounter them at a ball.'

'The Duchess of Archester is an old friend of Lady Summerfield's,' Dell told him. He knew this from the Season he'd spent so much time with Lorene. Her Grace the Duchess had made it a point to speak to Lorene about her mother. Dell was surprised to see Lorene in their party, though. And in the company of her mother.

Still, she looked lovely in a gold gown that shimmered in the candlelight. One glance at her face, though, showed her discomfort. His old protectiveness of her was roused and it was all he could do to keep from hurrying to her side.

As it happened, it did not take long for Lady Summerfield and the Count to be swept away by interested old friends. Dell watched Lorene retreat to a corner of the room. He crossed the room to her.

'Good evening, Lorene,' he said, bowing.

'Dell.' Her voice was a whisper.

He remembered, then, that moment he'd almost kissed her. How easy it would be to do so again.

Instead he inclined his head to where her mother and the Count stood. 'I am surprised.'

She sighed. 'Not as surprised as I was. She just appeared yesterday and now she and Count von Osten are staying in my town house.'

'You invited her to stay?' He was surprised.

'No, not precisely. She...just came. And here I am at a ball when I said I did not want to attend any part of the Season and now I do not see how I will be able to sell the town house with everyone in it.' She seemed to catch herself. 'But I am burdening you with my troubles again. Forgive me.'

It was as though she suddenly pulled away.

'I asked, Lorene.'

She averted her gaze for a moment before facing him again. 'And how do you fare, Dell? You did not stay long in Lincolnshire.'

'Not for lack of wanting to stay.' He'd torn himself away from Summerfield House before he settled in and became as great a recluse as Lord Tinmore had once been.

She gazed back at the ballroom guests, either clustered around her mother or sending curious glances her mother's way. Unfortunately, a few curious glances came their way as well.

'We are seen together,' Lorene said in a tense voice. 'Will there be talk?'

'I do not think so,' he said. 'There was very little mention last year of Tinmore's death, as far as I knew. And none at all about you and me.'

'I hope that is true,' she said. 'I do not want to be the object of gossip ever again.'

They were silent for a while until Lorene asked, 'Did you object to anything at Summerfield House?'

'No objection at all,' he immediately answered.

She looked relieved. 'I was not certain how you would feel. Lord Tinmore always pooh-poohed any idea I had about decor.'

Dell was eager to reassure her he was not like Tinmore. 'On the contrary, it looked…cared for. It was quite splendid. I found it difficult to leave.'

Her face filled with pleasure. 'You did not mind the changes?'

'Fresh paint? Upholstery? Curtains? It all seemed fresh. I very much approved of all you did.'

She smiled. 'I am so glad. I did enjoy it very much. I've made some improvements in the town house, too. Painting and plastering, mostly. I hope enough for it to sell.' She paused. 'If my mother and the Count ever leave.'

The butler announced, 'The Marquess and Marchioness of Rossdale. Mr and Mrs Glenville.'

Lorene's sisters and their husbands. Soon he would have no reason to remain at Lorene's side.

After they greeted the host and hostess, Ross and Genna walked over to speak to Ross's father. Glenville and Tess came straight to Lorene. None of them missed the spectacle that was Lady Summerfield.

'I never expected to see you here,' Tess said to Lorene.

'I was rather bullied into it,' Lorene responded.

Tess's brows rose. 'By whom?'

'Our mother.'

'Mother?' Tess tossed a scathing look towards her mother. 'However did that happen?'

'It happened after she and the Count invited themselves to be guests in my town house,' Lorene responded.

'They invited themselves to stay?' Tess looked horrified. 'And you let them?'

'Think about it, Tess,' Lorene said. 'Think what gossip there would be if I had refused her.'

Dell could leave now instead of being on the periphery of this family group. Lorene would no longer be alone. But he did not move.

Ross and Genna walked over.

Genna was already in high colour. 'Did you see her?' she asked her sisters.

Ross came to Dell. 'I am surprised to see her here.'

'Lady Summerfield?'

Ross laughed. 'Well, her, certainly, but I meant Lorene. She was adamant about not accepting any invitations. Believe me, we tried to change her mind.'

'Her mother compelled her,' he responded.

'It cannot be easy for them, having their mother show up after all this time.' Ross frowned. 'Genna pretends she doesn't care, but she has been rather touchy since she first encountered her.'

'When was that?' Dell asked.

'Yesterday.'

Dell tried to imagine what it might be like to suddenly encounter a parent one had not seen for over ten years. Even one who had abandoned them. He was not, however, the one to empathise. He would give anything to have a long-lost parent— or any relative—show up.

The butler announced, 'The Marquess and Marchioness of Brackton and Lady Alice.'

His spirits sank. Lady Alice's arrival was a reminder that he ought to excuse himself from the Summerfields, much as he wanted to stay.

Lady Summerfield breezed over with the Duchess of Archester in tow and Count von Osten following. 'My beautiful daughters! All here together! What a lovely picture they make, do they not, Louisa?'

Lady Summerfield made a lovely picture herself. Tall, but not quite as tall as Genna, with Genna's colouring and a great deal of similarity in their features. She also seemed totally oblivious to the obvious discomfort on the faces of all three of her daughters.

Her face lit with recognition when she turned to Tess's husband. 'Mr Glenville! How delightful to see you. You look even more handsome than I remembered.' She turned to her escort. 'And you remember Count von Osten, certainly.'

The Count extended his hand. 'Delightful to see you again, Glenville.'

Lady Summerfield looked from Ross to Dell. 'Am I to be introduced? One of you is Lord Rossdale, I suspect.'

Her daughters seemed paralysed to make the introductions.

Ross stepped forward and bowed. 'I am Ross-dale, ma'am.'

'I am delighted to meet you, sir!' Lady Summerfield smiled. 'I have longed to see this husband who will make my daughter a duchess some day.'

Her friend, the Duchess of Archester, gestured to Dell. 'This is the Earl of Penford, Hetty.'

The lady's glance turned to Dell. 'Penford?

'A pleasure, ma'am.' He bowed.

'The Earl is a Summerfield, Mother,' Lorene piped up. 'He inherited Summerfield House and all of Papa's entailed property.'

She looked from Lorene to Dell. 'Oh?' She smiled. 'But you are so handsome!'

'We shared an ancestor a few generations back,' Dell said.

Her smile grew wider. 'That does explain it, then.'

She introduced Dell and Ross to von Osten.

'See how well my daughters have done, Ossie,' she exclaimed loud enough for others to hear. 'Genna will be a duchess. Tess, a viscountess. And Lorene had the good fortune to become a wealthy widow.'

Lorene winced at her words.

Dell took a step closer to her. 'She says what comes into her mind, does she not? Do not let her words touch you.'

She gave a painful smile. 'That is difficult advice to follow.'

'Lorene!' Her mother gestured for Lorene to come closer.

Lorene glanced towards him.

'Do not trouble yourself about me.' He bowed. 'I will take my leave. There are others I must speak to here, in any event.'

Lady Alice, he supposed.

Lorene watched Dell walk away and could not ignore her dismay when he sauntered off to greet a pretty young lady she remembered seeing during her last Season.

Of course, better to pass the time with a reputable young lady than the scandalous entourage of Summerfields. Lorene could not miss the disapproving glances of about half the ball's guests, including the older couple next to Dell's young lady—her parents, perhaps.

More mystifying were those who greeted her mother and von Osten as long-lost friends. The Duchess of Archester took the lead and many of her friends followed.

Lorene, Tess, and Genna had to pretend to be happy about this reunion, although Genna failed completely at this task. Her husband must have noticed, because he excused them from the group as soon as he possibly could and took her off to greet his father. Their mother dragged Lorene and Tess from one group of old friends to another, always bragging about their beauty and the successes of their marriages. At least in the shadow of this brilliant star, no one much attended to her or to Tess.

Of the disapproving side of the guests, there were many who had been guests of her late husband. Not one of these people approached her, though. No one made an effort to offer condolences, although, perhaps, they, like her mother, considered his death her good fortune.

When the dancing began, her mother and von Osten were among the first to take their places in the line of dancers. Lorene used this chance to withdraw. She told Tess she needed the ladies' retiring room and she hurried out of the ballroom.

But even the ladies' retiring room seemed a place that might be fraught with curious questions and disapproving stares. Instead she looked for a quiet room to collect her thoughts.

'Lorene?'

She turned.

Dell stood behind her. 'Is there anything amiss?'

If it had been anyone besides Dell she would have been embarrassed, but he was the one person she felt would understand her without judgement, no matter what.

She smiled. 'Nothing. To own the truth, I am looking for a quiet place to hide.'

He nodded, his expression serious. 'Come with me.'

He led her to the library, tucked behind the dining room on the ground floor. From the fire in the grate, he lit a candle and placed it on a table between two large comfortable chairs facing the fireplace.

'How is this?' he asked.

'Perfect!' She sat in one of the chairs. Even if someone peeked into the room, they would not immediately see that the chair was occupied.

From the floor above they could hear the orchestra and the dancers' footsteps, but, like the private dining room they'd shared at the inn, it felt as if there were only the two of them in the world.

Would he leave her now? She hoped not.

He settled into the other chair, but immediately she felt ashamed of herself for wanting his company.

'Do not feel you have to stay with me,' she said. 'I would despise myself if I ruined your time at the ball.'

'You do not ruin it.' His voice was low, and, although he was clean-shaven, he seemed as rakish as that night in the inn.

'Do you not miss the dancing?' she asked.

He faced her. 'Do you?'

She wrapped her arms around her and tucked her feet under her. 'I did not expect to dance, but I thought you might.' With that pretty young lady he'd greeted as soon as walking away from her.

'I remember you were a very good dancer,' he said.

She smiled. 'My goodness, that seems so long ago.'

He stood. 'Come. You enjoy dancing. I remember you do.'

She shook her head. 'I just want to stay here for a little while.'

'Then let us dance here.' He extended his hand.

She hesitated a moment, but finally took his hand and let him assist her from her chair.

They could still hear the music, albeit faintly. 'The Duke of Kent's Waltz,' he said. 'We can dance these figures.'

They faced each other and joined their right hands. They stepped forward and back and forward again, this time with Dell twirling her under his arm. Then they switched hands and did it again. Next, hands joined moving in a circle and back again, then facing each other and holding both hands, stepping to and fro, releasing each other and circling around to take hands again. They danced the figures over and over again, silent, gazes locked upon each other. It was a light-hearted dance, but he did not smile and neither did she. She liked too much the touch of his hand, the joining with him, the *being* with him.

She remembered dancing with him two years ago when he'd taken pity on her because Tinmore always left her in a ballroom alone. How lovely it had been and how exhilarating that such a young, handsome man had chosen her.

But she much preferred how it felt to be alone with him, calming and thrilling at the same time.

His moves were as graceful here in the dimly lit library as they'd been two years ago in the ballroom. An easy grace, as if it came as naturally to him as walking. It had thrilled her to dance with him. This night, it stirred her even more deeply. She thought of that moment in the inn when she'd been almost certain he'd meant to kiss her.

The music stopped suddenly. Their hands were still clasped and they did not release them right away.

Finally she curtsied. 'Thank you, sir,' she said as if they were in the ballroom.

'My pleasure,' he responded, but his voice had turned low and smooth, stirring her in a different manner.

He released her and she returned to her chair. He returned to his. Their silence stretched even further, until he asked, 'How is it to see your mother again?'

She was surprised at his question. 'I hardly know.' She stared into the glowing coals in the hearth. 'She has not given us time to decide how we feel. No warning of her arrival. No chance to think about it. And—and she acts as if she's been gone a month instead of most of our lives.'

'Do you resent her?' he asked.

She straightened in her seat. 'Of course I resent her. But that is not all. I obviously feel something—an obligation, perhaps. I've allowed her to move in. Allowed her to make me attend this ball. I am certain if I were Genna I would have sent her packing.'

He nodded. 'I noticed Genna's displeasure.'

'She was so little when Mother left.'

'Still.' His tone was careful. 'Before yesterday it was as if you did not have a mother and now you do.'

'Yes. And I do not know how I feel about it.'

His countenance was so serious, she did not know what to think of him either. Except...

She leaned towards him. 'I am so sorry. I am complaining and you are thinking of what you would give to have your mother walk back into your life.'

He glanced away and she feared she had taken a liberty she should not have taken.

Finally he said, 'You are correct.'

She wanted to reach over and touch him, but

there was too much distance between their chairs. 'I do not forget what you have lost.'

'I am easier with it now,' he said.

She did not believe him.

'In fact, I am considering rebuilding the town house.' He did not have to tell her what town house he meant.

The one in which his family died in a horrific fire.

'I did not realise the house was still in disrepair,' she said.

He shrugged. 'Last year I had the exterior walls repaired and the windows replaced so that the damage would no longer blight the terrace on which it stands. The inside was cleaned of damage, but it is an empty shell.'

'So you cannot live there at present.' Obviously not, if it was a shell. 'Do you wish to live there?'

'A year ago I would have said I'd never set foot in there again,' he responded. 'But now…perhaps. More likely I'll offer it for rent, though.'

'Where are you living now?' She realised she did not know. So much she did not know of him.

'With Ross's father and stepmother.' He shifted in his chair. 'I am grateful to them. They have made a home for me ever since—ever since the fire. Ross brought me there. The Duke has been an enormous help in my finding my way in the Lords, but, with Ross in his own house with

Genna, I think it is time for me to leave. It makes sense for me to go to a property that is mine rather than lease rooms somewhere.'

'Do you have a plan for the town house?' she asked. 'Do you want to restore it to how it used to look or make it into something new?' Either way seemed an exciting task. She envied him. Think what a challenge it would be.

'It can never be what it was,' he said, his voice low.

Her heart ached for him. This was grief, a grief she'd never felt for her husband, nor for her father. The closest she could come was the grief of her mother's abandonment. 'Then you must make it into something new and beautiful, but something that will make it seem like a home that is all yours.'

'I would not know where to begin.' He gave her a direct gaze. 'Help me with it.'

'Me?' Her heart pounded, not at the exciting challenge of designing his house, but from the intensity of his eyes.

He persisted. 'You did well with Summerfield House. Do the same for my town house.'

'That was merely repairing things and changing things here and there. I've no experience in designing a whole house.' She'd not expected as much even from whatever country cottage she ultimately moved into.

'Advise me, then,' he said. 'It would help to have another person's opinion.' His gaze met her eyes again. 'It would help to have *your* opinion.'

'Of course I will help, in any way you wish.' It would mean spending time with him. How could she not enjoy that? 'I have a book of architectural drawings that show what is in fashion now. Perhaps we could start there.'

He stood. 'I wonder if the Duchess has such a book here.'

They found Humphry Repton's *Fragments on the Theory and Practice of Landscape Gardening*, which included a before and after picture of a renovated parlour. It was not quite what they were searching for, but it started a discussion of colour and style and wallpaper and upholstery.

Lorene forgot about her mother and the disagreeable ballroom guests casting disapproving eyes. She forgot about wanting to flee the city and being forced to stay now that her mother had moved in. She forgot that she and Dell could generate gossip of their own if they were seen too often in each other's company. She forgot about that young lady who captured his attention. She simply enjoyed being with Dell.

From above them, the music stopped and the dancing footfalls were no longer heard.

Lorene sighed. 'I should return to the ballroom.' She stood.

Dell rose with her and together they walked back to the first floor. As they reached the floor, one of the gentlemen guests stepped into the hallway and saw them. Dell nodded a greeting.

'Oh, dear,' Lorene said after they passed him. 'We are seen.'

'Do not worry,' Dell said. 'Likely he will think nothing of it.' When they reached the door to the ballroom, though, he said, 'Enter first. I'll wait.'

Perhaps he was more worried about being seen together than he let on.

She started to do as he said, but he spoke again. 'Thank you for the dance.'

Lorene could not help but return a smile. She slipped into the room and searched for her sisters, who were looking unhappy in a corner of the room. She walked over to join them.

'Where have you been?' Genna asked. 'You quite deserted us!'

'I was hiding,' Lorene answered truthfully. There was no need to tell them where.

Or with whom.

Tess sighed. 'I wish I had thought of that!'

Genna inclined her head towards their mother nearby, wineglass in hand, talking to the Duchess of Mannerton and the Duchess of Archester. 'She remains the centre of everyone's attention.'

Their mother's voice carried. 'Ossie says that we should marry, but I am not so certain.'

'Not certain?' The Duchess Mannerton said. 'But you must marry!'

'Why?' her mother shot back. 'We have gone along very well without being married.'

'But you could not marry when your husband was alive,' the Duchess went on. 'Now you are free to do so. It would be very wrong of you to continue as you are when you are free to marry.' She turned to von Osten. 'Is that not so, Count?'

He lifted his hands. 'It is my wish, of course, but Hetty has not yet come around to the idea.'

Others joined the debate, everyone siding with von Osten in favour of marriage and the disapproving grumblings grew louder from those who were not so welcoming of their mother's return.

Rossdale and Glenville joined the Summerfield sisters, carrying glasses of wine that they handed to their wives.

'Lorene, would you like wine, as well?' Rossdale asked.

She shook her head. She was thirsty, but that seemed inconsequential at the moment.

Rossdale looked from one sister to the other. 'What is it?

'She is debating the value of marriage!' Genna groaned. 'For everyone to hear.'

Rossdale put his arm around his wife. 'Is she for or against?'

'One guess,' Genna said.

The orchestra began to play again and their mother led von Osten to the floor. Lorene's sisters exchanged glances with their husbands.

'Please dance, if you like,' Lorene told them. 'I am perfectly comfortable here.'

They also joined the dancers.

As they left her alone, she watched Dell escort the pretty young lady to the dance floor, as he'd done with Lorene two years before. The lady was perhaps as young as Genna, with brown hair of no special distinction but a very sweet face, a lady he could dance with in the light of the ballroom instead of the darkness of the library.

Chapter Ten

The next morning Lorene's mother and von Osten rose early enough to join her for breakfast. While her mother chattered on about the ball, von Osten read the *Morning Post*.

'My dear, they have written about you in the newspaper,' he said to her mother.

She brightened. 'They have? What did they say?'

He cleared his throat. *"'Lady S— and Count O—'"* He looked up from the paper. 'They have botched my name.'

'Go on,' her mother said impatiently.

"'Lady S— and Count O—, recently arriving in town from Brussels, entertained the guests at the D— of A—'s ball with a debate about marriage. With the decease of Lord S—in 1814, this couple, who have cohabited for over a decade, might at last desire to make their liaison legal in the eyes of God and society, but nothing Lady

S— does has the least whiff of propriety. Lady S— loudly declared her desire to continue their demeritorious arrangement."'

He looked up again. 'I warned that you must hold your tongue, Hetty.'

She extended her hand for him to pass the newspaper to her. 'They are making a mountain out of a molehill, are they not?' She read it and looked up. 'I believe they mention you as well, Lorene.

"'Lady T—, daughter of the notorious Lady S—, is out of mourning, but Lord P— spends as much time with Lady A— as with the wealthy widow".'

Her mother looked up. 'Who is Lady A—?'

Lorene's stomach twisted. Had the reporters noticed her because of her mother? Or was this because she and Dell were seen together coming back from the library? In any event, she had no intention of appearing at any further society events.

Even if it meant never dancing with Dell again.

When Dell joined Ross's father at breakfast, he was deep in his newspaper. Dell knew better than to interrupt him. Besides, he preferred to be alone with his thoughts.

It had been impulsive to ask Lorene to help

him design his town house. He'd intended to hire an architect and simply let him do whatever he wished. He'd used a young student of Sir John Soane's to oversee the work done so far. It would have been best simply to ask him back.

To have Lorene involved, though, meant he might not be required to enter the property too often. That held some appeal, but it would also mean spending time with her.

His worry about society's interest in Tinmore's death had greatly diminished. Over the last year, such an interest seemed non-existent, even when his heir took his place in the House of Lords. The man neither cut Dell nor spoke to him. Rather, he seemed uninterested in him, but, then, the new Lord Tinmore was a powerful Tory who spent many years as a Member of Parliament. Dell was a relatively new Whig just starting to be heard.

The real reason he should stay away from Lorene—and her sisters—was that he felt himself becoming more and more attached to them, even though the tie was as thin as one silk thread.

And, of course, there was that impulse to kiss Lorene.

His Grace rattled the paper. 'This is not well done. Not well done at all.'

'What, sir?' Dell asked.

'I knew she would be trouble,' the Duke groused.
'Who?'

The Duke finally lowered the newspaper. 'Listen to this. *"Lady S— and Count O—, recently arriving in town from Brussels..."'* He read to the end and lowered the paper again. 'Trouble! Why does she not keep her mouth shut and make her lover a husband so we can all pretend she is respectable?'

'I heard the conversation. Lady Summerfield was not that specific that her intention was not to marry,' Dell said.

The Duke slapped the paper against the table. 'What does that matter? She should not have been discussing it at all.' He made a derisive sound. 'I lament the day Ross attached himself to that scandalous family.'

Dell rose to his friend's defence. 'Ross and Genna are happy. That is all that matters.'

Ross's father shook his head. 'It is not all that matters. Not only Lady Summerfield, look at the other family he is now connected to. Lord Northdon is as ineffectual as a man can be and still hold a title. No one heeds him. The most one can wish is that he does not speak in support of a bill one wishes to be passed. His support is a death knell.'

Viscount Northdon was Marc Glenville's father and Tess's father-in-law. As far as Dell could see, Northdon was a decent man, but he'd made the mistake of marrying a commoner. Not only a commoner, but a French commoner whose family had been active in the Terror. The *ton* did not warm to persons whose relatives beheaded their relatives.

'It is not that bad, surely,' Dell said.

'Lady Summerfield is a blight,' his Grace went on. 'The whole lot of them are a blight. I have no use for that scandalous family.'

Dell stiffened.

The Duke returned to reading the paper. A minute later he groaned. 'Now this is what I mean.' He shoved the paper at Dell.

Dell took it and read. The paper connected him with Lorene. Dell's spirits sank. This is what Lorene feared. That they would become the object of gossip.

The Duke wagged a finger at him. 'See? You are already being associated with them.' He wagged a finger at Dell. 'You should keep your distance.'

Dell had hoped that merely speaking to Lorene would not be enough to cause comment, let alone wind up in the newspapers. The Duke was right. Lorene's mother must be the reason they attracted attention.

'If you intend to court Lady Alice,' the Duke went on. 'Lord Brackton will not approve of you appearing to be one of the Summerfield set. Or of having his daughter's name connected with a Summerfield in the newspapers.'

'Your son is one of their set,' Dell ignored the Duke's comment about Lady Alice.

The Duke rolled his eyes. 'If he would listen, I would give him the same advice.'

Dell knew that this time the Duke's advice was sound and he should heed it, but not for the same reasons the Duke stated. He was becoming too attached to Lorene. Merely hearing what was written about them gave him worry for her sake.

He needed not to care so much.

At least he had not told Ross's father that he'd asked Lorene Summerfield to design the ornamentation of his town house.

He took another sip of coffee.

He could withdraw the request without much fuss.

Later that day Dell walked to Brook Street to call upon Lorene. He had every intention of explaining to her how ill advised their town house plans would be. He could cite his need to move up in the House of Lords as the reason he should distance himself. He would not tell her that he feared becoming too close to her.

As he turned on to Brook Street, a lady and gentleman approached.

Lady Summerfield and Count von Osten.

Lady Summerfield tossed him a charming smile. 'Lord Penford, is it not? How delightful to see you.'

'Good day to you, sir,' the Count said, extending his hand.

Dell shook it. 'Good day.'

'Where are you bound, sir?' Lady Summerfield's tone was friendly.

'To call upon a friend.' She did not need to know he was calling upon Lorene.

'We are off to see Tess and my darling grandson!' she cried. 'I am simply elated at the prospect.'

'He is a sturdy little fellow,' Dell said.

'You have seen him?' Lady Summerfield sounded surprised.

'At the christening.' And other times he'd been a guest at Tess's in-laws' home.

'Come, Hetty.' Von Osten started to walk away. 'We should be on our way.'

She took a few steps, but turned back. 'I am planning a dinner party soon. For my family. You will come, too, will you not?' She grinned. 'Of course, Lorene does not know of this dinner yet!' She hurried to catch up with the Count.

The woman did exactly as she wished, apparently.

When she and the Count had finally turned
the corner and were out of sight, Dell walked up
to Lorene's door. He could hear music from a pianoforte coming from inside the house and his
heart warmed to her. Her music always moved
him.

He sounded the knocker.

The butler answered.

Dell gave him his card. 'Lord Penford to see
Lady Tinmore.'

'One moment, sir.' The butler left him standing in the hall while he knocked on the drawing-
room door. When he opened the door, the piano
music became louder, then stopped. A moment
later, the butler returned. 'Lady Tinmore will see
you.' He took Dell's things and gestured to the
drawing-room door.

Dell entered the room.

Lorene stood ready to greet him. 'Dell, what
a lovely surprise.'

'I am afraid I have interrupted your playing.'
He gestured to the pianoforte.

'I have plenty of time to play.'

He wanted to ask if that was true now that her
mother was here, but held his tongue. 'I remember your playing with great pleasure.'

She blushed. 'Thank you.' She walked over to
a sofa and two chairs. 'Do have a seat. I have ordered tea.'

'I do not intend to stay long.' He should just say his piece and leave, but she looked so lovely, so gentle and vulnerable and happy to see him.

He sat in one of the chairs and she sat across from him on the sofa.

'Why do me the honour of your visit?' she asked.

'I wanted to see you.' The truth came out of his mouth unheeded.

He glanced around the room. It was nicely furnished, but without the pretty touches she'd added at Summerfield House.

'I did not redo this room,' she said, as if reading his mind. 'I did not do too much to this house, only enough to make it appeal to a buyer.' She glanced away. 'Not that I can seek a buyer now.'

He smiled. 'It is not decorated as fine as Summerfield House.'

She lowered her gaze and her dark lashes cast shadows below her eyes. 'That was a labour of love.'

'It showed.'

He should stop staring at her and simply state what he'd come to say. That it would be better she not be involved in the refurbishing of his town house.

'I stopped by to see if you were at liberty to accompany me to my town house,' he said instead. 'I would like for you to see the inside of the house.'

'Now?' she asked.

'If you are able.'

Why had he not stuck to his guns?

It simply seemed impossible for him to tell her no.

'I would need a few minutes to become ready,' she said.

'A few minutes will do.'

No more than ten minutes elapsed before she appeared in hat, gloves and pelisse and not more than two minutes later they were outside on the pavement.

'It is not too far away,' he said. 'On Mount Street.'

As they walked past Grosvenor Square, he noticed Lord and Lady Brackton walking on the other side of the street. They looked at him with disapproval. He tipped his hat.

Lorene asked, 'Who is that?'

'Lord and Lady Brackton,' he replied.

He could have told her they were Lady Alice's parents. He could have said that he was thinking of courting Lady Alice.

Instead he changed the subject. 'I met your mother on my way to see you.'

'Did you?' she said without pleasure. 'I hope she showed some propriety.'

'She was amiable,' he assured her. 'But she invited me to a family dinner party at your house, a party of which she has not informed you.'

'A party?' She glanced up in surprise. 'At my house?'

'I gather she wished not to tell you of it, but I suspected you would prefer to be forewarned,' he said.

'Yes, I very much would prefer to be fore-warned.' Her colour was high. 'I wonder when she intended to tell me. When the guests arrived?'

Lorene could set aside her mother's presumptuous behaviour while walking with Dell. In some ways she could be at ease with Dell more than with any other person, even Tess. Her marriage to Tinmore had damaged her closeness to both her sisters and to her half-brother, Edmund, but almost from their first meeting, she'd felt comfortable with Dell.

And, at the same time, giddy with excitement.

She could say anything to him, she was convinced, and there was something she very much wanted to ask him, something that had bothered her since their time at the inn.

'You rode away from me,' she said. 'That morning in the inn. You did not say goodbye.'

He frowned. 'I rose early.'

Why she was bringing this up, she did not know, except it plagued her. Had he been angry at her? She'd thought so at the time. 'I was in the yard, waiting for my carriage. You rode off.'

He stopped and faced her. 'I did not see you, Lorene.'

'You were not angry with me?' she asked.

'Angry?' He shook his head. 'For what?'

For that almost kiss, she wanted to say. But suppose she had been mistaken? Suppose it had only been her romantic notions that made her think that was what he was about to do?

She smiled. 'I did not know a reason. I thought it had been a very pleasant evening we shared the night before that.'

He looked down into her eyes. 'It was very pleasant.'

They walked a few steps further before she broke the silence again.

'Who was the young lady you danced with at the Duchess's ball?' she asked.

He'd danced only one dance.

He did not answer right away. 'Lady Alice. Lord Brackton's daughter.'

'She was very pretty.'

'Yes.'

She wanted to ask many prying questions, but what right did she have to do so?

They arrived at his town house, which looked the same on the outside as the houses next to it.

Even its brick exterior was so close in colour as to be indistinguishable.

'They did a wonderful job with the outside,' she exclaimed.

The expression on his face was not one of admiration, however. It was akin to horror.

He pulled a key from his pocket with a shaking hand and unlocked the door. She felt his tension rise as they crossed the threshold.

Except for the marble below her feet, this was a house without walls or ceilings. Instead it was a cavernous space tinged with the faint scent of smoke and the aura of many tears.

He became silent and still. His eyes filled with pain.

She did not think; she simply put her arms around him. His arms circled her and held on tight as if he feared a great wind would blow him away if he let go. She'd hugged Edmund that way when he'd suffered an injury, but Edmund had been a little boy. Dell was a man.

'It hurts, I know,' she said soothingly, although she truly had no idea what pain there might be in losing everyone who mattered to you. She'd spent a night in terror that she'd lost Tess when Tess was caught in the storm the night Glenville rescued her. It must feel like that, only worse. Tess came home to her the next day.

He released her. 'Forgive me. I keep imagining them in the fire, unable to get out.'

She kept hold of his hands. 'Their suffering is over.'

He nodded. 'Mine continues, it seems.'

In that way his pain was like guilt. Lorene's guilt seemed always to be with her.

'I am so sorry,' she murmured, touching his face.

His eyes darkened and that same feeling came over her that had come over her that night in the inn. Was he about to kiss her?

The moment passed and he stepped back. She'd been wrong again.

She walked further into the space. 'What of the lower floor? The kitchen and the servants' rooms?'

'They did not fare as badly. The maids in the attic were—were killed, but the housekeeper, butler and footmen escaped. Do you want to see the lower floor?'

'Certainly.'

In the corner of the vacant space was another staircase, this one leading below. They descended the stairs and came upon several rooms, now clear of furniture. The kitchen's hearth and ovens remained, as well as a long work table.

'Do you still have the pots and pans?' she asked.

He nodded. 'They are packed in crates.'

'It would not take much to put the kitchen in order, then,' she said.

They returned to what had once been the hall.

'What do you think?' he asked. 'Will you help me with this, Lorene?'

She looked around again, at the empty space filled only by a marble stairway leading nowhere. 'I do not know of building walls and putting in floors.'

'I hired a student of Sir John Soane's to do the exterior,' he said. 'I could hire him for the inside, but I cannot depend upon his taste. If you could pick out the details, the colours, the furniture, the carpets, he could do the architectural work.'

She smiled at him. 'I could do that.'

She would love to do that! To design the rooms from top to bottom? It would be heaven. She would make the rooms bright with colour and light. She would use wallpaper, carpet and furniture to dispel the gloom and the memories.

'You must tell me what colours you like,' she said.

'No.' He shook his head emphatically. 'You decide. I do not want to involve myself.'

It saddened her that the exciting project brought him such pain. 'I would be delighted to help you, Dell.'

He extended his hand for her to shake. 'We have a bargain, then.'

She placed her hand in his. 'A bargain.'

Chapter Eleven

Lorene took her man of business into her confidence about assisting Dell in the refurbishment of his town house. Mr Walters accompanied her when she met with the architect and came along any time there were negotiations to be made. Her mother had not the least curiosity of where Lorene went during the day, so the secret was easily kept.

Because she refused to attend society events, the *ton's* curiosity about her seemed to have disappeared as well. Her name did not again appear in the newspapers, even though her mother and Count von Osten were regularly in print, usually for something outrageous her mother said or did.

Days passed and Lorene's mother still did not tell her about the dinner she planned. Not only had she heard of the dinner from Dell, but also from her cook and housekeeper. Her mother never spoke of it until Lorene caught her mother addressing invitations.

Lorene found her mother in an upstairs sitting room at a writing table, a stack of folded paper next to her.

'What are you doing?' She sauntered over to the table.

Her mother first made an attempt to cover her writing, but then seemed to reconsider. She smiled up at Lorene. 'I am writing invitations.'

Lorene lifted her brows. 'Invitations?'

Her mother seized her hand. 'My darling daughter, it was to be a surprise! I am giving a dinner party. Nothing grand. A family dinner party.'

'And where is this party to be held?' she asked, as if she did not know.

Her mother gave her an innocent smile. 'Why, here, of course.'

A memory flashed through Lorene's mind of Lord Tinmore telling her what dinner parties he had planned, parties he'd not bothered to tell her about until they were a *fait accompli*. She could say nothing of that, but her life was different now.

She withdrew her hand. 'Without asking me first?'

'It was to be a surprise for you, my love.' Her mother's voice was wounded.

'No surprises, Mother, please,' she stated. 'I insist on knowing what is happening in my house.'

Her mother stood and gave her a buss on the cheek. 'As you wish, my love.' She picked up the completed invitations. 'As you will see, it is merely family.'

'No more secrets.' She put her hands on her hips. 'Promise me?'

Her mother blinked. 'Oh, I promise. I do.'

'Good.' Lorene turned to leave.

'Will you come to the opera with us tonight, my love?' her mother asked. 'We will sit in the Duke of Archester's box.'

For a woman who had created scandal after scandal in the early years of her marriage, Lorene's mother never seemed to want for invitations, although her companions were reputed to be a fast set. She also persisted in trying to persuade Lorene to attend with her.

'Thank you, no,' Lorene said.

The dinner party was scheduled for the next week. Dell received an invitation as Lady Summerfield had promised. On the night of the party he stood at the window of the drawing room in the Duke of Kessington's Mayfair mansion, watching for the carriage to be brought around to take the Duke and Duchess and him to Lorene's town house.

The Duke and Duchess, also in the room, talked together over a glass of sherry.

'Are you certain I cannot beg off with a sick headache?' the Duchess asked her husband.

Ross's father's second wife had never been a favourite of Ross's and Dell could easily see why. Her interest had always been in the prestige and power of her husband's title more than in her husband. It was not a love match, but as a political partnership it worked well enough. Dell could credit both the Duke and Duchess with helping him fit himself into the political machinations of the House of Lords.

Dell could agree with Ross that the Duchess had an exaggerated sense of her own importance. Even though her rhetoric supported the rights of ordinary people, she did tend to look down her nose at anyone who had not reached her lofty heights.

'I cannot bear to be in the company of that woman.' The Duchess meant Lady Summerfield. 'Her name is in the newspapers nearly every day.'

'We cannot cry off,' Ross's father said. 'We are obliged to attend. Like it or not, she is Ross's mother-in-law.'

'Why Ross wanted to marry that woman's daughter, I will never know,' she went on. 'Goodness. Ross's wife planned to go into *trade*, selling *portraits*, of all things. I shall never hire Vespery to paint another portrait for us. He will not be forgiven for taking her on as a student. And her sisters are quite as bad. We shall have to sit at the table with Lady Northdon, as well.'

Dell did not turn from the window, but he made his voice heard. 'Your Grace, may I remind you that I am Ross's friend and all these people are important to him? I do not like to hear them be maligned. Besides, I share a surname and some ancestors with the Summerfield sisters, so you might say I am related.'

'Well, not to *her*,' the Duchess shot back, meaning Lady Summerfield. 'And most probably not to the sisters either, if one can believe the rumours of their paternity.'

'Constance!' The Duke raised his voice. 'That is quite enough. You do not need to become bosom beaux with any of them, but you will attend this dinner and keep a civil tongue in your mouth.'

Dell turned and nodded approvingly to the Duke, who inclined his head in response.

The Duke took a sip of his sherry. 'Let us be glad that we do not have to cosy up to that windbag Tinmore.'

The Duchess lifted her chin. 'Hmmph! You scold me, but listen to you speak disrespectfully of the dead!'

The Duke still had the glass against his lip. 'He was a windbag.'

Dell turned back to the window. 'The carriage is here.'

Dell and the Duke donned their topcoats and hats, the Duchess, her cloak, and they were soon taking the short trip to Lorene's town house. They arrived and were announced. Ross and Genna were already there. Lorene made the introductions to her mother and von Osten.

She managed a smile for Dell.

He walked over to where Ross and Genna stood.

'I'm pouring claret.' Ross lifted the decanter.

'Pour a glass for me,' Dell said.

'He will not pour me another one,' Genna complained. 'And I need a second glass for this evening, do you not think so, Dell?'

'Indeed I do,' he said in good humour. 'As do I. The Duchess was in rare form tonight.'

'What was it?' asked Genna. 'Was she complaining about my mother or about me?'

Dell accepted a glass from Ross and took a sip. 'Apparently she has not forgiven you for wanting to support yourself as an artist, but her main complaint was needing to be in the presence of your mother.'

Genna rolled her eyes. 'My only consolation. My mother might soon drive the Duchess insane.'

Ross laughed. 'Perhaps Constance will meet

her match.' He left them to offer wine to his father and the Duchess.

A moment later the butler came to the door and announced Tess and Glenville and Glenville's parents, Lord and Lady Northdon, but a man walked through the doorway instead. Dell did not recognise him.

'Edmund!' Lady Summerfield cried and rushed over to him. 'You did come. You naughty boy. Why did you not write me you were coming?'

Edmund. Edmund was the sisters' half-brother, their father's bastard son.

Dell glanced at Lorene to see her response to this surprise. Her face was radiant with pleasure and her eyes sparkled with tears of joy.

Edmund laughed and gave Lady Summerfield a kiss on the cheek. 'You are not the only one who can arrange a surprise.'

Genna ran over to Edmund and threw her arms around him. Lorene held back, watching and waiting. Tess, Glenville and Lord and Lady Northdon entered the room, all smiles. A lovely young woman about Genna's age was with them. Edmund's wife, Dell presumed. Edmund's wife was Glenville's sister and the Northdons' daughter.

Genna let go of Edmund and turned to give his wife an exuberant hug. Edmund strode up to Lorene.

'Lorene.' He enfolded her in his arms and held

her there a long time. When he released her, she wiped her eyes with her fingers.

She turned to greet Edmund's wife, who, tall and blonde, looked more like Genna's sister than Genna looked like Lorene's. Tess joined them.

Genna pulled Ross over. His father and the Duchess followed.

Dell was outside this family group, this joyous reunion. He closed his eyes against the sight. He must not care. He must not remember that he once had a family to embrace.

Someone touched his arm. He opened his eyes. Lorene.

'Come meet my brother.' She looked happier than he'd ever seen her.

He let her lead him to her brother.

'Edmund,' she cried as they came near. 'This is Dell—the Earl of Penford. He inherited Summerfield.'

In Dell's opinion, Edmund should have been the rightful heir of the Summerfield estate, but Edmund was illegitimate and, therefore, could not inherit the entailed property. Instead the family line needed to be traced back three generations to find Dell's father—and a few months later, Dell.

'I am pleased to meet you.' He shook Edmund's hand.

Edmund's expression turned serious. 'I have heard of you, of course. You have been very gen-

erous to Lorene. To all the sisters. I am indebted
to you.'

Dell assumed this man knew all about Tinmore's death and Dell's unwitting part in it. No
one ever spoke of that out loud, though.

Dinner was announced and they formed by
rank, leaving Edmund and his wife at the end,
which seemed wrong considering they had travelled all the way from the Lake District to be
there.

Count von Osten as the host sat at the head of
the table and Lady Summerfield at the other end,
another protocol that rankled with Dell. This was
Lorene's house, was it not?

Dell did not complain, because the seat-
ing arrangement put him between Lorene and
Lady Northdon, whom he liked enormously and
whose manners were head and shoulders above
the Duchess's. The first course was served and the
first conversation at the table was about grand-
children. Lady Summerfield and Lady Northdon
enthused about Edmund's and Tess's boys. Lady
Summerfield started the conversation in French,
which seemed to Dell a notable and respectful ac-
knowledgement of Lady Northdon's background.
Edmund and his wife had their son the year before. The boy would now be a year old, a few
months older than Tess and Glenville's son.

Two sons and heirs. *Deux fils et héritiers.*

Dell thought about having children with Lady Alice, sons to carry the family name and to carry on the family legacy. He might be able to separate his emotions from Lady Alice, but a child of his own—and his family's—blood? What a risk to have a baby to love. Babies so easily died.

After the cleverness and delights of the grandsons were documented in great detail *en français,* the Duchess spoke up, directing her comment to Lady Summerfield.

'You attended the theatre last night, did you not, Lady Summerfield?' the Duchess asked.

Lady Summerfield smiled. 'I did indeed. Were you there?'

'His Grace and I had a more important engagement.' She let that barb prick before delivering another one. 'I read about it in the *Morning Post.*'

The *Morning Post* had noted that scandalous Lady S— had appeared in the Prince Regent's box and was obviously manoeuvring to become the next lady under his protection. It was just the latest gossip. It seemed her name reached the papers every time she ventured out.

Lady Summerfield laughed. 'How silly was that?' She gave a loving glance to von Osten. 'To think I would be unfaithful to my Ossie. It would never happen. Besides, Ossie was with me in his

Royal Highness's box. I do believe the newspapers left that part out.'

The Duchess returned a very sceptical look, then feigned an innocent one. 'I suppose the papers believe such nonsense when it is known you do not intend to marry the Count.'

'Is it known?' Lady Summerfield countered in a clipped voice. 'Because I do not know it.'

'Are you going to marry, then?' the Duchess pressed.

The rest of the table went silent. Not even one fork clattered against a plate.

Lady Summerfield made a sly grin. 'Perhaps we will. Perhaps we will not. I dare say it is for the Count and me to decide. Not the newspapers.' She stared directly at the Duchess. 'Or their readers.'

'You and the Count are thinking of getting married?' Edmund broke in. 'I would be happy for you. What good news.' Edmund's obvious sincerity cut through the Duchess's vitriol.

Edmund, Dell knew from the Summerfield sisters, had corresponded with Lady Summerfield for many years. He had briefly lived with Lady Summerfield and Count von Osten before and after the Battle of Waterloo. Unlike his sisters, he seemed totally at ease with her and obviously very fond of her.

This was a man Dell would be interested to

know. He rather liked what he'd seen of Edmund so far.

The second course was served.

'You have a sheep farm, I understand,' Dell said to Edmund after the food was on their plates.

Some wariness appeared in Edmund's eyes. 'We do. In the Lake District. And a more beautiful place in the world there cannot be.'

His wife spoke up. 'It is not a country house, but a working sheep farm. I could not imagine a life more different than London, but I cherish every day we are there.'

The Duchess looked appalled. 'Do not say you *work* on the farm?'

'Of course we do!' she answered. 'That is the joy of it!'

Edmund gave his wife an adoring look. 'Yes. Amelie has become quite adept at hay-making and sheep-washing. And there is no one better to tend to the lambs.'

'You *work*?' the Duchess cried. '*Farm* labour?'

'Yes, Your Grace,' Amelie responded proudly. 'I quite thrive on it.'

'Believe me,' Edmund said. 'I never figured myself a farmer. I was a soldier—'

'He was wounded at Waterloo,' his wife broke in. 'And my brother rescued him and brought him back to Brussels.'

'Where we nursed him back to health, did we not, Ossie?' Lady Summerfield added.

'Indeed, we did,' the Count agreed. 'Edmund and several other soldiers, as well. There were so many and we had a great house to shelter them.'

The Duchess's smile froze on her face. How was she to take all this? A war hero who became a farmer? A scandalous lady and her lover nursing the Waterloo wounded?

Dell caught Ross's eye. He was enjoying the moment as well.

'The farm has prospered beyond anyone's expectations,' added Lord Northdon. 'Edmund has increased its profits twofold.'

'We are so very proud of them,' Lady Northdon said.

'I am so very proud of my daughters as well as my Edmund.' Lady Summerfield smiled. 'They have all chosen well.' She slanted her gaze towards Lorene. 'Well, perhaps except Lorene, but that all worked out in the end.'

Dell felt Lorene stiffen at her words.

'Mother, really,' Genna said disapprovingly. 'What a thing to say.'

Lady Summerfield gave her that innocent look Dell was becoming familiar with. 'It is true, is it not?'

From beneath the table, Dell found Lorene's hand and squeezed it.

Tess spoke up. 'Lorene has always taken care of us, Mother. We are all grateful for it.'

The Duke cleared his throat. 'And you, Glenville. What are you about these days?'

'I do some work for Lord Greybury from time to time,' he responded.

'Greybury?' The Duke repeated. 'A Tory, is he not? Heads some committee.'

'That is correct,' responded Glenville.

From that point, the guests conversed more with those nearest to them.

Lorene spoke in a low voice to Dell. 'I have not told anyone of your town house, except for Mr Walters, my man of business. He accompanies me and makes certain the men listen to me.'

'That sounds wise,' he said. 'How is the construction faring?'

'Mr Good has workmen building walls on the ground floor. Next he says they will build the floors to the first floor, then the second. He has had the chimneys repaired.'

'I thank you, Lorene.' He did not want to see it, not until it was finished and looked nothing like he remembered.

She smiled. 'It is my pleasure, truly.'

Finally the dinner was over and the ladies retired to the drawing room, leaving the gentlemen to their brandy. Only a short time to go and the whole evening would be over and Lorene could seek the refuge of her bedchamber.

When the ladies entered the drawing room, Lorene looked longingly at the pianoforte. What she would give to simply sit down at the keys and drown out everything with music. But, even though her mother had claimed herself as hostess, this was Lorene's house and she felt responsible for the guests.

Genna and Amelie were already deep in an animated conversation.

'I never knew you were an artist!' Amelie exclaimed.

Genna laughed. 'I never knew you were a shepherdess!'

'Even I did not know that,' Amelie said. 'How was I to know how delightful it could feel to do something useful?'

Lorene knew that as well. She was delighting in helping refurbish Dell's town house, but she didn't want to tell any of them.

'I admit I was looking forward to earning my own money.' Genna sighed. 'Not enough to give up Ross, though.'

'Of course not,' muttered the Duchess. 'He will be a duke some day.'

Genna sent her a scathing glance, but did not engage with her.

Lady Summerfield crossed the room to Genna

and gave her a hug. 'I had no idea you wanted to be an artist. How exciting for you.'

Genna looked as if she tolerated the hug, but did not like it. 'Well, you were not around.'

'Edmund and Tess knew where I was. You could have written to me,' Lady Summerfield said.

Genna faced her. 'Why, Mama? You never wrote to us.'

Lady Summerfield stiffened. 'Your father refused my letters to you.'

Genna, Lorene, and Tess exchanged glances. None of them ever conceived of that possibility.

Lady Northdon, Tess's mother-in-law, spoke up. 'We can do nothing about the past, no? It is best to start from what we might do today.'

If anyone knew this it must be Lady Northdon. Her family's past, her humble status, were things she could not change.

'*Vraiment*, Lady Northdon?' The Duchess spoke the French word mockingly. 'Does not the past affect the present? Surely you know it does.'

Lady Northdon met her eye. 'The past affects the present, *c'est vrai*, Your Grace, but as we cannot change it, we must do what we can with what we are able to change.'

'So true, do you not agree, Lady Summerfield?' The Duchess smiled patronisingly at Lorene's mother.

Her mother lifted her chin. 'I do believe one must take the reins of one's life, yes.'

'Then certainly you will marry Count von Osten,' the Duchess said.

'Why do you harp on that subject, Your Grace?' her mother snapped. 'Surely it can be of no concern of yours?'

'Oh, but it is my concern,' she countered. 'My husband's son—the future duke—is tainted by your scandalous behaviour. You make yourself the object of gossip and that reflects on your daughters, one of whom is married to the future duke.'

'Your Grace,' Lorene said sternly. 'Let us not discuss this.'

'Oui, madame,' Lady Northdon added. 'It is not suitable for polite conversation.'

'Oh?' The Duchess raised a brow. '*You* would know?'

'Please,' Lorene tried again.

'No, I want to discuss this,' her mother flared. 'I fail to see how whether I marry or not reflects on my daughters.'

'Don't you, Mama?' Genna cried. 'Do you not realise that we have lived with the scandal of your behaviour our whole lives? The scandalous Summerfields! Do you not know that is what people called us? Call us even now?'

'Genna—' Lorene attempted.

'Why should what I have done have anything to do with you?' her mother said.

'Why?' Genna's voice became even more shrill. 'Because it has! It does! Do you not think that people now whisper at us as we go by, "There is the daughter of Lady Summerfield. Did you see what was said of her in the newspaper?"'

'I cannot help what people say of me!' she protested.

'You can behave with more propriety,' the Duchess said.

'This is nonsensical.' Her mother turned to Tess. 'Surely you do not see it that way, do you, Tess? Surely no one even remembered me from those early days.'

'We were always tainted by your scandal,' Tess replied. 'And by Papa's behaviour, too. When he died, what prospects did we have?'

'You made out very well,' her mother huffed.

'I dare say we found happiness in spite of the scandal that tainted us, but it did taint us,' Tess said. 'It was not easy. Look what Lorene had to do to try to help us.'

'Marrying that old lord?' her mother said. 'Well, she came out better than all of you. She is a wealthy widow, the best circumstance of all.'

Lorene felt her cheeks burn.

'Lady Summerfield,' Lady Northdon said in a

soft voice, 'perhaps you had better stop talking of this. Your daughters become very upset.'

'Oh, my darlings!' She walked from one to the other, kissing them on the cheek. 'I do not wish to upset you!'

'Then you will become respectable,' the Duchess said so quietly only Lorene heard.

The gentlemen entered the room then, talking of investments.

The Duke was having a tête–à–tête with Count von Osten. 'Will you come to my club tomorrow so we might talk more of this? I am intrigued.'

Edmund scanned the room and frowned. No doubt he sensed something was wrong, as did Ross and Glenville. They each went to their wives.

Lorene rose. 'Pardon me.' She hurried out of the room into the hallway where she leaned her forehead against the cool plaster.

'What is it?'

She turned. Dell was there.

Without thinking she walked into his arms. 'Oh, Dell! There was such a nasty quarrel!'

He wrapped his arms around her. 'The Duchess?'

'She started it, but my mother—my sisters— everyone quarrelled.'

'Not Armageddon then,' he murmured, rocking her slightly. 'Merely a quarrel.'

'I am not so certain,' she said. 'It may have been Armageddon.'

He loosened his grip and put a finger on her chin. 'No. No real harm done. You are still as beautiful as ever.'

Her eyes widened in surprise. 'Oh, Dell.' She put her arms around his neck and embraced him, clinging to him. How could it be that Dell was the one person to make her feel right?

'We had better return to the drawing room,' he said as they broke away. 'Are you quite recovered?'

She wiped her eyes and attempted a smile. 'Quite recovered.'

She gazed at him, so handsome, so caring. She was at great risk of becoming infatuated with him again, filling her head with romantic notions. Look what had happened when she'd felt like that before. She'd almost got him hung for murder.

'Let us go back,' she said.

Chapter Twelve

After the night of the dinner party, tensions worsened. As the month wore on Lorene's mother's outrageous behaviour seemed to escalate. She and the Count attended a ball given by those on the very fringe of society and the newspapers covered every bit of it. Her name was attached to a different gentleman each night. A satirical print was sold showing her flirting with the Prince Regent while the Count was depicted as a hapless buffoon.

She and the Count began to quarrel.

'Must you flaunt yourself wherever you go?' he asked at breakfast, throwing the newspaper down in front of her.

'Flaunt?' Her eyebrows rose. 'I do not flaunt. I am merely enjoying myself. I'll not allow any newspaper man to dictate how I ought to behave, nor will I allow you to do so.'

'You must consider that your behaviour affects more than you alone,' he went on, ignoring her admonishment. 'It affects me as well.'

'You have been with me for over a decade and now you complain about how I behave?' She looked affronted.

'You have never acted like this.' He lowered his voice. 'What is wrong, Hetty?'

'Nothing is wrong!' she protested. 'I am merely enjoying the entertainments that the Season affords. It has been many years—'

He leaned forward, an earnest look on his face. 'I urge you to stop this at once before you alienate everyone who should matter to you.'

Lorene sat in silence, watching and listening to this exchange and wishing she had taken her breakfast in her bedchamber. Too many memories returned of her mother and father shouting at each other.

Her mother turned to her. 'Am I alienating you, Lorene?'

Her mother spoke the question as if demanding Lorene to make the answer she desired.

'It is difficult to talk to you, Mother,' Lorene said truthfully.

'Difficult?' Her mother's colour was high. 'I am not difficult.'

Her mother fended off any criticism with denial.

Lorene knew that Genna and Tess were experiencing the effects of their mother's scandalous behaviour.

'Tess and Genna say they receive fewer invitations than last Season,' Lorene told her.

'That is not my fault!' her mother protested.

'But it is, Hetty,' the Count broke in. 'You know how people are.'

She crossed her arms over her chest.

'Tonight, Hetty,' the Count went on, 'please behave yourself. Lord and Lady Northdon are very good people and will not complain of you, but it will be so much pleasanter if you remain on good behaviour.'

'Northdon?' she cried. 'We are attending the theatre tonight with Lord Alvanley.'

Lord Alvanley was a member of the Prince Regent's set and a man young enough to be Lady Summerfield's son.

'No. Tonight is the Northdons,' he said patiently. 'A dinner for Edmund.'

She waved a hand. 'We can go to the theatre afterwards, then.'

Lorene dreaded this party. The last time the family gathered together, tensions had been high and tempers had flared. Her mother was already primed for losing her temper.

Anything could happen.

* * *

Dell shared a drink of claret with the Duke of Kessington in his library in the late afternoon.

'Come to the opera tonight, Dell,' his Grace said. 'The Duchess and I have some important people sharing our box. It should be a productive night.'

Dell took a sip of his wine. 'I cannot, sir. I am engaged.'

'Oh?' the Dukes brows rose. 'Is there some other event of which we are not aware?'

The Duke was always alert for the most advantageous social events during which to pursue his political aims. Not that Dell's commitment would fit that description.

'A small party,' he explained. 'I am invited to dinner at Lord and Lady Northdon's.'

'Northdon!' The Duke's voice rose. 'He is a pariah. Whatever induced you to accept that invitation?'

'It is on behalf of Edmund Summerfield. He is leaving soon.'

'Edmund Summerfield is not a connection that will do you any credit at all,' the Duke told him. 'You would be better off coming to the opera with the Duchess and me. There are always alliances to be made during the interval.'

'Another time, perhaps,' Dell said.

His Grace made a derisive sound. 'I suppose that abominable woman will attend as well.'

'Abominable woman?'

'Lady Summerfield.' The Duke shook his head. 'There is gossip about her in the newspapers every day, it seems. She's been fraternising with the Prince Regent's set. Men of the town, the lot of them. You should distance yourself from them, my boy. Cannot allow their reputation to damage yours.'

'It is to be a family gathering,' Dell responded. 'No newspaper men allowed.'

'You jest.' The Duke lifted his glass to his lips and sipped his claret. 'I do not know why you are included. You are not family.'

He should keep his distance. By God, he'd never questioned why he was invited to a family party. They were making him feel as though he belonged with them.

Dell finished the last of his wine.

It was a losing battle warring inside him not to become attached to the scandalous Summerfields. As much as he resolved not to attach himself, he was drawn to them.

'Where are you off to now?' the Duke asked.

'I am taking Lady Alice for a turn in the Park.' Although it felt more like duty than pleasure.

'Well done, my boy!' the Duke exclaimed. 'The Duchess will be very pleased.'

'Do not raise her hopes,' Dell said. 'I am not at all certain I am ready for a courtship.'

'Better now than later.' The Duke saluted him with his glass. 'You never know what can happen.'

Dell knew. In an instant a flame could go out of control and fire could consume all that was dear.

A short time later Dell was admitted into Lord Brackton's drawing room. Lady Brackton was already seated there.

Dell bowed. 'My lady.'

'Penford!' the lady said eagerly. 'Lady Alice will be down shortly. Do sit down and have some tea with me.'

He sat and allowed her to pour him a cup of tea.

She enquired as to his health. Discussed the weather and what the public would soon learn about Brackton's views on the next bill coming up for a vote.

'Lady Alice will be delighted to take some air this afternoon. It is such a fine day.' She repeated a review of the weather.

Lady Alice finally arrived. 'Forgive my lateness, Penford.'

'Indeed,' he said. 'It is of no consequence.'

She was not really a plain young woman. Pleasant was how he'd describe her. She lacked Lorene's intensity, though.

Was that to Lady Alice's advantage? Lorene drew him to her and he did not want to be drawn.

They proceeded to his high-flyer phaeton waiting outside. He assisted her into the seat.

'This is an impressive carriage!' Lady Alice exclaimed.

It had been his brother's and apparently brand new at the time of his death.

But Dell did not bother explaining that to her.

Her conversation was almost exactly like her mother's. Enquiring as to his health. Discussing the weather and politics.

They passed Berkeley Square and started down Mount Street. He could tell her he owned a town house on this street, but that would involve explaining about the fire and the renovation and he was not interested in discussing either with her.

But as they neared the house, the door opened and Lorene stepped out with her man of business. She looked directly at him and nodded as he passed. He touched his hat.

'That was Lady Tinmore, was it not?' Lady Alice asked.

'Yes, it was.'

'Mama told me she lived on Brook Street,' she went on. 'I wonder who the man was with her. Was it his house, do you suppose?' Her tone was disapproving and it rankled with Dell. Lorene had obviously been checking on his town house, doing nothing that required censure.

'He is her man of business,' he responded. 'And it is my town house they were leaving.'

'Your town house?' Lady Alice cried. 'But you live with the Duke.'

Surely her mother had informed her about the fire. 'The town house is undergoing a complete refurbishment. Lady Tinmore is in charge of it.'

'Lady Tinmore?' A line formed between her eyebrows. 'Why should she be in charge?'

'Because I asked her,' he said curtly.

'Oh.' Her voice turned small.

By the time they neared the Grosvenor Gate to Hyde Park, he took pity on her. 'Lady Tinmore refurbished one of my country houses. Her taste is impeccable, so I asked her to help me with the town house.'

'I see,' she said blandly. 'How nice of her to help you.'

They entered the park, which was crowded with other members of the *ton* who ventured out to see and be seen at this fashionable hour.

'Look how many carriages there are!' Lady Alice cried. 'We shall see several people we know here.'

They greeted several people as they passed them on the road circling the park.

At least Lady Alice was enjoying herself. Dell

found the outing a complete bore. To see and be seen was not enough of a reason for him to enjoy a carriage ride. Out in the country it made more sense. The fresh air. The scenery. Giving the horses their heads. They were slowed to a snail's pace. It was more difficult to keep the horses from charging ahead.

'Oh, look!' she cried for the hundredth time it seemed. 'There is Mr Holdsworth.'

He was walking on the footpath.

'Yoo-hoo, Mr Holdsworth' she cried.

He walked up to the carriage. 'Good afternoon, Lady Alice.' The young man looked miserable. 'Lord Penford.'

Dell nodded to him and tended to the horse while Lady Alice engaged him in conversation—about more than health, weather and politics—and with more animation than Dell had seen heretofore.

'A friend?' Dell asked.

'Yes.' Her voice rose an octave. 'I have known him my whole life.' She added sadly, 'He is a younger son.'

Lorene had dreaded the dinner at Lord and Lady Northdon's, not because she did not desire to see Edmund and her sisters, but because her mother already had become a tinderbox, ready to flame with little provocation, and it seemed that some provocation came whenever she met with her daughters.

Luckily a visit with Edmund's and Tess's babies eased the uncomfortable atmosphere. Nothing like babies to make a person smile. She was so happy for Edmund and Tess. They each were obviously as proud as they could be of their sons. The happiest in the room were the grandmothers, Lorene's mother and Lady Northdon.

Lorene sat with Dell as the babies played with each other. Edmund's son toddled around the room and Tess's little one tried his best to keep up by crawling.

'How dear they are!' Lorene said to Dell.

She glanced at him and saw that the sight was not as delightful to him. He looked as if in pain.

'Are you feeling unwell?' she asked him.

He blinked as if surprised at the question. 'I am very well.'

'You look as if someone is poking you with a dagger.'

His expression turned to dismay. 'I was thinking…'

'About your family?' she asked gently.

'About how easy it is to feel someone's importance,' he said cryptically.

She was puzzled. 'I do not comprehend.'

He smiled. 'There is no need for you to comprehend.'

But she wanted to understand. His countenance was so often unhappy that *she* experienced pain when she looked at him. Why could she not make happy those she cared about? Why could she not make *him* happy?

She glanced back at the babies and grasped at straws. 'Do you wish you had a son, Dell?'

She felt his body tense. 'Do you?' he asked.

She sighed. 'Yes. I do. Or a daughter. It used to be a dream of mine.'

'You could still have children,' he said.

'No.' She shook her head. 'I'll never marry again.' That dream had died. Marriage had been a misery to her. She'd never let a man have such control over her. 'And I will not have children without marriage.' She glanced at him again. 'What of you?'

'Why plague me with this conversation, Lorene? I do not wish to discuss it,' he snapped.

He'd never spoken sharply to her before.

Stung, she turned away and watched her mother and Lady Northdon in their dinner dresses down on the floor playing with the babies.

Tess's son started to cry and soon Edmund's son wailed along with him. Tess and Amelie scooped them up in their arms. 'Time to go back to the nannies and be put to bed.'

Lorene liked that Tess and Amelie were both attentive mothers. She'd always known it would

be so of Tess. She and Tess had once shared the
same dreams. To marry for love and to have babies to cherish. To have happy families.

Although the babies had left the room, Lorene's
mother and Lady Northdon repeated every charming thing they'd done.

This was a part of her mother Lorene could
like, her genuine delight in the grandsons. Had
her mother cherished her and her sisters when
they were babies? Did she have love pouring from
every pore like she did for these little ones?

If so, how could she have left them?

This was not the time to ask her and Lorene
hoped Tess and Genna realised it as well. The
happy glow from the babies was already wearing
off. Soon the tension would return.

Lorene darted a glance to Dell, who seemed
totally preoccupied. She could not count on him
to ease her discomfort or her fears tonight. Perhaps it was time she stopped thinking of herself
and thought of him instead. Perhaps he was the
one in most need tonight.

He must have sensed her looking at him, because he lifted his head and met her gaze with a
smile that felt nothing but sad to her.

'Wine?' Lord Northdon offered.

Dell asked her, 'Would you like a glass?'

'Yes, thank you,' she responded.

He rose and crossed the room to take two filled

glasses from Northdon's hand. He brought one to her and sat back down to sip the other.

She desperately wanted to pull him out of his withdrawal. 'The house is coming along very well,' she said.

'I am glad of it.' He did not sound glad.

'The walls and floors are finished,' she went on. 'Now it simply wants paint and wallpaper and furniture.'

'Do what you want with it,' he responded. 'I'll see it when it is through.'

'I thought to stop you today to look at it,' she said. 'You and the lady with you. That was Lady Alice with you today, was it not?'

'Yes.'

'She looked lovely.'

He glanced away for a moment, then turned back to her. 'I had to tell her about you and the town house. She was spinning a story of you having a tryst with your man of business.'

'Goodness!' She did not need that. 'So she knows I am helping you?'

'She does.'

'I suppose we should simply tell everyone, then,' she said.

His gaze swept the room. 'Not today.'

That suited her. She liked sharing that special knowledge with Dell alone and it spoiled it somehow that he'd told Lady Alice. This was the second time she'd seen him take special notice of the young woman.

She worked up her courage and asked, 'Are you courting Lady Alice, Dell?'

'No,' he responded.

Why should that gratify her? She wanted to see him happy above all things.

He added, 'But I am considering it.'

She made herself smile. 'How nice.'

Over in another corner of the room, her mother's voice rose. 'Why must everyone plague me?'

'I did not plague you, Mother,' Genna said. 'I merely asked you a question.'

Oh, no!

'Why I left you?' Her mother's voice was shrill.

Lorene rose from her chair and hurried over to them.

'I will tell you why I left you.' She glared at Genna. 'I had to make a choice. Run away with the man I loved and be happy or stay with a husband who loathed me and made me miserable. I was never very important to you in any event. You had nannies and a governess. You did not need me.'

Von Osten came to her mother's side and put his arm around her. 'There now, Hetty,' he said in a loving murmur. 'Do not upset yourself.'

She burst into tears, shocking everyone.

Lady Northdon came to her side. 'Come with me, dear. Let us go away from here.'

Her mother allowed Lady Northdon to lead her out of the room. Von Osten followed them.

'Genna, why did you speak to her like that?' Lorene asked, peeved that her youngest sister could not sense that this was not the time or place.

'Why, Genna?' Edmund joined in.

Ross stood beside Genna.

'I am sorry, Lorene!' Genna cried. 'I am sorry, Edmund. I do not know why I do such things. It is just that she pretends it was just fine that she left us and it wasn't!'

Now Genna looked ready to cry.

Ross held her. 'She will calm down. Do not worry.'

They had not even been called into dinner yet.

Several minutes later, Lady Northdon returned. 'Lady Summerfield apologises for her absence, but she is suffering from the headache and was compelled to go home. Count von Osten accompanies her.' She looked apologetically at Lorene. 'They have taken the carriage.'

'That is of no consequence,' Lorene said. Using the carriage had been ridiculous. Her town house was only a street away. 'I trust she will feel better soon.'

'Now I feel even worse,' Genna said.

'I do not feel it is entirely your fault, Genna,'

Lorene said. 'Our mother has been quite excitable lately. The Count remarked on it this very morning.'

Edmund frowned. 'I have noticed it, too. She is not herself. She is typically steady and in excellent humour.'

'And I made her worse.' Genna looked miserable.

Lady Northdon waved a hand in a typically French manner. 'We ladies must be allowed our moods.'

Her husband handed her a glass of wine. 'Then we have two fewer guests for dinner.'

Lady Northdon smiled as she accepted the wine. 'I have given instructions to take two places from the table.'

Dinner was announced and it turned out to be a surprisingly pleasant affair. It was delightful to have Edmund all to themselves, so to speak, without their mother to stir up emotions.

When it came time to leave, Dell offered to walk Lorene home.

'I would be delighted,' she said.

A moment later they were outside. The night was as fine as a spring night could be.

Lorene took hold of Dell's arm, but they did not speak and she felt the chasm between them had grown since their earlier conversation. She was at a loss.

They reached her town house. A rush lamp was burning at the doorway.

She took her key from her reticule. 'Goodnight, Dell,' she said. Her voice sounded strange after the silence between them.

He pulled her out of the light into the servants' entrance. She could barely see his face it was so shrouded in darkness. His eyes shone through, though.

'I am sorry, Lorene.' His voice rasped.

His intensity took her breath. 'For what?'

'For...' He paused. 'For being churlish.'

As she had done that night in the inn, she touched his face and felt his suffering. 'No need to apologise to me, Dell. Not you. You have always been my rock when I needed you.'

'Not tonight,' he said. 'Not tonight.'

'You have much on your mind,' she said, grasping at the only reason that made sense to her, the one that somehow made her insides twist. 'Making the choice to court a young lady or not would weigh on any man's mind.'

He drew back. 'I have not yet made a choice.'

She suddenly felt as if she were treading on thin ice. 'I did not mean you should.'

Just as quickly he came close again, even closer than before. She could feel his breath on her face as his eyes pierced hers. 'I do not want anyone to be important to me.'

'A wife would be important,' she agreed.

'That is not—' He did not finish what he was about to say. Instead he stepped back again. 'I should bid you goodnight.'

'Would—would you like to come in? I'm certain we have brandy. Would you like to come in and have some brandy? You could tell me—' She wanted to be of help to him.

'No!' he said sharply. 'I have said too much already.'

He'd said nothing—nothing that made sense.

She walked back to her door. He held out his hand for her key and unlocked the door for her. He opened it and placed the key back in her hand, keeping hold of her hand for longer than needed.

'Goodnight, Lorene,' he said.

She made an impulsive move. She stood on tiptoe and kissed him on the cheek. 'Remember, Dell. I am always here if you need a friend.'

Chapter Thirteen

The next morning an elderly man with a cane called upon the offices of the *New Tatler,* one of London's printers of pamphlets. He'd researched the possibilities carefully and learned that this publisher relished a scandalous story.

'I should like to speak with the editor, please,' the man said.

One of the workers responded, 'What about?'

'About a story,' he said.

The workman gestured for him to follow and led him to an office in the back of the shop where two men sat. Both looked to be in their prime. Forties, Dixon would guess. One was heavyset and bald; the other, thin as a whip with long dark hair that nearly touched his shoulders.

The workman inclined his head. 'Mr Addison and Mr Steele.'

The man leaned on his cane and looked from

one man to another. Neither said who was the editor and who was not. 'Yes. Well. I am Dixon. I have a story for you. A true one that will make you and me a fortune…'

Dixon had stewed over this for over a year. He had, of course, been pensioned off and sent packing as soon as the new Earl of Tinmore settled himself on the estate. It wasn't as if the old earl had not provided for him. He could have a comfortable living. It was just that he had served Lord Tinmore at Tinmore Hall for over half a century and now he was booted out of his home.

Because of *her*. That upstart. That fortune hunter.

When the Earl's wife and son died and the Earl retired as a recluse, Dixon had run the household. Wicky had been the Earl's valet for even longer and Filkins had served him as secretary for at least forty years. The three of them had made certain the Earl's needs were properly met. How many times had m'lord said he'd be lost without them? The Earl had been content.

Then she came, calling uninvited and offering herself like some Covent Garden strumpet. Promising him who knew what. If he'd marry her, she'd make his life heaven. And the old lord fell for it. He started to act as if he were twenty years younger. Inviting guests. Attending Parliament. All sorts of exertions.

She was behind it, Dixon knew. Driving m'lord to be running around London when he ought to have been resting. Heaven knew what parties and routs she made him take her to during the Season. Then bringing her fancy visitors to Tinmore Hall—a duke's son and Lord Penford. M'lord was always impressed by the loftiest titles. That sister of hers was another fortune hunter, snaring that duke's son into marriage. And the Earl of Penford—who did he think he was, charging into Tinmore Hall and confronting m'lord!

No matter what the Earl of Penford said at that inquest, Dixon knew his lordship had died from foul play. Penford pushed him, no doubt of that. If the magistrate was not willing to try Penford for murder, Dixon would see that he was found guilty in the eyes of society.

The two men in the office exchanged glances.

One said, 'You will have to tell us more than that.'

The other said, 'And tell us what payment you expect.'

Dixon gave what he hoped was a sincere smile. 'I would ask for a mere ten pounds…and fifty per cent of your profits.'

'Then you will have to tell us a very good story indeed,' the first man said.

Dixon shifted his weight. 'It is a very good story. A story about how one earl murdered the other for a woman, the murdered earl's wife! How an up-and-coming Whig rid the House of Lords of an esteemed senior Tory.' He lifted the cane. 'This very cane may have been the instrument of death!' Dixon had asked for and had been given the Earl of Tinmore's cane, the only personal item of Lord Tinmore's that he possessed.

He launched into the story, making it as dramatic as possible, just as he rehearsed it.

He came to his dramatic end. 'So this magistrate, a known Whig supporter—' his investigation discovered that fact '—saw to it that his compatriot got off scot-free.'

The idea of a political conspiracy was inspired, if Dixon said so himself.

'You claim this is true?' asked the first man.

'I know it to be so,' Dixon replied. 'I was there. I was butler to the late Earl of Tinmore.'

'You saw the murder?' the second man asked.

'I know it to be true,' Dixon prevaricated. 'I seek justice.'

He waited.

The two men exchanged glances again.

One said, 'True or not, it is a good story.'

'We may be opening ourselves up for a suit of libel,' his companion warned.

The first man shrugged. 'So we disguise the names just enough. If we publish this correctly, we stand to make a lot of money.' That sounded excellent to Dixon. 'It could be the sensation of the Season. Make our newspaper the most sought after in London.'

The other man rubbed his chin. 'If we publish it in pamphlet form, perhaps we can distribute it countrywide. Think of the profits then.'

The whole country against them? Dixon could hardly contain his excitement.

'We'll do it!' the first man said.

The other nodded with a smug smile.

His companion said, 'Let us have you sit down with one of our writers. Tell the story to him and we will go from there.'

Dixon frowned. Did they think he was a fool? 'First pay me my ten pounds and write out a contract for the fifty per cent.'

'Indeed,' one said, gesturing to a chair. 'Have a seat and we will do precisely that.'

The other man said, 'Let us also send a man to check on these two today, see what they are up to. It can only enhance the story. Show how they are living without the consequences of a murder.'

Excellent! thought Dixon.

A week later Lorene's only solace came from working on Dell's town house. Her mother was still often in the newspapers and still quarrelling with Count von Osten, and he was spending more time away from her.

One morning after the Count stormed out of the house, Lorene tried to talk with her mother, who looked as if she were preparing to go out, as well.

'Where are you going, Mother?' she asked.

'To call upon a friend,' her mother said tersely. '*He* cannot tell me who to see and who not to see.'

'Who did the Count tell you not to see?' she asked.

'A certain gentleman—you do not need to know who it is.' She pulled on a glove.

'Mother!' Lorene was shocked. 'Do not tell me you are unfaithful to the Count!'

Her mother sank into a chair and looked miserable. 'How could I be?' she asked. 'Ossie is everything to me. Everything.'

'Then why do you quarrel with him?' Lorene did not understand her mother at all.

'I do not know.' Her mother waved away her maid who had brought over a bonnet that perfectly matched her walking dress.

'He is concerned about you. That is what I see. He does not understand why you apparently seek the attention from the gossipmongers.' Lorene could not believe she was defending the man who took her mother away, but everything he did convinced her he was devoted to her mother.

She pulled her glove off again. 'This coming to England has been a disaster! My children despise me. My friends disapprove of me. The only people who like me are those who land me in the newspapers.' She dropped her head in her hands. 'And all Ossie talks of is getting married. I was all right for him before this, now suddenly even he disapproves of me!'

'You have apparently been acting outrageously,' Lorene said.

She looked up, eyes flashing. 'Now you disapprove of me, too! You and Tess and Genna.' She made a wounded, resentful sound. 'Genna.'

Lorene lowered herself so she could look into her mother's eyes. 'Mother, calm yourself. Give us time. It would help if we would not be dismayed about what we read of you.'

'Not all of it is true,' her mother said in a lowered voiced. 'I've not been unfaithful.'

She put her hand on her mother's arm. 'Do me a favour, then. Let me gather my sisters and Edmund and let us just talk together.'

'I do not know.' Her mother looked away. 'I do not wish to have you all yelling at me.'

'We would not do that to you,' Lorene assured her.

'How do I know there won't be a repeat of that horrid dinner?'

At the Northdons, she meant.

'I do not think Genna would repeat that.' She hoped. 'But perhaps you could listen to Genna a little. She is outspoken, but sometimes she speaks a truth we need to hear.'

If she'd confided in Genna before marrying Lord Tinmore, would she have gone through with it? She'd deliberately kept it a secret so her sisters would not stop her. Perhaps that was a trait she shared with her mother, sneaking away to do what she wanted to do.

'Arrange it if you wish,' her mother said tersely.

She squeezed her mother's arm. 'Thank you, Mother. Do you want your bonnet now?'

Her mother shook her head. 'I changed my mind. I am not going out after all.'

She kissed her mother's cheek. 'That is for the best, I think.'

Except Lorene was expected at Dell's town house and now she felt she could not leave her mother alone. She could not bring her mother with her without betraying the secrecy she and Dell had agreed upon.

Even if he had betrayed it by telling Lady Alice.

It was silly of her to think of it as a betrayal. He did not owe her secrecy. And she had told Mr Walters, but then, she needed Mr Walters's help.

'Excuse me a moment,' she said. 'I must speak with Mr Walters. I will be right back.'

She found Mr Walters in the library, poring over a ledger.

He stood at her entrance. 'Good morning, ma'am. I was reviewing our expenditures on furnishings.'

'And?' Would he criticise her? Say she spent too much? Or too little?

Why was she worrying about the opinion of her man of business? He was not her husband who'd criticised almost everything she said or did.

'And,' he responded, 'I will make a copy of it for Lord Penford along with the envelope containing the bills.'

She almost laughed. He wasn't judging her. He was merely doing his job.

'Excellent, Mr Walters.'

'Do you wish to go to the town house now?' He closed the ledger and stacked it upon another.

'I cannot go today,' she said. 'Something has come up. But I need for you to go and receive the furnishings that will be arriving today.'

He looked dismayed.

'You are not required to know where to put them,' she reassured him. 'I think you know which rooms the items go in. Place them in any order you wish. We can move them later.'

'Very well, ma'am.' He bowed. 'I will leave directly.'

'Thank you, Mr Walters,' she said. 'I am so grateful to you.'

His face flushed with pleasure. 'Pleased to be of assistance.'

She hurried back to her mother's bedchamber only to find her mother's maid helping her with her bonnet.

Her spirits sank. 'Did you change your mind about going out?' she asked.

'I did,' said her mother in a firm tone that was new to Lorene. 'But I have decided we should call upon Genna.'

This sounded ominous.

'Never fear, my darling.' Now her mother sounded more like herself. 'I will listen to Genna.' She smiled. 'And she will listen to me.'

Lorene was not at all certain that confrontation was the best way to handle Genna. If one pushed, Genna tended to push back even harder. But with any luck she would be able to keep both of them civil to each other.

'I'll order the carriage and get my things.'

When Lorene and her mother left the house, Lorene noticed a man loitering at the corner of Grosvenor Square. She'd seen him there a couple of days before, too, and that seemed odd. When their carriage drove by him, he left his spot and seemed to walk behind it. By the time they reached Chapel Street, she could see the man no more.

The carriage took them on to Hill Street, where Genna and Ross leased a small town house that featured a sunny second-floor bedchamber that Genna converted into a studio. The house had no rooms grand enough for entertaining great numbers of people and that suited Genna very well. She and the Marquess of Rossdale did little entertaining.

When Lorene and her mother were admitted to the small hall, they were told that the Marquess and Marchioness were in the drawing room one floor above. They had to wait until the butler attending the door received permission to announce them. Lorene surveyed the space and mentally began to refurbish it. She would make it brighter, perhaps exchange the wooden bannister of the staircase for a wrought-iron one made in pleasing shapes.

'Imagine one of my daughters being called a marchioness!' Her mother broke her reverie. 'And a duchess some day.' Her mother laughed.

Such good humour puzzled Lorene. Her mother's emotions seemed as changeable as a British winter. Cold and freezing one day, balmy the next.

The butler returned. 'The Marquess and Marchioness will see you now.'

They followed him up the stairs and waited at the door of the drawing room until he announced them.

'Mother!' Genna cried nervously before they had cleared the threshold. 'Lorene. What a surprise.'

She and Rossdale rose from the sofa.

Across from them stood Dell.

Rossdale immediately crossed the room. 'How good it is to see you. Come. Sit.' He gave them each a buss on the cheek.

Genna seemed frozen in place, but she managed, 'We are having tea. Would you care for a cup?'

'How very nice!' their mother said too brightly. 'Tea would be lovely.'

As Ross escorted them over to the sofa and chairs, Dell bowed. 'Good day, Lady Summerfield.' His blue eyes captured Lorene's. 'Lorene.'

Lorene had not expected to see him here, had not seen him since the Northdons' dinner party when he walked her home and seemed so disturbed. She was not prepared for the emotions that erupted at the sight of him. The giddiness of her schoolgirl infatuation. The worry over his welfare. The fear that he'd made up his mind to court Lady Alice.

'Delighted to see you again,' her mother gushed, saving her from a need to say something when words seemed hard to form. 'Is the Lords not in session today?'

'Not today, ma'am,' Dell said.

'Why are you calling upon us, Mother?' Genna asked in her outspoken manner.

Lorene winced inside. Genna looked prepared for battle.

Her mother gave Genna a charming smile. 'I called so you and I could have a little chat. Will that not be simply enchanting?'

Genna looked as if she'd rather have a tooth pulled. 'Enchanting.'

The butler brought a tray with two more cups and saucers and Genna poured tea for them.

'What a charming little house,' their mother said, glancing around.

Lorene thought the room lacked colour. Its walls were white with pale green plasterwork, the chairs and sofa the same pale green.

'It suits us for now,' Genna said. 'And it has a good room for my studio.'

'I would very much enjoy seeing your room and some of your paintings.' Their mother was trying so hard to be nice. Lorene's heart melted for her.

She glanced at Dell, whose eyes darted to her mother and back and gave her a look that seemed to understand what she was feeling.

How she'd missed seeing him. 'How are you, Dell?' she asked.

'Faring well,' he responded politely. 'And you?'

Goodness. They were talking as if strangers.

They all chit-chatted about the weather, about each other's health, about the tastiness of the biscuits served with the tea, but it seemed to Lorene that tension swirled through the room like the morning mist through woods. She could hardly stand it.

Her mother placed her cup and saucer on the table. 'Well!' she said. 'Now that we have performed the niceties, I should like to speak with Genna alone.'

Genna looked stricken.

'Alone?' Lorene said. 'Surely I should join you.'

'No. Just my baby girl and her mother.' She smiled sweetly.

'Then why make me come with you? I had other things to do.'

'You may go do them now,' her mother said in a dismissive tone. 'I'd prefer you not wait for me. I will see myself home.'

'Very well.' Lorene was stunned. 'I will have the carriage wait for you. I will walk back.'

Her mother smiled gratefully.

'Genna, do you want this?' Rossdale asked.

Genna's expression turned to resolve. 'Of course I do. Mother and I have much to catch up on.' She turned to their mother. 'Shall I show you to my studio? We may speak in private there.'

'Delighted!' exclaimed their mother, rising from her chair.

The others rose, too.

Rossdale turned to Genna. 'I am expected at my father's shortly, but I will delay if you prefer.'

She gave him a fond look. 'No, I actually prefer you go. All of you. Let Mother and me talk.' She walked over to her mother. 'Come, Mother. I will show you to my studio.'

The two ladies walked out of the room, arm in arm.

Rossdale said, 'Dare I leave?'

'I feel the same,' Lorene responded. 'I do not know if we should leave them alone.'

Dell spoke up. 'They are not children. Do not treat them as such. Let them take each other on.'

Both she and Rossdale looked at him sceptically.

Rossdale took in a bracing breath. 'You are right, of course. I must be off to my father's. Are you bound there as well?' he asked Dell.

'No.' Dell turned to Lorene. 'Shall I escort you home?'

She did not expect that. 'It is not necessary, but, yes, I would appreciate your company.'

'Well,' Rossdale said. 'Let us go, then.'

Chapter Fourteen

When they reached the outside, Rossdale walked towards Piccadilly. Lorene and Dell headed in the opposite direction.

It was a crisp spring day with blue skies and new green leaves on the trees, a lovely day to be walking on a handsome gentleman's arm, but there was no ease between them and Lorene missed that acutely.

'Where was Count von Osten today?' Dell asked. 'I have never seen them apart.'

They turned right on Audley Street.

'They had a quarrel and he stormed out,' she told him. 'Mother was so upset I was afraid to leave her alone.' She glanced back as if she could see them behind her. 'That is why I was reluctant to leave Genna alone with her.'

He laughed. 'I dare say you do not have to worry about Genna. She is made of stern stuff.'

'I am not as certain about Mother, though,'

Lorene admitted. 'She has been moody and un-reasonable since...well, since that dinner party she arranged.'

'She seemed calm enough to me,' he said.

'I know!' she cried. 'That is why I am worried. It was a big change.'

His voice turned serious. 'It is up to them to fix whatever is wrong between them, Lorene. Not up to you.'

Was that a scold? She could not tell. For a minute she felt their old camaraderie, but now the chasm between them returned. They walked in silence until they reached Mount Street.

She stopped at the corner. 'I—I must say good-bye to you here. I want to check something at the town house.'

She felt his body tense. He let her slip her arm from his.

'I bid you good day, then,' he said sombrely.

She started to walk away, but turned back. 'Wait a moment, Dell. I want you to come with me.'

He frowned. 'It is completed?'

'No, not completed,' she admitted. 'But I want you to see what we've done so far. It—it won't be quite as settled as I wish, but you should see it.'

He looked as if he wanted to walk on, but finally he said, 'Very well. If you insist.'

She hoped she was not making an error.

They walked to the town house and she tried

the door. It was unlocked. She turned to let Dell
open it when she noticed a man passing by at the
corner of Mount Street and Audley. It was just a
glimpse, but it unsettled her.

'Shall we go in?' Dell said, standing at the open
door.

'Yes.' She walked into the hall and turned
around to see his reaction.

The marble floors were partly covered with
oilcloth to protect them from the furniture that
was to be moved in. Only one bare table graced
the hall and Dell placed his hat and gloves upon
it. The walls of the hall were papered in silk the
colour of the sky on this fine spring day, with
faint stripes in the weave making the space look
larger and taller. The marble steps of the stairway
had been scrubbed and polished to their original
white, but Lorene had the wrought-iron bannister painted in a shade of orange that she'd seen
in a print of the Prince Regent's Carlton House.

She could not help but ask, 'What do you think
of it?'

His gaze circled the area. 'It is certainly different.'

Faint praise, but at least *different* had been what
he'd asked for.

She gestured to the walls. 'Mr Good, the architect, said he was familiar with the floor plan
of these town houses. He said there was not much

we could change, because of the confines of the space, but he did manage to move doorways and such.'

She pointed to the left. 'There will be a small drawing room there where callers can wait, but behind the stairway will be the servery and the cloak room, such as was probably there before. Behind that is the morning room.' She turned to the right. 'The room in front can be a library or a drawing room. The dining room is behind it, but come see this.'

She led him to the morning room. 'Look,' she said, spinning around. 'Mr Good put in larger windows and a door here. See all the light in here!' The windows looked out on to the small garden in the back of the house. The door opened on to the garden. She could imagine this space some day planted with flowers and shrubs, with a little room for a kitchen garden as well.

The curtains in the morning room were a sky blue similar to the hall wallpaper, trimmed in the orange also featured there. The walls were papered with Chinese birds and flowers against a pale blue background. In the centre of the room was a round table, with four chairs around it upholstered in the orange of the curtain-trim. The carpet contained myriad colours in an oriental pattern.

'This room is done,' she explained. 'Except for

paintings on the walls. I thought you might want to pick those yourself. Perhaps bring some from your country estate.'

They heard footsteps and voices in the hall. It would be Mr Walters and the men who brought in the furniture that was to arrive today.

Mr Walters was in the hall, indeed. He stood with some sturdy-looking workmen.

'My lady,' Mr Walters said with surprise. 'You are here.' He gestured to the men who pulled on their forelocks. 'We were just about to leave. Do you want to see if the rooms above are arranged correctly?'

'No, I do not wish to keep you if you are ready to leave.'

Dell joined her in the hall.

Mr Walters bowed to him. 'Lord Penford.'

Dell nodded.

'Thank you all,' Lorene said. After Mr Walters and the workmen left, she turned to Dell. 'Let me show you the upstairs.'

They walked up to the first floor.

The architect had warned her that the floor plan of this floor would also be similar to how the rooms were configured before, but he changed whatever he could. He made the doors to the drawing room double the size of ordinary doors. The room was spacious and continued the blue theme. This time a lovely blue damask covered the walls. The same fabric was used to upholster two couches and several chairs were covered in gold damask. A gold filigree outlined the new white marble fireplace and the white trim around the doors. Above the fireplace was a huge gold-framed mirror that rose to the ceiling.

The chairs sat in the middle of the oriental carpet in a haphazard way, not at all arranged in any sensible order.

Lorene walked over to them. 'These will not do. Help me place them where they should be.' She picked up a chair.

He took the chair from her. 'I will move the furniture; you tell me where.'

The sofas were already in place against their matching walls. They arranged the chairs in front of them and the tables between. Against other walls were cabinets and tables meant for vases of flowers and such.

She surveyed the room. 'It needs decorative items. Perhaps a card table. Or a pianoforte. But otherwise it is done.'

It was a beautiful room, Lorene thought, with a great deal of impact, but perhaps he did not wish for such vibrancy. She turned to see his reaction, her heart pounding.

'It is nothing like I remember,' he said.

'One more room to show you,' she said, this time forcing her enthusiasm.

* * *

Dell took one more look at the drawing room before following her across the hallway to another closed door.

He was stunned by what she'd shown him. The house he remembered had white or pale green walls with plasterwork trim, like so many houses influenced by architects like Robert Adam. The bold colours Lorene chose were nothing like that and nothing like she had done at Summerfield House.

She opened the door and walked into the next room. He followed her.

It was the bedchamber. Not blue, but a golden yellow that reminded him of sunshine. The curtains were in the same silk fabric as the walls, a striped pattern similar to the hall downstairs. In this room everything seemed to be in its place. A washstand with basin and pitcher. A mirror. A chest of drawers. Chairs. Tables.

The mahogany bed dominated the room. Its posters were carved into spirals. Its bed curtains were gold fabric with a different pattern than that on the walls.

Lorene crossed the room and opened a door. 'The—the dressing room is here.' He could see mahogany shelves and drawers.

He closed his eyes and tried to remember what this space looked like before.

Nothing like this.

'I can always change anything you do not like,' she said. 'I'll pay for what you don't use, of course.'

Pay? He would not make her pay.

His gaze swept the room again. 'It is nothing like I've seen before,' he said.

She lifted her chin. 'I will do it over.'

He strode over to her. 'No. No. You misunderstand. It is so very different. All the colour.'

'It is what the magazines show. Like the interiors of Carlton House.' She was still trying to explain, but it was he who should unravel his emotions upon seeing what she'd done.

He could say he wasn't used to this new idea of bright colours on the walls and the furniture and the carpets, but that was really of no consequence to him. He liked the colours she chose.

Was it the loss of the old house that bothered him? That was another part of his life that would never return. It was the intruding vision of the fire and of his family and those poor maids trapped in it that pained him. He had not realised that he would miss the house as it used to be. It made no sense, though. It wasn't even a house he ever considered home. Home was Penford, but he couldn't bear the memories that were sparked in every part of that house and estate. He'd asked Lorene to change this sad place. He'd asked her to erase the old house. She did just that, so how could he complain?

These rooms would never make him think of his family, but they would make him think of Lorene. He'd see her in every corner, in every shade of blue and yellow, every choice of table and chair.

How could he tell her that? How could he bring another woman—Lady Alice, perhaps—into these rooms and not be thinking of Lorene? How could he even think about bringing another woman to that bed, when it was Lorene he could picture there?

He put his hands on her shoulders. 'I like what you have done,' he told her.

She looked up into his eyes. 'Truly?'

'Yes.'

Her expression relaxed and the worry left her eyes. 'I am so glad.' She spun away from him. 'It is ready for you, Dell, if you choose to move here.' She extended her arms as if to encompass the whole room. 'There are enough rooms ready that you could live here now. You have a drawing room to receive guests, a bedchamber to sleep in and the morning room will do for dining until the dining room is ready. The kitchen is complete, as well, and rooms for the servants below stairs. The other rooms merely need furniture and wall coverings, but all that can be done while you live here.' She continued to circle the room. 'You'd need servants, of course, but not many at first. A cook. A housekeeper. A butler or simply a footman. A maid of all work.'

He gazed at the sunshine she'd placed on the walls. He'd been plunged in darkness when he first met her, but she'd always been a bright light in his life. Lately he'd been trying to stave off the darkness by not letting anything—or anyone—matter to him. At that dinner party, the one where her mother broke down in tears, he'd realised how much the Summerfields *did* matter to him—the Summerfields, the Northdons, Glenville, Tess, even Ross's father. He'd realised that Lorene mattered most of all.

She danced up to him, extending her arms for him to grasp. 'What do you say? Would you live here?'

He could not answer. Their gazes caught and he pulled her closer until his arms reached around her.

Seeing her so happy made his heart swell. He'd always had to dampen his attraction to her—when she was married; when her husband died—he'd not even admitted it to himself how much he desired her.

Now he could allow desire to overtake him.

He lowered his head and touched his lips to hers.

She stood perfectly still, like a young girl unschooled in lovemaking. Or one who disliked his liberty.

He backed off. 'Forgive me, Lorene. I should not have done that.'

Her eyes were huge and still focused on him.

'Why did you?' she whispered.

'Because I have long wanted to,' he answered honestly.

'Then why did you stop?' Her gaze remained fixed on his.

'You seemed not to desire it.'

She lowered her lashes. 'I—I did not know how to respond. I am unused to such things.'

'Unused to kisses?' Did not Tinmore kiss her?

'My husband's kisses were nothing like that,' she said breathlessly.

He took her in his arms again. This time she rose on tiptoe and met his kiss.

His lips felt wonderful, not cold and lifeless like the pecks Tinmore sometimes bestowed. Lorene pushed any thought of Tinmore out of her mind. Nothing mattered but that it was Dell kissing her.

Her old romantic dreams burst forth. Why hold back? Dell's kiss was even more than she could have imagined. Why not give herself to it?

She pulled off her bonnet and threw her arms around his neck, answering the press of his lips with eagerness. He urged her mouth open and she readily complied, surprised and delighted that his warm tongue touched hers.

He tasted wonderful.

She plunged her fingers into his hair, loving its softness and its curls. She liked his hair best when it looked tousled by a breeze. Or mussed by her hands.

He pressed her body against his and the thrill intensified. How marvellous to feel his muscles, so firm against her. And more. She felt the hardness of his groin, most thrilling of all. One hand slid down from his hair to his arm to his hip. How wanton was that? How like her mother she must be to want to touch him.

But she was a widow, was she not? Was not everyone telling her she had licence to do as she pleased? It pleased her to touch him. Although she was not quite brazen enough to touch that hard part of him that thrilled her most of all.

'Lorene,' he groaned as his hands pressed against her derrière, intensifying the sensations in all sorts of ways. 'We should stop.'

She did not want to stop. 'Why?' She kissed his neck. 'I am a widow. Are not widows permitted?'

'Do not tempt me,' he said, though his hands caressed her.

She moved away, just enough that he could see

her face. 'If you do not want this, then, yes, we should stop, but I do desire it, Dell.'

For a long time, she realised. Since she first met him. He was the man she had dreamed about in her youth, a good man, kind, honourable, handsome. But something more, something that made her want to bed him.

His lips took possession of hers once again and he lifted her into his arms and carried her to the bed. She kicked off her shoes and he pulled off his boots. She'd never thought of clothing as a barrier, but it felt so now. He might think her terribly fast, but she was a widow. Did not gentlemen have affairs with widows without anyone blinking an eye?

She unbuttoned her pelisse and slipped it over her shoulders, tossing it aside. As if following her example, he removed his coat and leaned over her to give her another kiss. She managed to work the buttons of his waistcoat and he soon shed that as well, all the while his lips tasting hers.

His hand cupped her breast and she rued the fabric of her dress in the way.

She sat up and turned her back to him. 'Unlace me?'

He untied her laces and loosened them until she could pull her dress over her head and let it flutter to the floor. Even her corset and shift seemed like too much between them, but, as his hand slipped under the fabric and caressed her bare breast, she suddenly was filled with need.

She pulled up the skirt of her shift and his hands slipped down to where her body ached for him. She wanted this—this coupling now. Needed it now. As he touched her legs, her fingers unbuttoned his trousers. He stopped long enough to pull them off and his drawers with them.

She glimpsed his male member and thrilled at the sight. It meant joining with him, being one with him. That, she realised, was what she'd dreamed of from their first meeting.

His fingers explored that female part of her and the sensations they produced brought pleasure so acute, it was akin to pain.

Without volition she made urgent sounds. 'Dell, please!' She dug her fingers into the firm flesh of his buttocks to urge him on.

That seemed to be all he needed. He rose over her and plunged inside her.

She cried out.

In pain.

Chapter Fifteen

Dell withdrew. 'I've hurt you?'

She'd felt a sharp pain inside and could not help but cry out.

It was not supposed to hurt, was it?

'Lorene?'

She sat up, hugging her knees. 'I must have done something wrong. I never—'

He cut her off. 'Never done this?' He glanced down at the bed linen. Blood stained them. 'Do not tell me. Tinmore did not—?'

She partially hid her face behind her knees. 'Tinmore tried. Twice. He—he could never get inside me. I do not know how to explain it, but he made me promise to tell no one and he left me alone after that. It…suited me.' She shuddered from the distasteful memory.

He reached for his drawers and put them on. 'Then we should not have done this.'

'Why not?' She released her knees and sat cross-legged.

'Because you are a virgin.' He stood next to the bed.

But she was a widow. Did that not make it acceptable?

She reached for his hand. 'Not any more.'

He stepped back and his rejection stung.

She curled up again, hiding her face.

The two times Tinmore had tried to bed her had been nightmarish. She'd believed she would never experience the pleasure that could exist between a man and a woman, the pleasure she assumed played a part in her mother choosing a lover over her own children. Until this day, in this room—a room she created—she'd believed that dream dashed. But then this chance arose to be alone with Dell and he'd said he wanted her.

Now he pushed her away.

'We should get dressed,' he said, but he made no move to put on his trousers.

Lorene felt as if she'd lost her best friend, the one person she thought she could always depend upon, the one person she could always confide in. But she'd ruined it all simply by wanting him in this carnal way.

'Lorene?' He spoke as if trying to wake her from a sleep.

She lifted her head.

He could abandon her like her mother and even her father did, but she refused to continue to be that dispirited person Tinmore turned her into.

She met his gaze and held it. 'I spent most of my life trying to please other people, but here, now, the one time I try to please myself, you become appalled?' She shook her head. 'Merely because my elderly husband could not consummate our marriage? Would you rather he had done so?' She rose to her knees. 'Because I certainly did not regret that he could not perform.'

He stood stiffly. 'I could never bear to think of him touching you.'

'Then, why castigate me now?' she asked.

His eyes flashed. 'I do not castigate you.'

She felt like throwing up her hands. 'Then what is it? I am a widow. I wanted you. You wanted me, too, did you not?'

He nodded.

'Then why must you stop? Why wound me that way?'

'Wound you?' he echoed. 'I mean to protect your honour.'

'What nonsense! What honour do I have after marrying an old man for his money?' What difference did it make that she was—had been—a virgin. 'A widow's honour is in being discreet, is that not so? I did not plan to tell anyone.'

'You could get with child,' he said.

Now that really would be a dream come true. To have a child by the man she loved. What could be better?

'If so, I would do what other widows do when they have a child by a lover.' She was not certain what that was precisely, but she could figure it out.

His expression turned severe. 'Do you mean get rid of it?'

Goodness, no! 'I would never do that. Suppose Edmund's mother had done that!' She thought quickly. 'I could travel to the Continent or somewhere far away to have the baby. Then I would bring the baby home and figure out some fiction to tell the world so they could pretend the obvious did not happen.'

But that would never be, because he would not bed her. All because her husband could not bed her.

She leaned against the bed board and turned away from him. This was too painful. It did not bear more discussion. 'Just leave, Dell.'

'Your dress?' he asked.

'I'll lace it up myself and cover it with my pelisse. I only have a short distance to walk. I do not need you.' Her last words made her feel like weeping, because she did need him.

Well, she had needed a mother, too, and had done without. She'd even done without a father, since he never bothered much with his daughters. She would learn to do without Dell, too.

She heard him moving around and assumed he was putting on his clothes, getting ready to walk out on her. Instead the bed creaked. He climbed on to the bed and turned her around to face him. He'd undressed again. Completely.

The murals and statues in her late husband's country house had shown many a naked figure of a man. Gods, they were supposed to be, but none was as fine as Dell. Broad-shouldered, narrow-hipped, strong-armed, his muscles so well defined no sculptor could have created a finer image of a man.

He lay her back against the mattress and rose over her again. 'This time,' he murmured, kissing her neck. 'This time we will take it slow so it doesn't hurt you. This time I will show you what it can be like.'

She threw her arms around him and simply clung to him.

He'd stayed! Dell had not left her.

Dell sought her lips and kissed them as hungrily as before. What had he almost done? He'd almost walked out on her. He'd almost left her alone with all her emotions and unspent passion. He'd almost been cruel and he never wanted her to feel cruelty again.

'Forgive me, Lorene,' he murmured. 'I was taken off guard.'

He was glad Tinmore had not forced himself on her. He could hardly bear to think of the man's hands all over her trying to consummate the marriage. He'd been so fevered with desire for her before that he'd thought only to slake his need, to reach that pinnacle of pleasure within his reach. This time, though, he'd make love to her. He'd show her all the pleasure that lovemaking could bring. That he could give her.

He sat her up again and loosened the laces of her corset, pulling it off her. Her shift came next. She lay in front of him in all her naked beauty. His gaze drank her in like a man who'd almost died of thirst. Her full firm breasts, her deep pink nipples, narrow waist, fuller hips.

She did not cover herself, but gazed back, catching his eyes whenever he tore them away from her smooth, creamy skin. His gaze travelled to the triangle of dark hair at the apex of her legs and his desire surged as before.

He hurriedly kissed her, to at least stave off some of his hunger for her. Then he slowly explored her, stroking her skin, feeling every curve. He felt her muscles relax under his touch. First he would free her body of tension, then he would build her desire. Only then would he enter her, this time slowly so her body accepted him with pleasure, not pain.

As her breathing slowed and contented sounds escaped her mouth, his lips sought the tender skin beneath her ears. He filled one hand with her breast and savoured the sensation. He scraped his palm over her nipple. Her hips rose off the bed in response.

His hand slid down between her legs. Very gently his fingers gently stroked and stretched. It was difficult to bank his own feelings. The desire to plunge inside her again was nearly impossible to resist, but resist he did.

Pleasure, not pain.

Beneath his fingers her flesh became as supple as putty and she was wet with desire for him. He positioned himself over her and, with gentle strokes, eased himself inside her.

He moved in and out, in and out, in a rhythm that mimicked The Duke of Kent's Waltz. In. Out. Come together. Go apart. Like the dance.

She followed the dance perfectly, increasing the tempo as his passion intensified. He could feel hers building, as well. She stayed with him until she cried out and convulsed around him. It was all he needed to unleash his own passion. His climax erupted with more force than he could ever remember. They held on to each other as their bodies tensed and the pleasure washed over them.

Now he was reduced to putty as he slid off her and settled next to her. She turned towards him and nestled against him.

It took a while for him to speak. 'Did I hurt you this time?'

'No. On the contrary, that was…' She pressed her lips to his skin. 'Indescribable.'

He held her closer.

'Is it always that way?' she asked.

'No,' he said, but added, 'For you and me, yes.'

She smiled and he kissed her.

He held her and felt more content than he could remember. The sense of being alone washed away, but with it an encroaching anxiety. He was at great risk of needing her, loving her, having her matter to him. He felt the fear of losing her, heard the crackle of flames as if fire would take her away as it did his family.

He fought the anxiety, the fear. *Do not think of it now*, he told himself. Enjoy the moment. Savour her now.

His lips sought hers again and sparked a return of desire. This time he was unable to be so careful, so controlled, because he needed to forget himself in the pleasure of her. This time her body would remember and accommodate to him. This time they both would know what was to come.

To his great gratification, her desire was aroused as quickly as his and she was as impatient as he was to rush to that moment of pleasure. His hands explored more aggressively, but she responded in kind, her fingernails scraping his back. This dance was more Scottish Reel than Waltz, faster, rougher.

The rhythm they established grew faster and faster, as did their desire. Her climax came a moment before his and they writhed together once more, crying out from the intense pleasure.

This was happiness. *She* was happiness.

But as he'd always known, this moment would be fleeting.

Reality set in.

'I think I must return home,' Lorene said. 'I do not want to, but I should. Who knows what the outcome of my mother and Genna's little talk will be? Or what will happen when the Count returns.'

What faced him at home was wine before dinner with whoever the Duke and Duchess had invited for the evening, a dinner filled with political discussion and a trip to the opera to see and be seen by more men who the Duke hoped to sway to vote his way.

Could he return there and pretend nothing had changed? His insides twisted. She'd broken down the wall he'd erected around his heart. Dare he allow her to become so important to him?

Dell sat up. 'I'll help you dress.'

He gazed around the room. Even in the afternoon light, the room seemed lit by sunshine. He could see himself waking every morning in this room.

He would awaken every morning thinking of her.

A few minutes later they were outside and the town house locked.

Lorene elected to take the soiled linens with her. Certainly she would have an easier time explaining a spot of blood on linens than would he. She folded it into an innocuous bundle that was easily carried.

'I will be at the town house tomorrow,' she told him as they walked the short distance to her town house. 'Mr Good and I will meet in the afternoon to plan more rooms.'

Her question was implied. Would he come there as well?

He should say no. He should say they ought not to repeat what happened between them today.

'I will be at the Lords tomorrow,' he began, but added, 'My morning is free.' How could he not want her again? And again? 'Will you meet me at the town house in the morning?'

'Yes.' She smiled. 'At ten o'clock?'

'Ten o'clock,' he repeated.

They walked on.

Her countenance turned serious. 'Dell, I do not

want you to think I expect more from you than—than the lovemaking. We are free to have an affair, are we not? I—I do not expect marriage. I never want to marry again, as you know.'

No commitment? Yes. That would do nicely. If they both remained independent—separate—there could be no devastating loss when—when they could be together no more.

'An affair,' he repeated. 'For as long or as briefly as we wish it.'

'Yes.'

A built-in time to say goodbye. He could do that.

They reached her house and he bid her goodbye cordially, although he really wanted to take her in his arms and kiss her one more time. They were not private, however. A man stood nearby as if waiting for someone.

After she disappeared behind the door, he started towards Ross's father's town house.

Perhaps he would move into his own house, as Lorene suggested, Dell thought. The ghosts of his family were gone and he thought he could handle the pleasant memories he was making with Lorene there.

He'd let the Duke know this evening.

He glanced up to see a gentleman waiting at the end of the street. When he came closer, he recognised the man as Lord Brackton, Lady Alice's father. Had Brackton seen him walking with Lorene? Probably. But what did it matter? Dell knew now he could never pick Lady Alice.

He tipped his hat to the man. 'Good day, Brackton.'

'You were with that Lady Tinmore.' Brackton made it sound like an accusation.

'Yes,' Dell responded, his response questioning as if to say, *Why do you remark upon it?*

Brackton continued in the same tone. 'This is not the first time you have been connected to her.'

He certainly was not going to discuss his feelings for Lorene with Brackton.

'Her sister is married to Rossdale.' Everyone knew he and Rossdale had been fast friends since schooldays. 'That puts us in each other's company from time to time.'

'But you dishonour my daughter!' Brackton cried.

Dell kept his voice even. 'I do not dishonour Lady Alice. I hold her in high esteem. Walking with Lady Tinmore has nothing to do with your daughter.'

'You court my daughter and gallivant with that scandalous widow?' Brackton's face turned red.

Dell gave him a direct look. 'Sir. I have danced with your daughter. I have taken her for a turn in the Park. If it had been my intention to court her, I would have asked your permission first.'

'My daughter said you are courting her. She says you made her an offer of marriage.' Brackton peered at him with suspicion. 'Have you trifled with her?'

This was outrageous. Impossible. He'd been careful never to lead Lady Alice on.

'I would never dishonour your daughter in any way.' Dell tried to speak calmly. 'I cannot explain why Lady Alice would say I am courting her. I never discussed such a matter with her. I certainly never offered her marriage.' How could he convince this man? 'You might ask the Duke of Kessington. He has been privy to my thoughts on this subject.'

'My wife has spoken to the Duchess,' Brackton shot back. 'Her Grace assured my wife that you did, indeed, mean to marry my daughter.'

The Duchess. Was she behind this? She was always trying to manoeuvre others to her ideas of what should be. In politics, Dell had no complaint about this. But this was his life. He'd had enough of the scheming woman. First agitating Lady Summerfield, then insulting Lady Northdon. Now this.

'I do not take her Grace into my confidence.' Dell fought to hold his temper. 'There is no truth in this, sir. I give you my word.' He looked Brackton directly in the eye.

Brackton, at least, looked less certain. Still, he

puffed up his chest. 'We shall see about that!' He marched away.

Dell remained where he was, waiting for some sense of composure to return. He knew the Duchess tried to stop Ross and Genna from marrying, but it had never occurred to him that she would take even the smallest interest in manipulating his life.

Had she or Lady Brackton shared this falsehood with others? If so, there was sure to be gossip, even scandal. And, if he shared openly his intended relationship with Lorene, the scandal would fall upon Lorene, as well, and as undeserved as ever.

He strode off at a quick pace. He'd have it out with the Duchess and he would not spend another night in her house.

Chapter Sixteen

When Dell reached the Duke's house, he asked the footman attending the door where the Duke and Duchess were.

'In the drawing room, m'lord.' The footman took his hat and gloves.

Dell went directly there and found Ross with them. Ross was often there. He'd taken on many of the Duke's duties in the last two years, ever since the Duke had a seizure of the heart.

They were all having a glass of wine.

'Ah, Dell! Glad you are here,' the Duke said. 'Come have some claret.'

Dell crossed the room. He did not look at the Duchess who was seated on the sofa. He accepted the glass of wine and drank half of it in one gulp.

'Is something amiss?' Ross asked.

Dell swivelled around to face the Duchess. 'I encountered Lord Brackton on the street. He said you told Lady Brackton that I had decided to marry Lady Alice.'

'Lady Alice?' cried Ross. 'No, Dell!'

Dell put up a hand to silence him. 'Did you say such a thing to Lady Brackton?'

The smile froze on the Duchess's face. 'Why, Dell, did you not say you would court her?'

He glared at her. 'You know I did not.'

Her expression turned all innocent. 'Why, I am certain you did.'

'I know my own mind, Your Grace,' Dell told her through gritted teeth. 'You and the Duke were keen on my marrying Lady Alice. I did nothing more than consider it.'

'Thank God,' Ross said.

'Now, Dell.' The Duchess spoke to him as if he were a child. 'You know you did more than consider it.'

He leaned into her face. 'Do not try to manipulate me, ma'am. You had no right to speak to anyone about our private conversations, let alone tell falsehoods about me.'

The Duke put down his wine glass. 'Constance, what have you done now?'

She tossed her husband a defensive look. 'Well, we both know Dell will come up to scratch in the end. The Bracktons were considering other gentlemen. I was merely helping matters along.'

This still did not explain why Lady Alice said he was courting her, though, Dell thought.

'You have exposed an innocent girl to gossip and me, as well,' Dell said.

She blinked up at him. 'Then you will simply have to marry her and the gossip will have no teeth.'

'Constance! Damn your infernal meddling!' the Duke said sharply. 'Dell is our friend.'

'I'm doing this for Dell,' she protested.

The Duke shouted, 'I am out of patience with you. I expect you to return to Lady Brackton and tell her you lied.'

She blanched. 'I will do no such thing!'

The Duke glared at her and pointed to the door. 'Leave us! Immediately! I will deal with you later, but, rest assured, you will do as I say.'

Likely it would not matter. Once a scandalous story reached society's ears, it persisted in spite of a dozen protestations that it was untrue.

After she flounced out, Dell turned to the Duke. 'I hope you realise, sir, that I can no longer stay here.'

'Yes. Yes.' The Duke nodded.

'Come stay with us.' Ross clapped Dell on the arm.

Dell felt the friendship. 'I appreciate your invitation.' Indeed it warmed him deeply. 'But I am not going to disturb that idyll you and Genna have together. I've meant to go back to the town house, even before this.' A decision made within the last hour.

'The town house!' Ross exclaimed. 'It is a shell.'

He was not ready to tell Ross about Lorene managing the renovations. Ross would ask too many questions. 'I started renovations,' he said vaguely. 'Enough rooms are done for me to take residence, at least in a few days. I'll stay at Stephen's Hotel in the meantime.'

'No, Dell,' the Duke broke in. 'Stay here in the meantime. I'll keep the Duchess out of your way. If you go to a hotel it will cause talk. Make matters worse.'

That made sense. 'Very well.'

He ought to have spent the rest of the day in mellow bliss, savouring the memory of making love with Lorene. Instead he was faced with a manipulative duchess and some addled young woman who decided to invent a proposal where none existed.

Lorene had hurried up to her bedchamber. She wanted to change clothes right away lest someone notice her dress was a bit wrinkled, but instead of trying to untie her laces herself, she collapsed in a chair.

She could not hide it from her maid. And what was she to do with the soiled bed linens?

Moreover, what was she to do to prevent getting with child? Her words to Dell were brave, but a child out of wedlock had a hard road growing up. She'd witnessed what it had been like for Edmund. Who was she to ask what to do?

Tess? Genna?

She wished to tell Tess and Genna eventually, but for right now she wanted this special time with Dell without anyone knowing or talking among themselves about it. Tess and Genna would keep her secrets, but they would discuss it with each other and with her. At the moment it seemed too precious to share.

But she could not engage in this affair without addressing the risk of a baby.

Nellie, her ladies' maid, walked into the room. 'Oh! Beg pardon, m'lady. I did not know you were at home.'

'No need to apologise,' Lorene said, trying to sound calm, when she did not feel calm inside.

Her maid peered at her. 'What is amiss, m'lady? Are you ill?'

Yes, she could not hide from Nellie.

She looked up at the girl, younger than herself by at least two years. 'May I depend upon you, Nellie?' she asked.

'Of course you can!' Nellie squatted down to look into her face. 'What is it, m'lady?'

'You must promise to tell no one.'

'I promise,' Nellie cried. 'I would never talk about your private matters.'

'Well.' Lorene glanced away. Who else could she talk to? She took a breath. 'I have taken a lover.'

Nellie broke out into a smile. 'Oh, that is wonderful, m'lady! Who is it?'

She did not expect that question. 'I would rather not say.'

'That is all right,' the maid said. She gave her sideways glance. 'I'll wager it is Lord Penford.'

Lorene's cheeks burned. 'Why do you say so?'

'Oh, at Summerfield House we used to wonder why he let you stay. We thought he might be smitten with you.' She grinned. 'It will make us all happy.'

'You cannot say so to them!' Lorene said.

Nellie lifted her hands. 'I will say nothing. I already promised.'

'I need your help, Nellie. I do not have anyone else to ask.'

Her maid nodded. 'I will help you.'

She rose from the chair and walked over to where she had dropped the bed linens. 'I need to have these laundered without anyone knowing.'

Nellie looked puzzled, but took the bundle. 'I will do this, certainly.'

'But there is more,' Lorene said. 'I need to know how—how to prevent a baby.'

Nellie looked aghast and Lorene wavered. Had she gone too far in confiding in Nellie?

Nellie's eyes were wide. 'Do you mean, you do not know?'

Lorene shook her head. 'In spite of my being married, I have no experience in such things.'

'Well, we must get you a sponge—' Nellie seemed to know all about this.

The maid explained how to use the sponge and promised to bring her one before the next day.

When she finished, Lorene hugged her. 'Thank you, Nellie! What would I do without you?'

Nellie's grin erupted again. 'You could ask your mother, perhaps?'

Lorene gasped at the thought. She did not know her mother well enough to trust her and what she knew made her question her mother's judgement.

'Speaking of my mother,' Lorene said. 'Is she at home?'

'Yes, m'lady, but Count von Osten is not.'

Lorene presented her back to the maid. 'Then help me dress, Nellie. I should probably speak with her.'

Lorene found her mother in the drawing room seated in a chair, a glass in hand and a nearly empty crystal decanter on the table beside her.

'Mother?'

Her mother raised her glass as Lorene approached her. 'Lorene, my darling daughter. Haven't you been gone a long time?' Her words were slurred. 'Not as long as some, though.' She laughed.

Lorene picked up the decanter and received a strong whiff of brandy. 'Are you drinking the Count's brandy?'

'Why not?' Her mother drank the remaining contents of her glass. 'Ossie will not need it.'

Lorene had no idea what that meant. 'You've had quite a bit of it.'

Her mother poured the last of it into the glass.

'Did something happen with Genna?' If so, it must have been a terrible row.

'With Genna?' Her mother seemed to struggle to recall. 'Oh, with Genna. She scolded me for leaving when you were children and scolded me for coming back and scolded me for causing more gossip. Disagreeable girl. Perhaps I should have been around to teach her some proper manners.'

'Genna is outspoken,' Lorene said. 'It is one of her most admirable traits.'

Her mother laughed again, though it was a dry sound. 'And one of her abiding faults.'

'So you quarrelled?' She feared they would quarrel.

'Oh, no,' her mother said, taking a sip from

her glass. 'I was all properly contrite. Shedding tears and all, so she had to agree to be friends.' She stared into the glass as if reconsidering. 'Not *friends*, precisely. She did make me agree not to cause any more scandal, but I do not know how I can do that when I don't cause scandal. Other people merely like to gossip about me.'

'When you accept invitations from Lord Alvanley and others of the Prince Regent's set, you are causing gossip.'

'Now *you* are scolding me,' she pouted, putting the glass to her lips again.

'Are you upset about Genna?' Lorene asked.

Her mother made a scornful face. 'No. She will get over her sulks.'

This was becoming more confusing. 'Then why are you drinking a whole decanter of brandy?'

Her mother leaned forward, almost losing her balance and slipping off the sofa. 'Because, my darling daughter, Count von Osten has left me.' She shoved a piece of paper at Lorene.

Lorene unfolded it and read silently.

My dear Hetty,
I have had all I am able to endure. I came to London to marry you, not to stand around while you flirt with a gentleman of question-able character.

I return to Brussels. Fabron may pack my things and follow me, but I am already gone. Yours, et cetera,
O.

Lorene looked up from the letter.

'He has left me!' Her mother flung herself down on the sofa and had a fit of weeping.

Lorene came to her side and tried to comfort her, even though she secretly felt her mother was at fault. The Count might have been the reason her mother abandoned her children years ago, but he'd always seemed like a decent man. His devotion to her mother was evident, but his decision to stand up to her was admirable.

'Now, now, Mother,' Lorene murmured. 'Perhaps you can go after him. I will send you in my carriage.'

'Run after him?' Her mother sat up and looked aghast. 'Never! I have done nothing wrong.'

'Mother.' Her tone was direct. 'Really. You have treated him shabbily since you arrived here.'

'I have done nothing of the sort!' Her mother tried to stand, but lost her balance and collapsed on to the sofa again.

'Mother, this is the man you love, is he not?' Did she not love him more than her own children?

'Doesn't matter,' her mother muttered. She tried to stand up again, this time bracing herself against the sofa to keep her balance. 'I am not going to chase after him!'

'Where are you going, then?' Lorene asked.

'Out,' her mother said haughtily. 'To call upon my friend.'

'The gentleman of questionable character?' She used the Count's words.

'Why should I not call upon him?' Her mother lifted her nose indignantly.

'Because the Count asked you not to.' And because calling on the gentleman would undoubtedly put her name in the newspapers yet again.

'Ossie is not my husband. He cannot dictate who I call upon and who I do not!' She'd spouted the same refrain that morning.

It seemed so long ago. 'Now, he did not dictate, did he? He simply asked you.' It would not have been like the Count to forbid.

She took a swaying step. 'I am going out anyway.'

'You will *not* go out!' Lorene stated firmly. She took hold of her mother's shoulders. 'You are in no condition!'

'I will do as I please!' Her mother wrenched away, but had to grab Lorene again to keep from falling.

'Not this time, Mother.' Lorene pulled her away.

Her mother used a table to help keep her upright.

Lorene crossed the room and tugged on the bell pull.

Her mother staggered her way towards the door, leaning on the furniture as she went.

Lorene's butler appeared at the door.

She gestured for him to enter. 'Trask, help me take my mother to her bedchamber. She needs to rest.'

'As you wish, ma'am.' Trask hurried to her mother's side.

Lorene put one of her mother's arms around her shoulder and Trask took the other one. She protested loudly the whole way to her bedchamber on the same floor, but did not resist.

Her mother's lady's maid was in her room.

'Marie, my mother needs a nap,' Lorene told her. 'Help her, will you?'

'Of course, *madame*,' Marie said.

Trask left the room and Lorene and Marie helped her mother undress down to her shift.

'Come, Mother,' Lorene murmured. 'Sleep now.'

They helped her into bed.

When Lorene walked back into the hallway, she leaned against the wall. The happy glow of her time with Dell had faded, dimmed by the drama her mother created.

The next morning her mother elected to remain in bed. Likely the effects of the brandy were preying upon her. Lorene prevailed upon her mother's maid and Mr Trask to keep her mother inside while Lorene went on her 'errand'.

Dressing for the day was difficult. Lorene wanted to look her best for Dell, but she also did not want it to be obvious she had fussed with her appearance.

Nellie solved the dilemma. 'May I suggest, m'lady, a gown you can take off and put on by yourself?'

Practical Nellie.

Nellie had also provided the sponge Lorene had first learned about the day before. Who knew why Nellie was so knowledgeable?

Lorene had told Mr Walters that she would meet him at the town house at one in the afternoon. Mr Walters was to see that Mr Good, the architect, was informed of the one o'clock time as well.

She walked unaccompanied the short distance to Dell's town house and used the key to let herself in. She arrived before the time she and Dell agreed upon so she could put the freshly laundered linens on the bed.

When the time neared for Dell to arrive, Lorene paced the hall. Would it be as she remembered? Would he be as she remembered? Or would what they'd shared together somehow change things between them?

She already felt changed.

Through the window she saw him walk up to the door, carrying a basket. Before he could sound the knocker, she opened the door. Her uneasiness grew.

He stepped into the hall, dropped the basket and immediately pulled her into his arms, capturing her lips as if his first meal in a week. Her hands held his face, holding him in the kiss for fear he might stop and separate from her again. The kiss was more than eager, more than intense, more than any kiss could possibly be.

'I have missed you,' he murmured, finally moving away just enough to be able to speak.

She smiled. 'I missed you, too.' At least she'd missed him when her life gave her the luxury of thinking about him.

They kissed again. Lorene captured the moment in her mind. She would remember the feel of his lips against hers, the taste of him, his scent.

Still pressing his lips against hers, he lifted her and she wrapped her legs around him. He carried her up the stairs to his bedchamber and, like the day before, set her on the bed.

She looked up at him. 'I am prepared this time.'

He nodded approvingly while she unfastened the front of her dress and he tore off his coat.

Soon they were naked and his flesh was pressed against hers.

Another moment to savour. The feel of his body against hers. The intimate touching.

This lovemaking was eager, as eager as the greeting kiss had been. He entered her and they rushed to their climax as if they'd already waited too long when they'd been apart.

The next time was slow and sensuous. Dell stroked her body until Lorene thought she would shatter with desire. The waiting, the slow build, worked a magic she never expected. Her pleasure intensified and seemed to roll on for ever.

Dell's desire was sated and his body languorous after. He focused on those feelings rather than admit to himself how hard it would be for this idyll to come to an end.

He left the bed still naked and walked downstairs to retrieve the basket he'd bought at Fortnum and Mason before coming to the town house. Sitting cross-legged on the bed and facing each other, the basket in the middle, they drank wine and nibbled on a selection of cheeses and sweetmeats while Lorene shared her ideas about the next rooms to finish.

'I have decided to move into this house,' he told her, popping a piece of cheese into his mouth.

'You did?' Her lovely face brightened. 'I am so glad.'

'When do you think it can be accomplished?' What went in to setting up a new household? He'd never been faced with this problem. 'How might it be accomplished?'

'First thing is to hire servants,' she said.

Having servants in the house would change things, he thought. Other gentlemen might entertain all sorts of women under the noses of the servants, but Dell could not see compromising Lorene's privacy like that.

That thought depressed him. 'When servants are hired, we will not be able to meet like this.'

He watched dismay come over her features.

'Not without risking talk, I suppose.' She put on a brave but sad smile. 'I suppose I always knew we could not continue for long.'

He lowered his voice. 'I do not want this to end now, Lorene. Not because of a town house and servants.'

'I do not want this to end now either,' she said.

He smiled. 'Servants must have a day off.'

Her eyes sparkled. 'They do indeed!'

'We might have a whole day together.' He filled her wine glass. 'Perhaps I will purchase a pianoforte and you will play for me.'

'As I did at Summerfield House that first time we met.' She smiled and took a sip. 'You so politely allowed me to play my old music on the pianoforte that I grew up playing. I was so touched when you gave me that music later.' Her eyes grew huge. 'It was you. You sent me the Mozart Quintets!'

'I thought you might like it,' he said.

That first Season after they'd met, he'd seen her at a musicale. She seemed to enjoy the music performed more than anyone else in the room, so the next day he combed the music shops until he found piano sheet music for the Quintets, possibly the last copies in London. He'd sent them to her anonymously. It seemed too presumptuous a gift for a single gentleman to send to an elderly earl's new wife.

She put down her wine glass and moved the basket from between them. She placed her hands on both sides of his face and carefully kissed his lips.

'That was the kindest thing anyone had ever done for me.' Her voice was raspy with emotion. 'They are my favourite pieces of music. Now I shall treasure them even more.'

He kissed her back and felt the flaring of desire, but he had delayed long enough what he must tell her. He nestled her against him, his arm around her, his fingers playing with her hair.

'There is something I must tell you.' He'd delayed long enough.

He must have sounded ominous, because her voice turned wary. 'What is that?'

'Lady Alice has apparently told her parents that I was courting her and that I had made her an offer of marriage.'

Lorene slid back to her seat opposite him.

'It is not true,' he quickly told her. 'I danced with her at balls and I took her for one ride in the park. That is all. I do not know why she said what she did. But apparently the Duchess of Kessington has been meddling as well. She told Lady Alice's mother that I intended to offer for their daughter. The Duchess knew very well that I had decided no such thing. She was manipulating.'

Lorene covered herself with the bed linens.

Dell felt the bleakness creeping back. 'I am hopeful that Lord and Lady Brackton will not risk their daughter's reputation by disclosing any of this, but we shall have to see.'

'Has this become common knowledge, Dell?' she asked.

'Not yet, apparently,' he responded. 'But I wouldn't put it past any of them to open their mouths about it.'

'I will not expose myself to scandal. I cannot. Imagine if we are seen together.' She averted her gaze and he felt as if he'd lost her this second.

She climbed off the bed. 'I should get dressed.'

Before she could pick up her clothes, he stood

and faced her, holding her by her upper arms. 'Stay, Lorene.'

She tilted her head up and looked him in the eye. 'You may be obligated to another. I cannot do this.'

He gripped her arms. 'I refuse to be obligated. I will not be manipulated into marrying a lady I do not love.' To think he'd been about to do that very thing.

Her face was inches from his. He kissed her again as passionately as before and with desperation, because he feared he'd lost her. She kissed him back with equal fervour, but with the aura of goodbye.

When he broke away, he rasped, 'I will not give this up without a fight.'

She shook her head. 'A fight would merely bring more gossip.' She touched his face. 'We will see what happens. That is the most I can say. But now we must return to the—the way it was before yesterday.'

He released her. And felt the blackness descend upon him.

Chapter Seventeen

The next few days were an agony for Dell. He saw Lorene at the town house when she met with Mr Good or the workers. Her man of business accompanied her and there was no opportunity to speak privately. He'd engaged an agency to find him servants and had to interview the applicants for butler at the town house. Once he hired the butler, he'd trust him to select the other servants.

He would have liked Lorene to sit in on the interviews and tell him who she thought would be best, but under the circumstances, how could he?

This day was the last of the applicants for butler. After the man left, Dell found himself unexpectedly alone with Lorene in the hall.

His whole body felt a pull towards her. His lips remembered the feel of hers. His fingers recalled the smoothness of her skin. But he stood apart from her. There were workmen papering his walls in rooms nearby and Mr Walters darted from one part of the house to the other. Someone might enter the hall at any moment.

'How are you, Lorene?' he asked, not out of politeness but a real need to know.

She looked into his eyes. 'It has been difficult,' she said in a low voice. 'My mother is bereft because the Count left her. She does not go out.'

'And you?'

She glanced away again. 'I am well.'

Mr Walters walked in. 'Sorry to keep you waiting, ma'am.'

She glanced back at Dell again. 'We are bound for an agent who represents properties in the country.'

To find her hideaway. She truly was leaving.

He nodded and she left with her man of business.

Dell picked up his own hat and gloves. This was ridiculous. All because of a foolish young woman and a manipulative older one, he'd lost this time with Lorene. They could have had part of these few days alone together, enjoying each other, free to indulge in the passion that he now knew had hummed between them ever since they first met. Instead he was paralysed.

And he was losing patience. He was not attending society functions, but the Duke reported there was no gossip about him. Dell refused to ask the

Duchess the same question. How could he be certain she would tell him the truth?

The Duke had informed him earlier that morning that Lord and Lady Brackton still considered him betrothed to their daughter. That was unwelcome news.

'You might as well marry her,' the Duke had said. 'Brackton is quite well connected with both the Whigs and Tories. A union with Lady Alice would give you many political advantages.' Ross's father was as bad as his wife in this matter, Dell realised.

A short while ago Dell might have listened to such nonsense from the Duke, but now he easily perceived how wrong it would be to consign that lively young lady to a marriage devoid of emotion. Foolish girl. As long as Lady Alice maintained the lie, she kept herself from considering other suitors. She might find a gentleman who would have a true regard for her if she gave this up.

He'd come close to offering her marriage. What might he have done to her life if he'd done so? She'd be feeling this desolation, what he was feeling now.

He set a brisk pace to the Brackton town house and was soon being announced to Lady Brackton. She was alone.

'Sir.' She sniffed indignantly. 'I am shocked you should show your face here.'

He bowed, trying to remember that Lord and Lady Brackton were convinced he'd wronged their daughter. 'Forgive my intrusion, ma'am. It is kind of you to receive me.'

She continued to look at him with distaste.

'I wish to bring this to some conclusion, for all our sakes,' he said. 'Would it be possible for me to speak with Lady Alice? With you present, of course.'

She straightened. 'I fail to see what that will do.'

He took a step closer. 'I do not know why your daughter told you and Lord Brackton that I was courting her. I assure you, I never spoke to her about marriage. Perhaps she will explain, if I ask her.'

'Have you not upset us all enough?' the lady said.

'The upset is not of my doing,' he insisted. 'May I not have the opportunity to speak to her about it?'

She waved a hand. 'Oh, very well.' She rose and rang for a servant.

A footman responded almost immediately.

'Find Lady Alice and tell her to come to me,' Lady Brackton said.

She did not speak to Dell while they waited. Neither did she invite him to sit.

Soon they heard footsteps hurrying to the door.

Lady Alice appeared in the doorway. 'You wished to see me, Mama?' She saw Dell and her face fell. 'Oh.'

'Come in, dear,' her mother demanded. 'Penford wishes to speak to you.'

She crept into the room, passing by Dell without looking at him and taking a seat next to her mother. She stared down at her hands folded in her lap.

Dell tried to speak as mildly as possible. 'You told your parents I had spoken to you about an intention to marry you, is that not so?'

She darted a glance at him and nodded.

'But it was not true, was it?'

This time she glanced worriedly at her mother and twisted her hands.

'It was not true, was it?' he repeated.

She suddenly appeared to build resolve. 'You spoke to me about marriage.'

'Lady Alice,' he said firmly. 'You know I did not.'

She gave him a look that was almost apologetic. Her mother looked smug.

She was lying and feeling regretful over it, he was certain of it, but he'd never convince her parents of it.

'Other people will be hurt by this.' Lorene had already been hurt over this, but he had no confidence this would make a difference.

Lady Alice could no longer look at him.

Lady Brackton sniffed. 'You must not bully her into saying what you wish her to say.'

'The truth is all I want,' he said.

Lady Brackton stood. 'Until you are ready to speak with Lord Brackton about marriage settlements, I suggest you take your leave.'

He bowed to Lady Alice and her mother and strode out of the room without another word. He grabbed his hat and gloves from the footman attending the hall and hurried outside. As he neared the end of the street he heard running footsteps behind him.

'Lord Penford!'

It was Lady Alice.

He stopped and waited for her to catch up to him.

Her hand pressed against her chest as she caught her breath. He waited for her to speak.

'I—I am sorry,' she said. 'I have caused you terrible trouble.'

'Undo it,' he demanded. 'Tell your parents.'

'I cannot tell them.' She took a deep breath.

'Why?'

She glanced down. 'I am not at liberty to say.'

'Not at liberty?' He raised his voice. 'If you think you can force me to marry you, you are gravely mistaken. I will never be manipulated into marriage.'

A gentleman crossed the street at that moment. Dell took her by the elbow and led her in the opposite direction from where the man headed.

Her eyes grew huge. 'Do you think that man overheard? My father will be furious if this whole thing is talked about.'

'This will be talked about,' he said. 'Someone always talks. Do you not realise what you've done? You've risked my reputation, but your own even more. You cannot accept another suitor, some gentleman who might actually want you.'

Her expression softened for a moment, then returned to looking distressed.

What game was she playing?

'What is it? Tell me. If you are in trouble, maybe I can help.' He'd do anything to extricate himself from this.

'I am not in trouble,' she said. 'Everything is fine.'

Dell was so angry he wanted to throttle her. 'I have nothing more to say to you.' He turned and strode away without looking back. He passed the gentleman who very well might have overheard him.

He slowed his pace as soon as he was out of her sight and walked slowly back to the Duke's town house where he no longer felt welcome, but must stay for another week or so before all the servants were hired. As he approached the house, the door opened and Ross walked out.

Ross peered at him. 'I would ask you how you fare, but I can see you are not well. What has happened?'

'I called upon Lady Alice and her mother,' he responded.

'That did not go well, apparently,' Ross said.

'Lady Alice is obviously lying. She even feels distress about it, but she will not recant and she will not explain why.' He paced in front of Ross.

His friend clapped him on the shoulder. 'Come home with me. Do you have dinner plans? You are welcome to stay for dinner, if you like.'

Dell actually appreciated the chance to be away from the Duke's house. 'An unexpected guest will not be a problem?'

'Not you, Dell,' Ross said. 'You are always welcome.'

Dixon was in the *New Tatler* office when the reporter came in with a grin on his face.

'Addison! Steele!' the man called out. 'Do I have something for you! You will not believe it!'

Dixon knew the difference between Mr Addison and Mr Steele now. Mr Addison was the bald one; Steele, the thin one. They were the joint owners and editors of the paper that specialised in scandalous stories.

Dixon sat with the writer assigned to tell his story of Lord Tinmore's death in as sensational a manner as possible. The writer had quickly written the first draft, but they'd been tinkering with it while waiting for the reporter to gather current information.

'Come in!' shouted Mr Addison to the reporter.

Dixon rose and hobbled to the office door to listen.

'So...he waits for this girl, you know. Couldn't have been more than nineteen. She's running after him and then they talk. I wanted to hear what they were saying so I crossed the street right when he says, *"Do you think you can force me into marriage?"* and *"I won't be manipulated."*' He grinned. 'I think the man has this respectable lady as well as the other one.'

'Did you hear that, Parham?'

Parham, the writer with whom Dixon worked, called back, 'I heard it indeed! The plot thickens!'

'Do we have enough?' Steele asked.

Addison clapped his hands together in delight. 'Any more and they will say we made up the story!' Which was what they would pretend to do so no one could sue them for libel. Very clever, these fellows.

That was why Dixon selected them. The *New Tatler* might not come out regularly, but when it did, it always caused a commotion.

* * *

The next afternoon Dell stopped by the town house after a meeting with the Duke of Kessington and other Whigs about the latest legislation. Mr Walters was there supervising the workers.

'Will Lady Tinmore be coming to the house today?' Dell asked him.

'No, sir,' replied Mr Walters, looking worried. 'She had to attend to an urgent family matter.'

Urgent family matter? What could that be? One of her sisters? One of the babies? He was immediately filled with concern.

'What family matter?' Dell demanded. If she needed help, he would go to her.

Walters shifted uncomfortably. 'I am certain she would not wish me to say.'

'Never mind.' Dell turned to leave.

Dell's desire to remain detached from the Summerfields was futile. He cared about them all. He cared about Lorene.

Dell opened the door and hurried out.

He all but ran to Lorene's town house, knocked and was soon admitted.

She stood in the hall, dressed to go out. 'Dell!'

He approached her. 'Walters said there was some family emergency. What has happened? Is someone hurt? Ill? How may I help?'

'Oh, Dell!' She looked close to weeping. 'Come in the drawing room and I will tell you.'

As soon as they crossed the threshold of the room, he said, 'Tell me now. What has happened?'

'It is my mother.' Lorene's face crumbled. 'She left in a carriage saying she is attending some masquerade tonight. I think she plans to be with Lord Alvanley and his friends. She might do anything! She is still despondent over the Count leaving her!'

He could not help it. He took her in her arms and held her, to comfort her. 'Do not fear. We shall figure out a way to stop her.'

She clung to him. 'That is not the worst of it. She told her maid she would dress as Iphigenia.'

Dell nodded. 'Like the Duchess of Kingston years ago.'

Over half a century ago, the Duchess of Kingston attended a masquerade dressed as Iphigenia, a princess in Greek mythology. The costume exposed her breasts and was still talked of today.

For Lady Summerfield to attend a masked ball wearing a costume that exposed half of her body at that ball would certainly affect the reputations of her daughters—of Lorene—even more than being in the company of dissolute gentlemen. Lorene had been hurt enough by her mother's excesses.

He released her. 'You were going out? Where were you going?'

She straightened her hat. 'To try to discover the

location of the masquerade, so I could be there to stop her.'

Dell's brow knitted. 'Who is going with you?'

'No one,' she responded in an uncertain tone.

'Not Ross or Glennville? Or your brother?'

'I do not want them to know,' she said. 'I just want to stop it.'

He seized her shoulders. 'You do not have to act alone, Lorene. They can help.'

She shook her head. 'I do not want them told! They will start hating her all over again. Edmund is fond of her and we have been getting used to her.'

He understood. It would be like losing their mother again.

'Very well.' He made her look at him. 'I will help you. I will always help you.'

She wrapped her arms around him and held on to him.

She abruptly pushed away. 'You should not help, though. We must stay apart.' Her eyes reddened. 'Because of Lady Alice.'

'Do not be nonsensical. I'll not allow Lady Alice's lies to keep me from helping you. Besides, we do not have to go out together. I'll go alone to find out where the masquerade is to be held and when,' he said. 'I'll ask at my club. Someone there will know. You ought to stay here in case she returns, in any event.'

She nodded.

He'd also visit some costume shops. Ask if Lady Summerfield might have procured the costume there.

Dell lifted Lorene's chin. 'I will not fail you.'

She met his gaze and seemed to look into his very soul. 'You never do, Dell.'

Dell went directly to Brooks's Gentleman's Club, where he was an infrequent patron of late. The club had been founded by prominent Whigs over fifty years ago and was still largely Whig. It was one of the places where Ross's father liked to spend his time, meeting with his political allies. Lord Alvanley was a member who frequently played cards there. The man was not present at the moment, though, but Dell hoped someone else would know what he was up to.

Dell joined several other gentlemen who were nursing brandies and discussing politics. He bided his time until there came an opening to mention the masquerade.

'Oh, yes,' Conversation Sharp said. 'It is tonight.'

Richard 'Conversation' Sharp, now wealthy from investments in the West Indies, was the son of a hatter. He was also a decent man, kind, good-tempered, sensible—and could talk on any subject.

'Where is this masquerade?' Dell asked.

'The Argyll Rooms,' Sharp answered. 'On Little Argyll Street. They are calling it the last hurrah before the Argyll Rooms are demolished to make room for Nash's New Street.'

John Nash, the architect for the Prince Regent's Carlton House, had conceived the idea for a new street running from Carlton House to Regent's Park.

'Of course,' Sharp went on. 'It is more of an excuse to hold a masquerade ball than a reason to do so. The demolition of the buildings has been delayed several months.'

Dell seized on this topic. 'Still, it does celebrate the Argyll Rooms, does it not?'

'Certainly,' agreed Sharp genially.

'I have not been there in an age. Nor to a masquerade. This cannot be missed,' Dell said. 'Do you know where I might get a ticket?'

'I believe Nugent has tickets.' Sharp inclined his head towards the card room.

Dell excused himself and walked into the game room, trying not to look too eager. Baron Nugent was deep in a game of whist. Dell tried to wait patiently until the game was over.

Luckily Nugent won, which put him in a good mood.

'I heard you have tickets for a masquerade tonight,' Dell said. 'I haven't attended a masquerade in years. Might I procure some at this late date?'

In their youth, he and Ross caroused with the best of them, until Dell went off to war and everything changed.

'How many do you need?' Nugent asked. 'One for you; one for Rossdale?'

Let them think Rossdale came with him. 'Yes. Two.'

With tickets purchased, Dell left Brooks's and headed for Jackson's Habit Warehouse, a costume shop in Covent Garden.

The shop had several customers—all men— looking for costumes. Dell picked out a black domino and black mask as did most of the customers.

He spoke to the clerk. 'These are for the masquerade tonight.'

'Do tell,' the clerk responded unenthusiastically.

'I am eager to attend,' Dell said. 'I heard one lady is coming as a bare-chested Iphigenia.,'

The clerk did not rise to the bait. 'Indeed,' he said.

It took three shops before Dell heard what he'd hoped to hear.

'Oh, yes,' this clerk said. 'A lady came in with Lord Alvanley. Older woman, but still a beauty. Could have been his mother.' The clerk laughed. 'Don't suppose Alvanley takes his mother to a masquerade, though.'

Dell felt obliged to purchase something in exchange for this information. He picked out a leather Venetian mask painted white with gold-and-silver filigree. Perhaps he'd give it to Lorene if the search for her mother was successful. Perhaps it would be something for her to remember him by.

Chapter Eighteen

It seemed to take for ever for Dell to return. Lorene paced, played her pianoforte and paced again until it approached eight o'clock. What could possibly take him so long? What if he could not discover where the masquerade was to be held?

Finally Trask announced his arrival and Dell strode into the drawing room.

Lorene rose from the piano stool and rushed towards him. 'What did you learn? Do you know where it is to be?'

He lay down two wrapped packages and took both her hands in his. 'The Argyll Rooms at ten o'clock.'

Relief washed through her. 'Then we do not have much time. We must go there and stop her before she enters the building.'

He squeezed her hands. '*I* will go. Not *we*.'

'I must go with you!' she insisted. 'One pair of eyes may not be enough.'

He gave her a sceptical look. 'Were you not planning to go there alone if I had not shown up?'

'Yes, but that was different.' She set her chin. 'I had no other choice, but now I am able to go with you.'

'No,' he said.

Her brows rose. 'Do you think you can refuse me?'

She could not sit alone waiting and wondering, not another second.

He rubbed her arms. 'It is no place for you, Lorene. A masquerade is a raucous, debauched place.' Especially this one, he feared.

'I want to go,' she said firmly. 'It will draw a crowd and everyone will be masked. It will be difficult to see her, will it not? You will need an extra pair of eyes.'

'I will take your butler, then,' he said.

'You will not take poor Trask!' she cried. 'I insist. Take me with you. If you do not, I will come anyway.'

'You have to wear a costume. If you are not masked, you will reveal yourself and your name will land in the newspapers.'

'You won't have a costume.' If he went without, so could she. If he revealed himself, so could she...except they should not be seen together.

Never mind. The scandal her mother would create would be so much worse. She would have to risk some gossip about her and Dell together.

He picked up one of the packages. 'I have a domino and mask. That is all I need.'

'Then I can make a mask! I'll wear a cape or something. That's all a domino is, really.'

Once she would have been cowed by the demands of a man—Tinmore's demands—but no longer, not even Dell's. Tinmore's will might have made her wealthy, but it also made her independent. She could pay for what she wanted.

Dell turned away and her nerves almost failed her. Would he leave? Make her do this on her own?

Instead, he picked up the smaller package and handed it to her. 'Open it.'

She untied the string and unwrapped the paper. It was a mask! A beautiful mask!

'Oh!' Words failed her.

'I did not mean for you to wear it and come with me, but as you are determined...' He shrugged.

She ran up to him and kissed him on the cheek. 'I am determined!' She hurried to the door. 'I will have Cook serve us something quick to eat and have Nellie help me devise a costume. Do you mind waiting here?'

He smiled. 'Not at all.'

* * *

At ten o'clock their carriage stood in a line of several others and inched its way to the Corinthian pillars that graced the entrance of the Argyll Rooms. The chance to catch her mother at the door was lost. When it was finally their turn to disembark, they stepped into a crowd of gaily dressed guests all waiting their turn to pass through the doors.

There were plenty of men dressed in dominos like Dell, but others wore costumes from history—Medieval lords and ladies, Renaissance courtiers and noblewomen, Elizabethan jesters and clowns. Some dressed like shepherds and shepherdesses, or like Turkish sultans and Indian princesses. Or abstract concepts like curiosity or courage. Lorene, who wore a ball gown, a silk cape and the beautiful Venetian mask, searched only for ladies dressed as Greek goddesses.

They were difficult to see. At the doorway, most still wore capes or cloaks, like she. When they reached the inside and all the costumes were revealed it would be easier to spot them.

'We will find her,' Dell assured her. 'We have the whole night to search.'

Dell would not fail her. He never did.

They entered the lobby illuminated by gilt lamps and Lorene was struck with the enormity of their task. There were other rooms on this level. Three, she counted, and this was not even the main ballroom. Who knew how many more spaces there were?

'Stay with me.' Dell took her hand as they climbed the grand staircase.

Already the revelry surrounded them, squealing maidens chased down the stairs by men costumed as priests, exotic couples groping each other intimately as they made their way upstairs, others laughing, others ogling. The music from the orchestra competed with the din of a multitude of celebrating voices.

They reached the ballroom, a grand, oblong saloon, curved at each end. At one end the orchestra played. Above the entrance on each side were three tiers of boxes made private with scarlet draperies.

Lorene's sprits sank. Any could hide her mother.

The first tiers were decorated with bronze antique bas reliefs, the upper ones in vibrant blue, with faux-stone scrolls and gold mouldings. Along the walls were Corinthian pillars and long benches also covered in scarlet. Off the ballroom was another huge dining hall with tables laden with food and another room set up for playing cards, several tables already full of determined players. Above their heads in the ballroom were crystal chandeliers so abundant they lit the whole space.

And everywhere there were masked, costumed

people dancing, masked costumed people drinking wine and spirits, masked costumed people wantonly embracing.

'This is a mad house,' Dell muttered.

'There!' Lorene cried. 'Is that her?'

She glimpsed a blonde-haired woman draped in white, like the clothes on Greek statues, and ran after her.

Dell cried, 'Wait!'

But she couldn't. She reached the woman and looked her full in her mask-covered face.

'What, my dear?' A masculine-sounding voice came from the goddess's tinted lips. 'Never see a goddess before?'

She was stunned.

The man laughed and melted into the crowd again.

Dell reached her. 'Was it your mother?'

'It was a man!' She looked at him, incredulous.

'A man dressed as a woman. I've seen that done at a masquerade.' He scanned the crowd again.

They saw several more Greek goddesses, all fully clothed and none her mother. They strolled around the room, trying to look as though they belonged there.

'Perhaps she is late arriving,' Lorene said as the time ticked by. 'She would like being fashionably late.'

'We can watch near the door,' Dell said.

The scene before Lorene both attracted and re-pelled her. She envied the women their freedom from the confines of propriety. Because no one knew who they were while masked, they could act without restraint. Dance with abandon. Kiss their lover without fear of what people would say.

On the other hand, some seemed to make a mockery of love. Men kissed and touched sev-eral women in succession, and women did the same. Masked, how did they know with whom they shared such intimacies?

There was only one man she wished to kiss; only one man she loved. She could kiss him now, as passionately as she wished, and no one would know. In this setting no one would care. It was only those guests whose behaviour leaped into excesses of sensuality and drink who earned dis-approving looks.

She glanced up at Dell, so intent on their task, his eyes darting from one person to the other. The black silk robe that made up his costume made him look mysterious and dangerous, especially with the black leather mask that covered half his face. Still, she felt she would have known him instantly even if she'd encountered him here by chance. How could anyone not recognise the set of his jaw, his strong neck, his sensuous lips? Even if she merely saw him from the back, would she not have known him by the way he stood, the way he moved?

She shook her head.

This was no time to moon over Dell, nor to regret the loss of that idyllic time between them. She forced her eyes back to the people walking through the door.

One woman caught her eye. Not because she might have been her mother. She was dressed as a shepherdess, complete with a shepherd's crook on her arm. She was young, though, perhaps younger than Lorene herself. The girl walked tentatively into the ballroom. Her glance swept the room. Nervously, Lorene thought.

The shepherdess's gaze then fixed on Dell. She stared long and hard. Not an interested gaze, like young ladies at a society ball might engage in, but one of terror. Her hand flew to her face and the hook on her shepherd's crook caught her mask, pulling it down.

Lorene recognised her! The girl quickly put the mask back in place and retreated to the wall near the door.

Lorene pulled on Dell's arm. 'That was Lady Alice!'

He looked around. 'Where?'

She pointed to the shepherdess, nervously standing by the wall just inside the doorway. 'The shepherdess. Her mask came off and I saw her.'

'Come,' he said.

They walked directly to her.

Dell confronted her. 'Lady Alice. What are you about now?'

The young lady's eyes looked panicked. 'I—I am not—you have mistaken me.'

Dell leaned closer. 'I know it is you. What are you doing here?'

'Waiting for somebody?' she said uncertainly. 'Please do not give me away! It is vastly important that you do not give me away.'

'Are you in trouble?' Lorene asked, very concerned. She would not have felt safe in this place if not at Dell's side.

Lady Alice's expression relaxed. 'Oh, no. Not in trouble. Not at all.'

'You had better tell us right now what you are doing here or I will expose you. And see you taken back to your father.'

She seized his arm. 'You must not do that! My whole future happiness depends upon it.'

At that moment a shepherd came up. 'Are—are these people bothering you, miss?'

Lady Alice practically fell into the shepherd's arms. 'Oh, Frederick! I was afraid you would not come.'

'Who is this, Lady Alice?' Dell demanded in a tone so commanding her shepherd backed off in fright.

'You remember him, sir,' the girl answered. 'He is Mr Holdsworth.'

'Your friend from childhood?' Dell whirled on the young man. 'What sort of gentleman are you to meet this respectable young lady at a place like this?'

'I did not know it would be like this,' Mr Holdsworth said. 'Or I would have made another plan.'

'Plan?' asked Lorene.

The shepherd and shepherdess looked at her as if noticing her for the first time.

Lady Alice straightened her spine, but clung to Mr Holdsworth's arm. 'We are eloping to Gretna Green. Coming here was just a ruse to confuse my parents.' She turned to Dell. 'Like the betrothal with you, Lord Penford. That was a ruse, too.'

'Come.' Mr Holdsworth pulled her away. 'I have a carriage waiting.'

'Do not tell on me,' Lady Alice pleaded. 'I will write a letter to my parents explaining the whole thing. I'll tell them you never proposed to me.'

'Alice!' A booming voice sounded coming from the stairs. 'Alice!'

The young couple cowered in the corner while Dell peeked out of the door.

'It is your father,' he told them. 'With two other men.'

'Oh, no!' cried Alice. 'What will we do? He will kill me!'

Mr Holdsworth embraced her. 'I will protect you with my life.'

Dell pushed them. 'Move. Disappear into the crowd. Wait until you can get by them and make your escape.'

They nodded and, hand in hand, hurried away, joining the crowd and disappearing from view.

'Now we must go as well,' Dell said.

'Why?'

'If her father finds me here, he will blame this on me. He must not see me here.'

Dell led her to the stairway that led to the tiers of boxes. They looked through many, alarming some couples who were *in flagrante*. They finally found one that was empty.

Dell pulled her inside and immediately took her in his arms. 'Do you know what this means, Lorene?'

His arms around her, his strength, completed her. Since she sent him away, she'd felt like half of her had been wrenched away. She relished the embrace.

But did not understand it.

'What does what mean?' she asked.

He hugged her tighter. 'It means that I'm free of Lady Alice. In a few days her parents will know that I was telling the truth. We can be together again.'

Be with him again? Make love to him again? She wanted nothing more, but a pall of sadness covered her, as well. She still was leaving London. Her plans had not changed.

'We still have to find my mother,' she murmured.

'We will find her,' he said. 'I am certain of it.'

He gently removed her mask and his own, and captured her lips. His kiss brought her back to life, like bluebells in the forest after winter is done. When she left him, would the bluebells wither and die?

She did not want to think of that.

She rose on tiptoe to better kiss him back, threw her arms around his neck and held on. He released her, kissing her cheek, her ears, her neck. He lifted her off the ground and lay on top of her on the *chaise longue* provided there for couples like themselves. Her body flared with sensation and the need for him grew.

Was this not what she feared her mother was about? Copulating with some man in this near-public place? But she did not care, not as long as it was Dell whose hands touched her, whose lips kissed her. Filled with need, she pulled up her skirts and his hand slid between her legs. To her great surprise the sensations grew stronger, just as if he'd joined her. Her need built, higher and higher, until her release came, an explosion of pleasure.

He held her close as her the pleasure washed away into a satisfied languor.

'Dell,' she whispered, fighting the malaise

that would certainly come when she ended this affair.

A shouting voice sounded outside the box, coming closer. 'Alice! Alice! Are you in there?'

Lord Brackton was near.

Dell groped for their masks, but there would be no time to put them on again. He pulled pins from Lorene's hair which fell to her shoulders.

'Kiss me again,' he whispered.

He sat on the *chaise longue* with her on his lap, her legs wrapped around him. Her hair was like a curtain, hiding much of his face.

'Call me by another name,' he said.

Lady Alice's father's voice came closer, right next to them.

'John. John,' Lorene cried against his lips as the door to the box opened. 'I want you, John.'

The door closed again and the voice passed on.

They each released tense breaths.

He found their masks on the floor and handed hers to her. She set it aside until she tamed her hair a bit, pulling a piece of ribbon off her dress and using it to tie back her hair. Then she put her mask back in place.

Dell donned his mask and peeked out of the curtains to the ballroom floor below. 'We'll stay here until we see Brackton leave the ballroom.'

She stood next to him, her arm around his waist.

The music stopped and the orchestra left the platform. The dancers on the ballroom floor moved away, some to the dining hall, some to the benches against the wall. They watched Lady Alice's father search through the room again before leaving with his minions.

'We can go now, too,' Dell said.

But Lorene's eye caught a woman, draped in white, leading a man in a black domino much like Dell's by the hand down the length of the room towards the door.

'Dell!' she cried. 'That is my mother!'

He looked down to the ballroom. 'It could be.'

They hurried out of the box to the stairway, climbing down as fast as they could in hopes of reaching her mother before she left the room. As soon as they re-entered the ballroom, though, they caught her figure walking out the door arm in arm with the gentleman in black.

They just caught the tops of her mother's head and that of the man with her as they hurried through the guests on the stairway.

Lorene pushed her way through the crowd, breaking away from Dell. She ran after her mother, reaching the pavement outside just as her mother climbed into a waiting carriage.

As the carriage pulled away, her mother took off her mask and cried in surprise, 'Lorene, whatever are you doing here?'

Dell reached her and they both watched help-lessly as Lorene's mother's carriage disappeared down the street and around the corner.

'Did you see?' she asked Dell. 'Was she fully dressed?'

'All I could see was a great deal of drapery,' Dell responded. 'The man with her was not Al-vanley, though. Alvanley is quite stout.'

'What shall we do now?' Lorene asked.

'There is nothing to do now but go home,' Dell said. 'She could be anywhere.'

They walked the line of carriages until find-ing Lorene's carriage, which took them back to her town house.

Dell climbed out of the carriage and extended his hand to her.

She placed hers in his and let him help her from the carriage. She held his arm as he walked her to the door. She dreaded his leaving. She was almost as alone as when her husband died.

'Would you like me to stay?' he asked.

It was as if he'd read her mind.

'Yes. Please, stay.' She turned to the coachmen. 'You may take the carriage back to the mews. That will be all for tonight.'

'G'night, ma'am,' the coachmen said.

Trask opened the door and they walked in.

'We were not successful, Trask,' Lorene told him.

The butler frowned. 'I am sorry for it, ma'am.'

She handed him her cape. 'Could you bring some brandy to the drawing room for Lord Penford and some claret for me? And see if Cook left us anything to eat?'

She and Dell entered the drawing room. She sat on a chair and he slumped on to the sofa.

'I failed you.' He rubbed his face. 'If I had not kissed you in that box, we might have found her sooner.'

She rose and sat next to him, resting her head on his shoulder. 'If you had not kissed me, perhaps we would not have seen her at all. We cannot know. All we can hope for now is that her escapade does not reach the newspapers, but I do not hold out much hope.'

She put her feet up on the sofa and curled against him. His arm draped over her shoulders. He was her port in the storm. Next to him she could feel calm and peaceful and safe. Odd that what she sought in a small cottage somewhere was a place where she could feel calm and peaceful and safe.

Trask brought in the brandy and claret and some pieces of cheese and cold ham. As Dell sipped his brandy, Lorene told him of the day her mother drank too much.

'It was because of von Osten leaving her, but she drove him away,' Lorene said. 'She does not want to marry; that is the root of the problem.' And Lorene could understand that in her mother. A lover gives; a husband controls.

After a while they merely sat together until they dozed off.

When they roused, Dell said, 'I must leave or I'll be here all night.'

Lorene did not want him to leave. She wanted to fall asleep in his arms and wake up the same way, and this, perhaps, would be her only opportunity. Was that how her mother felt? Wanting to be in her lover's arms, but not wanting to be bound to him? A wife was the property of her husband; in the law, a wife had no identity separate from her husband.

But never had he spoken of marriage. Theirs was an affair, taking place in stolen moments. Tonight, however, she might have more.

'Stay with me,' she murmured. 'Just this once.'

Chapter Nineteen

The next morning Dell woke with the sunrise. He'd slept not more than an hour or two after making love with Lorene. Each moment of love-making drew him even closer to her until he felt incomplete when not in her presence. How foolish he'd been to deny how much she meant to him. She was as essential as the air he breathed.

He did not want to part with her. With Lady Alice's Gretna Green wedding, he was free. Perhaps now he and Lorene could forge something permanent between them. Perhaps he could overcome her determination never to marry again. Perhaps he could have a family again—with Lorene.

He watched her face, illuminated by the rising sun, relaxed and girlish in sleep as if nothing had ever caused her pain. He wished it was in his power to make it so, but the truth was he'd failed to do what he'd promised her—he'd failed to find her mother at the masquerade.

He should rise now, return to the Duke's house and change his clothes, then set out to purchase a copy of every morning paper. He tried to slip out of the bed quietly so as not to wake her, but her eyes fluttered open.

Her gaze fixed on him. 'Good morning,' she murmured.

She was too alluring, with her mahogany-coloured hair spilling across the pillows. He pulled her into a kiss and almost instantly he forgot anything else but the taste of her lips, the smoothness of her skin, the faint scent of rosewater that clung to her.

She climbed atop him, her legs straddling him, her breasts touching his chest as she leaned down to deepen the kiss. He guided himself inside her and they moved together as if this were a dance they'd practised over and over, instead of a new one danced the first time.

Dell lost himself in her, in the sensuality of her, building towards his release. His pleasure came in a crescendo and, with a cry, she joined him in her own release.

She melted atop him afterward and he held her, stroking her hair, until sounds of the servants moving about the house reached his ears.

'I must dress,' he said. 'I'll go home to change my clothes and bring back the newspapers to see what they've printed.'

She slid to his side. 'I feel I have woken from a lovely dream, back to the same problems. Do come back to me, Dell. I would like you to be with me when we discover what the newspapers say.'

Dell dressed quickly and hurried out without encountering any of the servants. They knew, of course, that he had stayed the night with her, but she trusted them to be discreet, so he would trust them, too.

The early morning was brisk and the several streets' walk to the Duke's residence felt bracing. When he entered the house, the footman attending the door, the Duke's butler and Dell's valet were all clustered together, worried looks on their faces.

'Thank goodness you are here,' the butler said.

Dell was alarmed. 'What has happened?'

'Lord Brackton,' the butler said. 'He showed up a few minutes ago insisting on speaking with you, saying I was to wake you and direct you to come down no matter what. But we discovered you were not here and were at a loss as to what to tell him.'

Dell supposed he should not be too surprised that Brackton called on him so early.

He blew out a breath. 'I suppose I must see him, then.'

Dell did not bother to change clothes or shave,

but went straight to the drawing room off the hall where the footman had asked Brackton to wait. When Dell entered the room, Brackton, who looked ashen and distraught and totally without sleep, strode up to him.

'Where is she?' Brackton demanded.

'Where is who?' Dell knew precisely of whom Brackton spoke.

'My daughter!' The man sounded frantic.

Dell was suddenly filled with pity for this man. It was a cruel joke his daughter played on him and her mother.

'I do not know where she is,' Dell said, keeping his tone mild. 'She is not home?'

'No.' The man collapsed in a chair and put his head in his hands. He lifted his gaze again. 'She is not here?'

Dell sat in a chair across from Brackton. He leaned forward so he was close to the man. 'She is not here. I assure you, sir, that I have no personal contact with your daughter. I have no connection to her, but if you tell me what this is all about, perhaps I will be able to help.'

Brackton nodded. 'She left the house last night without our knowing. Her maid found her missing. We suspected she had gone to that masquerade ball at the Argyll Rooms—' He stopped abruptly and seemed to notice Dell's appearance for the first time. 'Where have you been? Have you been with her?' He seized the lapels of Dell's coat. 'You have been with her. Where is she? By God, you will make right by her.'

Dell put his hands on Brackton's and gently pulled him off. 'Lord Brackton, upon my honour I was not with your daughter. I was with another lady, but I will not be so ungentlemanly as to name her.'

Brackton searched his face and must have believed him. He collapsed into a chair and rubbed his face. 'Where could she be?'

'Have you checked with her friends?' Dell kept his voice mild. He was genuinely concerned, more for the father, not the daughter. Sweet-faced Lady Alice was causing her father agony.

Brackton shook his head. 'I was certain she attended the masquerade with you.'

Dell lowered his voice further. 'She did not. I am nothing to your daughter.' Nothing but a tool to help her get what she wanted. 'I assure you.'

'Then something terrible must have happened to her.' The man fought tears.

Dell reached over and touched the man's arm in sympathy. 'It is more likely she is with a friend.' Her equally foolish Mr Holdsworth. 'Come. There are pen and paper in the library. We can make a list of her friends.' Perhaps with luck one of them would divulge Lady Alice's cruel plan and put this poor man out of this misery—and on to another one.

The scandal of a Gretna Green elopement.

After Brackton left, Dell went to his bedchamber to shave and change clothing. As soon as he could, he left the house again, this time to purchase as many morning newspapers as he could find.

Lorene was at breakfast when Dell arrived with the newspapers. The two of them sipped tea and pored through each paper to see if there was any mention of her mother. The masquerade was mentioned as the site of much debauchery, and most papers wrote about the frantic Lord B— who trolled through the crowd looking for his daughter.

'I cannot help but feel sorry for Lord Brackton,' Lorene said. 'His search for his daughter is now known to everyone.'

Dell lowered the paper he was reading. 'I saw him. The poor man was distraught. He came to the Duke's house, looking for me, thinking she was with me. I believe I finally convinced him I've had nothing to do with her.'

'Did you tell him she eloped?' she asked.

'I dared not,' he said. 'Lest he think I arranged it.'

'Those poor parents.' She remembered when Tess had gone missing. It had been terrifying.

They turned their attention back to the news-papers.

Lorene scanned the *Morning Post*.

'Oh, dear!' she exclaimed. 'Here is something— *"Lady S— once more entertains with outrageous escapades. Dressed as Iphigenia in sheer white muslin draped loosely about bare skin, she left nothing to the imagination except the identity of the gentleman who quarrelled with Lord Alvanley and won the lovely Iphigenia. And was that her daughter, Lady T—, disappearing into a box with another mysterious escort? Like mother, like daughter."'*

Lorene's face burned. Someone had recognised her and connected her to her mother.

She hated this. Hated seeing her name in the newspapers, knowing she would be discussed over breakfast tables and in gentlemen's clubs all over town.

She dropped the paper. 'Why could the *Morning Post* discover my mother when we could not?' She glanced up at him. 'And me. Why did they have to mention me?'

Dell looked distressed. 'I should have been more careful.'

She waved a hand. 'It is not your fault.'

She blamed her mother. If not for her mother, would any reporter have cared who she was? Certainly if not for her mother she would never have been in such a debauched place.

But her time in the box showed she was wanton enough to deserve such a mention.

She took a sip of tea. 'At least you are not identified.' That was some consolation.

He gazed at her, his blue eyes looking soft and loving. 'Do not concern yourself over me.'

She remembered the feel of his arms around her and wished she could be enfolded in his embrace at this moment. She wished he would kiss away all this unpleasantness.

But it would never go away.

She stared into her teacup. 'My whole life I've lived under this cloud of scandal caused by my mother and my father—and then by me for marrying Tinmore. I hoped it would end. I hoped everyone would forget about me. I've wanted that more than anything.'

He reached across the table and took her hand. 'It will pass in time.'

But in her experience it never passed entirely. Someone always remembered. Someone would always say, *Isn't she the daughter of that scandalous Lady Summerfield? Didn't she marry that elderly Lord Tinmore for his money? Did she not attend that scandalous masquerade ball?*

She averted her gaze. 'I wish my mother had never come here.'

She thought his expression turned somewhat disapproving. 'Have you no fondness for her?'

Had she not? She'd felt sorry for her when Count von Osten left and even when Genna spoke so harshly to her. But fondness? 'I do not know. It seems I have spent more time worrying about what she has done or will do than—than—'

'Getting to know her?' he offered.

She blinked, feeling a little guilty. 'Perhaps.'

Of course, her mother expended very little effort getting to know her or her sisters.

'Any word from your mother?' he asked, lifting his teacup to his lips.

'None.'

'Are you worried about her?' he asked.

She could easily answer. 'Not worried. I'm more angry than anything else. Does she think it is of no consequence to me to have no idea where she is or who she is with?' That rather sounded as if she did care about her mother.

He squeezed her hand. 'I promise to do whatever I can to help.'

But, really, what could be done?

After breakfast they retired to the drawing room. Lorene sat on the sofa and Dell joined her, putting his arm around her.

'We should think of what to do next,' he said.

Lorene sighed. 'What is there to do?'

He felt he must do something. 'I could ask at Brooks's. Try to discover where she has gone and who she is with.'

She shook her head. 'That would only encourage more talk.' He felt her body tense. 'I do dislike this. I cannot make plans until I know hers. I cannot leave this house, until I know whether she means to return or not.'

That was some consolation, Dell thought. She would not leave London.

'I want you to stay, Lorene.' He turned so he could look directly in her eyes. 'Now that this business with Lady Alice is resolved, I am free. I want us to be together.'

Her eyes flickered. 'What are you saying?' Her voice rose. 'Are you proposing marriage, Dell? Because I do not want marriage!'

He knew that, but if he could change, perhaps she could as well. 'We could be a family, Lorene.'

Her expression turned to panic. 'No, Dell! No—'

At that very moment, the sound of voices came from the hall.

Lorene stood and said impatiently. 'Who is it now?'

The door opened and her mother burst into the room, clad in a bright red cloak that opened enough to reveal she was still in her costume. Behind her came the biggest surprise of all—Count von Osten.

'Mama!' Lorene cried. 'Count!'

Dell rose. 'We were concerned about you.' He extended a hand to the Count. 'Good to see you, sir.'

The Count accepted the handshake with a smile. 'I have had quite the journey in more than one way of conceiving it.'

'Where were you, Mother?' Lorene demanded.

Lady Summerfield glided over to her and gave her a hug. 'Let us sit and we will tell you.'

The Count sat next to Lady Summerfield on one of the sofas and she twined her arm through his. 'My Ossie is the most splendid man.'

'Just tell us what happened,' Lorene said.

Her mother looked into the Count's eyes. 'Forgive me, Ossie, my love. I do not know what came over me. To be here—in London—I hardly knew myself.'

'You are back with me.' The Count patted her hand. 'That is what matters.'

'*You* came back,' she said. 'That is *everything*.'

'Mother,' Lorene tried again. 'Tell us why you went to that horrid masquerade.'

'Oh.' She drew out the sound dramatically. 'I was despondent about Ossie leaving me. That was losing *everything* to me.'

Lorene and her siblings were apparently not part of Lady Summerfield's *everything*, Dell thought.

Lady Summerfield straightened in her seat. 'Lord Alvanley was pursuing me; there is no other way to say it. I—I was amused. Playing along, you might say—'

Landing her name in the newspapers, you might say.

'Then everyone started telling me what I should and should not do. I felt quite like I used to feel when I was married. I could never do as I pleased when I was married—'

Dell's impression was that Lady Summerfield had always done as she pleased, even when married.

She went on. 'Then Ossie left me. What did anything matter then? The invitation from Alvanley came and I thought what did it matter what I did? Besides, I was angry and hurt. I'd be outrageous. That would show him.' She gave Count von Osten a contrite look.

'Is that why you chose this costume?' Dell asked.

'Oh, yes!' her mother said brightly. 'I wanted the most scandalous costume I could think of and I remembered the stories about the Duchess of Kingston. I said I'd dress as Iphigenia and have everyone wonder if I would bare my bosoms!' She laughed and wrapped her cloak around her a bit tighter. 'In any event, Alvanley was not a gentlemanly escort, I must say. He desired all sorts of debauched things. Honestly! With a woman of my age. I could not get away from him. I did not know what I would do!'

'Here is where my part comes in,' said the Count. 'When I left London I was determined to return to Brussels. I expected Hetty would chase after me and beg me to take her back.' He smiled. 'I made it all the way to Ostend before I woke up to the fact that Hetty would never beg anyone for anything. If I wanted her—and I wanted her desperately—' He took her hand in his and lifted it to his lips. 'Then I would have to go back to her.' He turned to Lorene. 'I did not come here, not knowing of my welcome. I secured a room at Mivart's Hotel and went in search of Lord Alvanley with the intention of making him give up his pursuit of Hetty or see me in a duel—'

Lady Summerfield gave him a worshipful look.

'I was told he was planning to attend a masquerade that night and that I would find him there. I knew Hetty would be there. I purchased a costume and attended the masquerade.'

'He found me in the nick of time!' Lady Summerfield cried. 'He told Alvanley that he was taking me home and that gentleman must have no more dalliance with me!' Her colour was high as she spoke. 'Alvanley backed down immediately and Ossie swept me out of the ballroom and out to a waiting carriage. It was so romantic!' She gazed into the air as if remembering, then she turned and focused on Lorene. 'What were you doing there, Lorene, my love?'

'I was looking for you, Mother,' she said. 'Dell and I tried to find you and bring you home before you did something to land your name in the paper again.' She glared at her mother. 'We were too late.'

Her mother smiled. 'That explains why your name was in the paper, too! I was puzzled over that, although I rather hoped you were headed for a romantic tryst with some gentleman.' She gave Dell a sly look. 'Or perhaps you were.'

Lorene ignored that comment and turned to Count von Osten. 'I am very grateful to you, sir, for taking Mother away from there before she did something worse.'

He nodded, but turned back to their mother. 'I have given up asking her to marry me, though. I know now that I want my darling in any way she feels happiest.'

'Given up?' Lady Summerfield squeezed his hands. 'I was hoping you would ask me one more time.'

The Count's eyes kindled with anticipation. In front of them all he slid off the sofa on to one knee. He still held Lady Summerfield's hands.

'My darling Hetty,' the Count said in a voice trembling with emotion. 'Will you marry me? Be my Countess at last?'

'Yes! Yes!' Lady Summerfield cried, leaning down to kiss him.

Dell glanced at Lorene. For a moment she appeared anguished, but she recovered and her eyes flashed.

'That is all well and good, Mother,' she said in a strained voice. 'But your outrageous behaviour, no matter how justified in your mind, landed my name in the newspapers.'

Her mother turned her gaze upon Lorene. 'You were the one discovered going into the boxes.'

Her mother had undoubtedly read the same papers Dell and Lorene had read.

Lorene stood. 'I would not have been there if not for you!' Dell watched her try to wrest control of her emotions. 'Count, you are welcome to stay here. Mother, I suggest you go to your bedchamber and change into a dress.'

Her mother made no effort to comply.

Lorene turned to Dell. 'Please stay. Just give me a moment.'

She crossed the room to the door. Dell wanted to go after her, but held back.

Chapter Twenty

Lorene hurried out of the drawing room, so filled with confusing emotions, she did not know what to do with them. Her mother's callous disregard for the effect of her behaviour was infuriating, but Dell's near proposal had her in turmoil, especially after witnessing the Count's romantic proposal and her mother's acceptance.

Could she take a chance, like her mother?

She walked out to the hallway and heard Trask admit some visitors. She looked over the bannister to see who it was.

Rossdale and Genna.

'Where is my sister?' Genna cried to Trask. 'I need to see her immediately! Immediately!'

Trask was taken aback. 'Of course. I'll announce you. One moment.'

'It is all right, Trask,' Lorene called from the landing. 'They can come up.'

Someone pounded on the knocker and Trask opened the door again. This time Tess and Glenville, Edmund and Amelie, walked in.

'We would see Lady Tinmore—' Edmund stopped when he saw Rossdale and Genna.

'Everyone, come to the drawing room,' Lorene, quite alarmed, called from the landing. As they walked up the stairs, she asked, 'What has happened?'

Genna handed her a pamphlet. 'Here!'

Lorene took it in her hand. 'The *New Tatler.*' She gaped at them, puzzled.

'They are selling these pamphlets up and down Bond Street! Everywhere. In print shops. Everywhere,' Rossdale said.

Edmund added, 'We found them as well. You cannot turn a corner and not encounter them.'

She led them to the drawing room. 'But, what is it?'

'You must read it,' said Tess.

They stopped in surprise when seeing Dell in the room. Her mother and the Count had also not moved.

'Dell!' Rossdale walked over to him. 'It is good you are here.' He had several copies of the pamphlet and he handed one to Dell, before handing them to her mother and the Count. 'Read it!'

Lorene looked down at the title.

Murder in Lincolnshire or
The Cuckolded Earl Meets His End

Her blood turned cold. She was aware of a gasp from her mother and another sound of surprise from the Count, but could not look away from the words on the front page.

This is a story of a murder in Lincolnshire—a murder in which the perpetrator was able to walk away with impunity. This is the story of what really happened and how privilege and wealth and cunning prevented justice from being served for the poor deceased.

Is this fiction or is it truth? Only you, dear Reader, can be judge and jury...

Lorene placed her hand over her mouth as she read on. Genna paced back and forth while the others read, too. The pamphlet was written in the style of a work of fiction. Names were changed, but there were enough hints as to who the true characters were. Lorene became Lady Moretin and her poor deceased husband, the Earl of Moretin. Dell was Lord Fordpen. Ross, the Marquis of Daleross. A child could figure it out.

The hero of this story was the butler, Ondix, who gallantly fought for justice for his beloved

master only to be crushed by those more powerful, more moneyed, more titled. The story continued after the inquest. It continued to London
where the two conspiring lovers reunited in a secret, but torrid love affair.

Where they met, when they met was related in
almost complete, but embellished, detail. Someone had followed them! It culminated in a tryst
at a masquerade where the lovers drank a toast
to their success. They had got away with murder.

A wave of nausea hit Lorene so strong that
she feared she might not be able to control it. She
glanced up at Dell, who also had finished reading and gazed back at her with an agonised expression.

Genna shook her copy of the *New Tatler*. 'This
makes it sound like the two of you are lovers. As
though you've been meeting at Dell's town house.'

Lorene and Dell exchanged another glance.

'Of course they are lovers!' Lady Summerfield
piped up. 'One has only to look at them. It is this
murder I do not understand.' She looked from Dell
to Lorene with what appeared to be admiration in
her eyes. 'Did you kill Lord Tinmore?'

'No, we did not kill Lord Tinmore,' Lorene
rasped. 'How can we fight this? It describes true
events, but twists them and embellishes them and
distorts what really happened.'

'Then what is true here?' Genna asked.

'Not the part about killing Tinmore!' Lorene cried. 'Not the conspiracy. None of that.'

'We know that. What about the lovers' part?' Genna persisted.

'Genna, maybe they do not want to say,' Edmund's wife Amelie spoke up. 'Surely the fear now would be that people would believe the false part if any of it were known to be true.'

That was it, Lorene thought. Just as they had to pretend not to be friends after Tinmore's death, now they must definitely pretend not to have been lovers.

Amelie turned to Edmund. 'Do you think we could go to where they sell these pamphlets and purchase them all? Then we could burn them.'

'No, love,' Edmund said. 'There are too many of them.'

To Lorene's surprise her mother rose and put her hands on Lorene's shoulders. 'Ignore it, my darling daughter. That is my advice. Ignore it and live your life the way you wish. Let them talk. Let them judge. You know what is in your heart.'

She was touched by her mother's intention, misguided as it was. 'I am to walk down the street and pretend that people are not saying, *There is the woman who had her lover kill her elderly husband?* Dell is to walk into the House of Lords and not have the others protesting that he is a murderer? I do not know how to do that.'

Her mother released her and made a flourish with her hand. 'You just do it. It becomes easier with time.'

'Why did you not tell us about you and Dell?' Tess asked. 'Why keep it a secret?'

Lorene evaded the question. 'See? You believe what you have read in that pamphlet and so will everyone else.'

'So you and Dell are not lovers?' Tess asked.

'Tess,' Amelie tried again. 'She does not want to say.'

'We've got to counter this somehow,' said Rossdale.

Trask came to the door. 'The Duke of Kessington,' he announced.

'Good God,' Rossdale muttered.

The Duke walked in flashing a pamphlet. 'Have you seen this?' He stopped, noticing all who were there. 'I see you have. Gathering to discuss this. Good. Good.'

'Why are you here, Father?' Ross asked.

'Well, we have to do something about this,' the Duke said.

'Your Grace, you need not concern yourself—' Lorene started.

He interrupted her. 'Of course I need to concern myself.' He waved the pamphlet. 'This slanders my son! Says he colludes with murder!'

Yes, Lorene must remember that others were

hurt by these lies. Her sisters. Their husbands. Perhaps even Edmund and Amelie.

'We have to get to Dixon. Make him recant,' Rossdale's father went on.

What would be the use of that? People would still believe the more sensational story.

Dell rose and led her to a chair. 'Sit. We will deal with this somehow.'

Genna moved over to them both. 'I do not care what Amelie says. I want to know. Are you two lovers?'

Dell answered. 'Yes.'

The discussion among the others stopped.

'Were you lovers back when Tinmore died?' Genna pressed.

'No,' Lorene and Dell said in unison.

Dell went on. 'Your sister would never be so disloyal, not even to Tinmore. So, no, we were not lovers back when Tinmore died. But I know now that I have loved her since that first meeting at Summerfield House.'

Tess broke in. 'This town house where it says you met, was that part true?'

Dell answered again. 'It was my family's town house. Lorene was working with the architect to refurnish and decorate it.'

Lorene winced. Their secrets were being shattered one after the other. 'Dell asked me to, because I had worked on Summerfield House.'

'Ha!' Her mother pointed a finger. 'That is where you have been going every day, you and your man of business. I am much relieved. I thought perhaps you had made your man of business your lover.'

Lorene glared at her. 'No, Mother. Not Mr Walters.'

Tess moved closer to her. 'You kept this secret, Lorene?' She looked hurt. 'You never used to keep secrets from me. We shared everything. Until Tinmore.'

'I did not want anyone talking about me. Speculating about me. Telling me what I should or should not do.' She was sounding like her mother. Her mother, though, had agreed to marry.

'Exactly so,' said her mother. 'You wished to do as you pleased without interference.'

Actually, that summed it up.

'You did it again!' cried Genna. 'You kept an important secret from us! You did not trust us. You didn't trust us back when you married Tinmore and you don't trust us now!'

'Genna,' her husband cautioned. 'Do not make her feel worse.'

How could she feel worse? Her beloved sisters were mad at her and she was once again alone. She lost them and lost Dell, as well. They could never be together, not even as friends.

All because of a mean-spirited butler.

Dell started towards the door. 'I'm going for a lawyer. I'm going to sue the paper and Dixon for libel.'

'You won't win,' the Duke said.

'Maybe not,' Dell said. 'But not to sue is like saying that the story written there is true.'

'I'll go with you.' Rossdale turned to Genna. 'Will you be able to get home without me?'

'Of course.'

'Everyone go,' Lorene said in a shrill voice. 'I really want to be alone. Mother, you can change into a dress. Everyone leave me now.'

Tess and Genna barely looked at her as they left the room. Dell was last out of the room.

He took her in his arms. 'I am sorry for this, Lorene. I am so sorry for this.'

'No, I am sorry.' She savoured the feel of him one more time. 'Because you came to my aid, all this is happening to you.'

'Come to the town house tomorrow morning,' he begged.

'What if someone is watching?' she asked.

'Please.'

One last time, she thought. 'Very well.'

Lady Summerfield and the Count retired to her room, but the others gathered in the hall. Ross asked that the footman go to the stable and request his carriage.

While they waited, the butler said, 'I am afraid there are some reporters outside. I asked them to leave, but they would not go.'

It had not taken the reporters long to figure out who the characters in the pamphlet were supposed to be. 'This is unacceptable!' the Duke said to Dell. 'You cannot have this kind of attention. You will have to sever your ties to this family—especially Lady Tinmore. Otherwise, libel case or not, this will hang over you. It will affect every aspect of your life, especially your effectiveness in government.'

'Father!' Ross cried. 'What a thing to say at such a time. Leave it be for now.'

The Duke lifted his chin. 'I'm thinking of you, too, Ross. You are implicated in this, as well.'

'Are you telling me to stay away?' Ross said. 'This is Genna's family.'

Genna looked stung.

Ross's father seemed to notice her presence belatedly and looked a bit contrite. 'I've said my piece. If you wish to discuss it more with me, I will be at my club.'

Dell said, 'See what the mood is at your club. It may help to know.'

'I will do that,' the Duke said. When the door opened and he walked out, they could see the reporters approach him. He yelled for them to be out of his way.

The butler quickly closed the door.

Glenville approached Dell. 'I am going to speak with Greybury. I've worked with him and he is knowledgeable about matters such as these. He may be able to help.'

Dell shook his hand. 'I would be very grateful.'

Edmund asked, 'Do you mind if I go with you to the lawyer? I am new to all this. We were not told of any of it, but I would like to lend my support.'

Dell was touched. 'I would like your support, Edmund. We can fill you in in the carriage.'

'I don't want to go out there and be accosted by those reporters,' Tess said.

'There is a way out the back I could show you,' the butler offered.

'Yes, let us go out that way.' She looked relieved.

The butler led them away and it was just Dell, Ross and Edmund in the hall.

'This is a terrible mess,' Ross said. 'The worse fix we've ever been in.'

'You were in the army, were you not?' Edmund asked Dell.

'Yes. The 44th Regiment of Foot.'

'Then you saw battle in the Peninsula, correct?' Edmund went on.

'Yes.'

'No matter how bad this is,' Edmund said, 'battle was worse.'

And Dell had survived battle. Many times. But then it was only his life at stake. This time the sabres were slicing into Lorene and Ross and other people he cared about.

When the carriage finally came, Dell, Ross, and Edmund stepped out of the house and on to the street, where the reporters ran up to them.

'Which of you is Lord Penford?' one asked.

Dell stepped forward. 'I am Penford.'

He'd decided not to shrink from the truth.

'What do you have to say for yourself, sir?' another asked. 'You've seen the story?'

'Yes, we have all seen the story,' he responded. 'It is a mix of truth and lies. There was no murder. No conspiracy to commit murder and no conspiracy afterwards. The document is libellous. We are going to go against the printers and the author of this piece. That is all I will say at the moment.'

He was the last one in the carriage, which immediately pulled away as soon as he was inside.

Lorene stayed in the drawing room after the others left. She curled up in her chair, holding her knees against her chest. She could still hear their voices in the hall and didn't move until it was quiet. She went to the window in time to see Dell talking to a group of men. Why were there men outside of her house?

They were newspaper reporters, she realised.

It obviously took them no time to figure out the characters in the pamphlet. The names were so thinly disguised.

She watched Dell speak with them. He looked so calm, when she was all turmoil inside. She watched him until he climbed into the carriage and it drove away.

A suit of libel was all well and good, but would it not merely keep people talking about them? They would have to prove that Dixon's account of Tinmore's death was false, but how could they? There were no witnesses.

She crossed the room to the pianoforte in the corner. She'd not played very much at all lately, but today she needed the music. She placed her fingers on the keys and closed her eyes, trying to block out what would happen next. More articles in London newspapers. The story reprinted in other towns and cities. And reprinted in the *Annual Register*, widening the audience and producing it in a form likely to remain for years on library shelves in countless homes.

It would never entirely go away.

The Mozart music sheets were on the piano, the sheets Dell had secretly given her after that musicale they'd attended two years ago. He'd been so kind to her.

She gently touched the music notes on the page

before letting her fingers fly over the keyboard.
The music both filled her and poured out of her.
The pain, the humiliation, the trepidation of this
day left her momentarily while she played.

After she finished, she played it all again and
after finishing the piece a second time, she played
all the music she could remember playing for him
the first time they'd met, when he'd invited Genna
and her to Summerfield House and Tinmore was
too ill to come with them. She'd been filled with
a jumble of emotion that day as well as this one.
Playing music for him had been a calm in the
storm.

She played Mozart's *Andante Grazioso* and
Beethoven's *Pathétique*. She played and sang.

I have a silent sorrow here,
A grief I'll ne'er impart;
It breathes no sigh, it sheds no tear,
But it consumes my heart.
This cherished woe, this loved despair,
My lot for ever be,
So my soul's lord, the pangs to bear
Be never known by thee.

She'd been so unhappy then and he seemed
to understand without her having to say a word.
Later, whenever she sang the words to that song,
she sang them about Dell.

When she finished the song, she put her arms across the keyboard and rested her head on them.

Even the music was not enough to quiet her this time. She wished she could go outside and run until she exhausted herself, like she did that day at Tinmore Hall, after the will had been read.

The cursed will. Her means of independence was now transformed into a motive for a crime. And who would believe she'd never asked for it or expected it?

She rose from the piano bench and returned to the window. The reporters had dwindled down to three. Would they stay there all night? she wondered. She certainly did not want them following her when she went to meet Dell in the morning.

She leaned against the window frame with the curtain obscuring her presence from the outside. Enough feeling sorry for herself. She had to decide how to proceed.

The door opened and she turned to see who it was.

Her mother. Dressed normally, at least.

She swept in. 'My darling daughter, was that you playing the pianoforte?'

'Yes, Mother,' she said.

'Why, it was quite skilled. I had no idea you were so skilled at the pianoforte. Or that Genna was so talented an artist.'

Had she stayed with her children, she might have discovered their talents.

'Come sit with me.' Her mother lowered herself on to the sofa and patted the area next to it as an invitation.

Lorene chose to sit in a chair nearby.

'I have done some thinking,' her mother said. 'I was unprepared to return to England, I believe. It was as if I turned into the unhappy woman I once was, the one who would do any silly thing to try to relieve the unhappiness.' She sighed. 'To think I almost drove Ossie away.'

Lorene averted her gaze. How like her mother to think of her situation and completely sweep aside the devastating thing that just happened to her daughter.

Her mother went on. 'I was terrified, you see, of marrying again, especially because everyone wanted me to do so. Before I married your father, my parents and everyone wanted me to marry him. We were mere gentry and he was a baronet. A step up for our family. What a mistake I made! I was fearful that marrying Ossie would be a mistake, too. I was afraid it would ruin everything. We've been so happy!'

At our expense, thought Lorene. 'I am sorry for your distress, Mother, but you have caught me at a moment in which I simply cannot listen. Why speak of this now?'

Her mother gave her a direct look. 'For one, to apologise.'

Lorene's brows rose. She had not expected that.

Her mother's expression turned serious. 'And to urge you to think about what will make you happy. Do not listen to other people, what they say. Do what makes you happy.'

For her mother to rally round her was unexpected.

There was a knock at the door.

Her butler opened it a crack and announced, 'The Duchess of Kessington to see you, m'lady.'

'Oh, lovely,' her mother said sarcastically.

'Send her up, Trask,' Lorene said.

'She is here,' he responded in anxious tones.

The Duchess strode in.

'What can she possibly want?' Lorene whispered under her breath.

'To make trouble, no doubt.' Her mother rolled her eyes.

The two ladies rose.

'Your Grace.' Lorene curtsied.

Her mother curtsied as well.

'Hmmph.' The Duchess eyed Lorene's mother. 'I did not realise you would be here.'

Her mother smiled condescendingly. 'I live here, Your Grace.'

'Do sit.' Lorene gestured to a favoured chair.

The Duchess looked at the seat suspiciously, as if it might not be worthy of her. She sat.

Lorene and her mother sat side by side on the sofa facing her.

'To what do I owe the honour of this visit?' Lorene asked. Although she had some idea.

The Duchess pulled out a copy of the pamphlet. 'I came about this.'

Lorene had been right. She'd read the pamphlet.

'What is that, Your Grace?' Her mother fluttered her lashes with feigned innocence.

'I am certain you know what it is, ma'am,' the Duchess snapped.

'Oh!' Her mother cried. 'That silly piece of libel.'

'I presume it is libellous,' the Duchess countered.

The Duchess probably wanted Lorene to protest her innocence and Dell's, but Lorene remained silent with her hands in her lap.

The Duchess went on. 'The Duke and I, of course, heard all about this from Dell and Rossdale after it happened.' She pointed a finger at Lorene. 'You were lucky it was not much talked about at the time—'

'Yes, Your Grace,' Lorene broke in. 'But I still do not understand why you called upon me.'

The woman made an attempt at an ingratiating smile. 'As you know the Duke and I are very fond of Dell—Lord Penford—I am here totally on his behalf.'

'He sent you?' Lorene's mother asked.

'Not precisely,' her Grace admitted. She turned an intense expression on Lorene. 'If you have the least notion of snaring Dell into marriage—or even a liaison—' She darted a scathing glance at Lorene's mother. 'Then I wish to make you aware of the consequences.'

Lorene stiffened.

'The only way to disprove this horrid story is for you to stay away from him. For you to engage in an affair with him, or, God forbid, marriage, will simply be seen as confirmation that you plotted to kill your husband. You have been left a wealthy widow. There will be other men to distract you—' Again she glanced at her mother. 'I am certain of that. You do not need to ruin Dell's life. He has a bright future in government. He could be a driving force for the reform the Whig Party strives for so valiantly. He could make a name for himself.' She looked directly into Lorene's face. 'If you continue to dally with him, scandal will plague him his whole life. Someone will always question whether he was indeed a murderer. No one in government will trust him. His contribution will be lost.'

'This is a packet of nonsense!' Lorene's mother cried.

'It is not nonsense!' snapped the Duchess. 'If he is free to marry a respectable woman, one worthy of him, it will make all the difference in his political career.'

She was still holding out hope for Dell to marry Lady Alice, Lorene realised. Wait until she discovered that Lady Alice could create a scandal all her own.

Lorene's mother half-rose from her seat. 'How dare you say my daughter is not worthy? Not respectable! How dare you?'

The Duchess glared at her. 'Well, her name continues to be linked with yours in the newspapers. A masquerade ball, indeed!'

'Do not believe everything you read, Your Grace,' her mother went on. 'My daughters are fine ladies. I am quite proud of them.'

'Well, since you know them so well...' The Duchess let that barb sink in before she stood. 'I have said my piece. I hope you heed my advice. It is kindly meant.'

'No, it isn't,' muttered her mother.

Lorene stood, as well. 'Good day, Duchess.'

The Duchess sent her mother a sneering look and strode out of the room as she had entered it.

Lorene's mother immediately turned to Lorene and held her by the shoulders. 'Do not you dare listen to that harpy! She is wrong. All that nonsense of being a success in government, it is meaningless. If you and Dell make each other happy, you must seize the opportunity to be together no matter what scandal tries to stop you, no matter how witches like her try to stop you.'

'No matter who it hurts, Mother?' she asked.

Her mother hugged her. 'I am sorry I hurt you and Tess and Genna. But I am not sorry I chose to go with Ossie. I have been happy, Lorene. That is no small thing.'

Perhaps her mother was truly sorry, but Lorene knew her choice had hurt her children. Unlike her mother, she could not turn away from the consequences. The scandal would not only ruin his future, but would hang a pall over all of them. The Scandalous Summerfields could add murder to the list of things people whispered behind their backs.

'Tell me you will choose happiness!' her mother cried.

'I do not know what I will do,' Lorene said truthfully.

Chapter Twenty-One

The next morning the newspapers were full of news about the story Dixon had created, all giving credence to the lies and distortions he presented. Dell had to evade the reporters waiting outside the Duke's house so he could reach his town house without anyone knowing.

He arrived before Lorene and let himself in. He sat and waited for her on the stairs, the original marble stairs he, his parents, his brother and sister used. He hadn't lit any lamps or candles so the hall was dark and the bright colours Lorene picked were muted into grey.

He could imagine their voices—his family. His father's voice, deep and booming, his mother's light and musical. He could still hear his brother yelling at him for tagging along wherever he went. He could hear his sister sing.

He buried his head in his hands as grief washed over him once more.

The sound of his sister playing the pianoforte seemed to echo through the newly built walls. Or was it Lorene playing the same pieces his sister played? Mozart's *Andante Grazioso*. Beethoven's *Pathétique*.

He risked losing Lorene, too. Because of one man's lies.

He'd done all he could think of to do. He'd set the wheels in motion for a libel suit. Through Glenville's Lord Greybury they would find Dixon and learn what there was to know about him. Ross volunteered to travel back to Tinmore Hall to try to learn more about Dixon and the other servants. Ross also planned on alerting the magistrate and the coroner about how their work on the death had been depicted as corruption and bribery.

Even if they could rewrite that story with the truth, though, he might lose her. He had to convince her to marry him.

He heard the key turn in the lock. He stood as the door opened and Lorene entered the hall. She looked up and jumped.

'Lorene.' He quickly approached her. 'It is I.'

She covered her heart with her hand. 'It was dark. You were like a shadow.'

He put his arms around her. 'Forgive me.'

She looked up into his face and rose on tiptoe. He dipped his head and ever so gently touched his lips to hers. The kiss was light and fleeting and when his lips left hers again, he held her close. They simply held each other.

Lorene pulled away a moment sooner than Dell desired.

'Shall we sit in the morning room?' she asked.

It would be the brightest of the rooms, even though the sky outside was as grey as his mood. Dell yearned for the intimacy of the bedchamber, but matters were so unsettled and emotions so high, he could understand that this was not the time for lovemaking.

'Of course,' he replied.

They walked to the morning room and Dell was struck again at how pleasant it was, a bright and cheerful place to start the day. This day, though, even this beautiful room lacked the capacity to cheer him. The morning light illuminated Lorene's face, which was pale and pinched. But she held her head up and put on a very brave front.

He held out a chair at the table for her and she sat. He sat across from her.

'Did you read the newspapers this morning?' she asked.

He nodded. 'I anticipated something like that.'

He wanted to reassure her that it would go away and all would be well, but likely they could expect more scrutiny and attention for fighting the story than leaving it alone.

'Let me tell you what we've begun...' He explained about the libel suit, about Ross travelling back to Lincolnshire, about looking for Dixon.

She nodded. 'It is good of you all to try.'

'I want to clear our names,' he said. 'None of us deserves this.' *She* did not deserve this.

She met his gaze. 'You realise it will never go away, even if you do clear our names. Someone, somewhere, will remember it and repeat it all over again. It will never go away.'

'I want the truth to be as public and widespread as Dixon's lies.' He vowed it would be.

'I am going away,' she said, her voice so low he hoped he had not heard her correctly. 'If we are not together, no one can say we committed murder to be together.'

Lorene's voice cracked and she felt in danger of losing control of her emotions. She'd stayed up half the night agonising over this. She'd come to the same conclusion as the Duchess had. They could not be together. Not as friends. Not as lovers.

If they stayed apart the story would lose its teeth. If the supposed motivation for the murder was for them to indulge in a love affair, then to separate took away that motive. The truth would be easier for people to believe then.

She tried to smile. 'I never wanted to be in London. You must be here, though. It is important.

You must be free to make a name for yourself, especially in these times when there is so much discord and strife. And suffering.' Her throat tightened. 'If I leave, I will soon be forgotten, which is what I want.'

The problem was, as she had tossed and turned that night, she'd realised what Dell meant to her. As a girl she'd dreamed of a man like him, someone who loved her and would never leave her, someone kind and strong. A man to admire. A man to depend upon. A man to believe in her. She and Tess used to stay up late into the night talking about wanting to marry a man like that. Like Dell.

She'd given up that dream when she married Tinmore; in fact, marriage to Tinmore made her give up dreaming of marriage altogether. Even after knowing Dell. Even after making love to him.

Until last night when she realised she loved him. Dell was the man she'd dreamed of in her youth.

'Edmund and Amelie are going back to the Lake District in a week. I will ask if I may go with them.'

She dared to gaze directly at him again. His face was ashen.

'I do not want this, Lorene,' he said.

'It is best, Dell.' She knew this was what she

should do. She now knew she loved him enough to do it. 'You told me once that you needed to carry on your father's causes in the Lords. You will not be able to do that if they believe you murdered Tinmore. Surely your opponents will use that against you.'

Dell heard her resolve. Never mind his career in the Lords, he did not want her to suffer from this scandal. He'd opened his heart again and lost, but he wanted her to be happy. He wanted her to be at peace. So he would not try to convince her to stay.

Instead he walked her to the door and put his hand on the door latch ready to open it.

She gazed around the hall. 'I wish I had got the chance to finish this for you.'

His eyes swept the room. Would he ever live here? Could he bear to?

Without her with him, the place would only be a repository of painful memories.

'I love you,' he said.

She flew into his arms and they held each other even more tightly than before, but it was the embrace of goodbye. He made himself release her. He made himself open the door.

He made himself watch her walk away.

Chapter Twenty-Two

One month later

Over the protests of her sisters and her mother, Lorene left London and travelled with Edmund and Amelie and their son to their farm in the Lake District. Genna had railed at her for sacrificing her own happiness once again. Tess pleaded with her to reconsider, to allow Ross and the other men to counter the lies before making a decision, but she'd been resolved. She'd be an impediment to Dell and she did not want to have him regret their relationship later because of the sacrifices he'd been forced to make.

Besides, it had always been her desire to live a retired life. Where could be better than this breathtakingly beautiful area?

She'd been here in the Lake District for almost three weeks and was still waiting to feel peaceful. Thus far she only felt grieved.

But she put on a brave front for Edmund and Amelie. Luckily they were very busy, so Lorene was free to take walks—or runs—across the hills where the sheep grazed. No one bothered her. Even though Edmund and Amelie were there in evenings, even though she often relieved the nanny of her little nephew, Lorene felt incredibly lonely.

Without Dell.

He was still constantly in her thoughts. How was he faring? she wondered. Had he moved in his town house as planned? Were the newspapers leaving him alone? Had the scandal abated since she was absent? Was he busy? What would he do when Parliament was dissolved? Where would he go?

She tried not to think of him so often, but, she had to admit, he was all she wanted to think of. She'd heard very little of him, though. Letters from Tess and Genna usually did not mention him, although once Lorene wrote and asked Genna how Dell was faring and Genna wrote back that they hardly saw him. That set off more worries about him. Why was he not often with them? He and Rossdale were such close friends.

Was he alone?

They wrote very little about the scandal, as well, saying only that they were still working on it. The London newspapers that reached Edmund's house still mentioned it, but less often. For a while the elopement of Lady Alice and Mr Holdsworth dominated.

Lord and Lady Northdon were expected to visit Edmund and Amelie any day now. They were to spend the summer with Edmund and Amelie. Lorene offered to find housing elsewhere, but they refused, insisting Amelie's parents would welcome seeing her.

When Lord and Lady Northdon arrived, Lorene controlled herself from asking about Dell first thing. They had been there several days when she happened upon Lord Northdon on a walk and fell in step with him.

Before she could ask, he said, 'You might wonder about that pamphlet business. I have news to report.'

'Yes?' she responded, even though it was not the scandal that concerned her the most. It was how it was affecting Dell.

'Everything came together shortly before we left town. Your Lord Penford, Glenville, and the others gathered a great deal of information for the libel case. Lord Rossdale tracked down Lord Tinmore's valet. It turns out that, though he did not witness your husband fall, he did witness the fact that the butler could not have seen the event.

Two other servants said the same. And then there was the butler's inquest testimony where he admits he did not see anything.'

Of course! Even she could have attested to that fact. She'd been on the stairway with full view of Dixon when Tinmore fell.

Lord Northdon continued. 'Rossdale gathered affidavits from the servants, from the valet, the magistrate and the coroner, who vowed that they were not asked for any favours and were paid no bribes.'

'Has that helped anything?' she asked.

'It helped a great deal,' Lord Northdon assured her. 'In exchange for dropping the libel suit against them, the *New Tatler* printed a strong correction, telling the true story and casting the butler in the role of villain. The correction went on sale the day before we left. The newspapers repeated the story the next morning.'

'But it does not mean the scandal goes away,' she added.

He stopped and took her hand. 'There are those who will only remember the false story. And those who will repeat it simply to delight in hurting others. You simply ignore them and point to the truth.'

In Northdon's case, the truth *was* the scandal and it never went away. It would always be said that Lord Northdon had married a French commoner whose family had ties to the Terror. Never mind that she was a lovely person.

'How have you managed, sir?' she dared to ask. 'You constantly live under scandal. Does it make you less effective in Parliament? Do not the other aristocrats in Lords ignore you?'

He laughed. 'I always have my vote.' His expression quickly sobered again. 'If you are asking me whether I would prefer more success in the Lords to being married to Lady Northdon, I would pick Lady Northdon every time.'

Pick happiness, her mother had said.

They walked on for several steps before she asked the most important question on her mind, 'Do you know how Lord Penford fares in all this?'

'I admire him,' Lord Northdon said. 'He pushed through the worst of it. Being booed in the Lords. Held his head up. Seemed less under the thumb of the Duke of Kessington than before and that is a good thing. He's his own man. Glenville said he was tenacious in dealing with the publishers, in getting the true story out.' He looked at her kindly. 'You will wish to know more personally how he fares and I regret to tell you that I do not know.'

To hear that Dell was booed in the Lords made her want to weep. How alone he must have felt!

She'd abandoned him, she realised. Abandoned

him the way her mother abandoned her children. She made the same excuses of how it was better to leave than to stay, just like her mother had done. If Lorene had stayed, though, Dell would not have had to go through this horror alone. She felt sick inside.

She stopped. 'Forgive me, sir, I—I must go back to the house.'

He smiled. 'Of course.'

She started off, but turned back. 'Do you know where Lord Penford is now? Is he in town?'

He shook his head. 'On the last day in the Lords, he said he'd go to Lincolnshire.'

To Summerfield House!

It took Lorene three days for her hired coach to reach her home village of Yardney where one of the wheel spokes broke and needed repair. She paid off the coachmen, but could not immediately find a carriage to take her on to Summerfield House. She could walk there faster than waiting for a coach. It was only a short walk, one she and her sisters had done countless times. She arranged to leave her luggage at the inn to collect later and started off.

Until she cleared the village she was stopped several times for greetings and welcomes home. With the village behind her, though, she was alone and soon she was at the part of the road that abut-

ted Summerfield land. The old break in the hedge-
row was still there, marking where she and her
sisters and brother used to take a shortcut through
the field. She would reach Summerfield House
more quickly that way.

With each step her nerves jangled more in-
tensely. Would he be glad to see her? Would he
forgive her for leaving him when he needed her
most? She lifted her skirts and tried to outrun
the nerves plaguing her. Her hat flew from her
head and was held only by the ribbon tied under
her neck. Pins fell from her hair and it tumbled
to her shoulders and blew in the wind, but with
each stride she was closer. She would know soon.
She would know by the look on his face when
she appeared.

Dell finished his morning ride and headed back
to Summerfield House at a quiet pace, cooling off
his horse gradually. From the corner of his eye
he thought he saw someone running, but the figure disappeared in a dip in the land. He turned
his horse to wait for the person to reach the crest
of the hill.

He saw her. A woman running in the direction of Summerfield House. It took only seconds
to recognise her.

Lorene.

He urged his horse to a faster pace to reach her,

though she kept disappearing behind the gentle hills. He dismounted at a place where she certainly would see him. She appeared at the top of the hill and stopped, so much like she had that day on a field near here after Tinmore's death. Her hair was loose, her colour was high. She was more beautiful than ever.

He dropped the reins of his horse and strode towards her, though she stood her ground, her chest heaving from the exertion of the run.

'Dell,' she exclaimed breathlessly as he came close enough to hear.

This was so far from his expectations that he could not make himself speak. All he could do was drink in the sight of her.

When she was close enough to touch, her expression became anxious. 'Dell,' she said again, taking quick breaths. 'I have much to say to you, if you will allow me—'

'Don't speak,' he managed. 'Not yet.'

He pulled her into his arms, so grateful to feel her body against him once again. She sobbed and clung to him.

'I did not know if you would welcome me,' she cried. 'I feared you would send me away.'

'Never,' he said.

Her voice turned raspy with emotion. 'I abandoned you. I am so sorry.'

He pulled away so he could look into her face. 'Abandoned me?'

'Left you to deal with the scandal alone,' she explained.

She was correct. He had been alone. More alone than when his family died, because he withdrew from Ross lest Ross be further drawn into the scandal. His only consolation was protecting them—protecting her—from the worst of it.

'I was glad you were not there,' he said. It had been that terrible—to be called a murderer wherever he went, even among his fellow Whigs who suddenly cut him completely. 'You were right to leave.'

'No,' she insisted. 'I was very wrong.'

'Have you heard?' He held her against him again. 'The *New Tatler* recanted. Now suddenly the truth is the story and the scandal is the lies Dixon told.'

'I heard,' she said. 'But it does not matter. Even if the scandal raged on, I would want to be with you. So you won't ever be alone.'

He took her face in his hands and savoured the light of love that shone through her eyes. He held her face while his lips descended upon hers. He'd not thought ever to taste her lips again, to hold her again. He'd told himself it was sacrifice enough to keep her out of the fray, but it was not enough. He needed her the way he needed air to breathe.

He lifted her into his arms and carried her to his horse. 'Come,' he said. 'Let us go home to Summerfield.'

Epilogue

Christmas 1818

They gathered there, the Summerfields. Ross and Genna. Tess and Glenville and their son. Edmund and Amelie and their son. They'd all gathered. Even Lord and Lady Northdon. Even Count von Osten and the new Countess von Osten, Lorene's mother.

This motley group was Dell's family now and he was pleased to share Christmastide with them.

Most important, though, was the woman at his side. Lorene.

His wife.

And the family they were creating together.

He and Lorene married as soon as the banns were called in the village church she attended when growing up. The family showed up that day, too, as well as well-wishing villagers, tenants, and servants. Ross and Tess were their witnesses and afterwards they celebrated at Summerfield House.

Now she was expecting a baby. Genna, too.

Dell's family was growing.

This was Christmas dinner, a lavish feast lovingly created by the servants who'd watched Lorene, Tess, Genna and Edmund grow up there. The servants even embraced their mother upon her return. This Christmastide was not a season for regrets or past injuries, but a season to celebrate the gifts of today.

Dell felt as blessed as he ever had been.

This meal was marked by toasts, spontaneously given throughout the courses. Ross toasted Dell, calling him his friend, closer than a brother. Lord Northdon toasted his wife for marrying him and forgiving him the years he did not show her how he loved her. Lorene's mother toasted her daughters and stepson who, as she said, might not have forgiven her, but who each filled her with admiration. Edmund, in return, toasted the new Countess, thanking her for caring about him and making him feel important when he was a boy. Tess and Genna stood up together and toasted Lorene for sacrificing herself for them. They also begged her never to do it again.

Dell rose. 'I have a toast,' he said, rising from his chair. 'Be patient. It is a long one.' He lifted his glass. 'To Lorene. My beloved wife. In my dark-est days she was a bright light who made me take my mind off my loss and think of her. In those dark days I thought I had lost everything when my father, my mother, my brother and my sister perished in a fire. I could not even see that I had a brother.' He pointed his glass to Ross, then back to Lorene. 'From my regard for Lorene came some-thing more.' He swept the glass over all of them. 'I'd lost one family, but another embraced me. All of you.' He turned again to Lorene. 'I toast you all. My family.'

They all drank to the toast.

After dinner and gifts when it came time to re-tire, Dell walked with Lorene to their bedcham-ber. Soon nestled in their bed with Lorene in his arms, Dell could not be more satisfied.

'I feel sad,' Lorene said.

'Sad?' He was surprised. 'Why?'

'I wish your parents and your sister and brother could be with us now. To see how happy we are.' She laughed softly. 'Of course, they would prob-ably not have liked you being linked to the Scan-dalous Summerfields. Who would?'

What could he say? They probably would have protested any connection with the Scandalous Summerfields.

'Let us name our children after them,' she said.

'Children?' He placed his hand on her rounded belly. 'Do you not mean our child?'

'No. Children.' She rose on an elbow and looked into his eyes. 'At least enough for all their names.'

He reached up and pulled her towards him for one of many kisses. 'If you insist,' he murmured.

* * * * *

If you enjoyed this story,
you won't want to miss the first three books in
THE SCANDALOUS SUMMERFIELDS
quartet from Diane Gaston

BOUND BY DUTY
BOUND BY ONE SCANDALOUS NIGHT
BOUND BY A SCANDALOUS SECRET

MILLS & BOON®

HISTORICAL

AWAKEN THE ROMANCE OF THE PAST

MILLS & BOON®

EXCLUSIVE EXTRACT

When aristocrat's daughter May Worth's life
is endangered, only one man can protect her:
government agent Liam Casek…the man whose
sinfully seductive touch she's never forgotten!

Read on for a sneak preview of
CLAIMING HIS DEFIANT MISS

Liam wasn't willing to chance it by letting May roam
free and unprotected. It infuriated him she was willing
to take that chance. She had blatantly chosen to ignore
him and vanish this morning just for spite. He knew
very well why she'd done it; to prove to him she didn't
need him, had never needed him, that he hadn't hurt
her, that indeed, he had been nothing more than a speck
of dust on her noble sleeve, easily brushed off and
forgotten. But that wasn't quite the truth. He had hurt
her, just as she had hurt him. They were both realising
the past wasn't buried as deeply as either of them hoped.

To get through the next few weeks or months they
would have to confront that past and find a way to truly
put it behind them if they had any chance of having an
objective association. The task would not be an easy
one. Their minds might wish it, but their bodies had
other ideas. He'd seen the stunned response in her eyes
yesterday when she'd recognised him, the leap of her
pulse at her neck even as she demanded he take his hand

off her. Not, perhaps, because he repulsed her, but because he didn't.

Goodness knew his body had reacted, too. His body hadn't forgotten what it was to touch her, to feel her. Standing behind her in the yard had been enlightening in that regard. He wasn't immune. He hadn't thought he was. He had known how difficult this assignment would be. His anger this morning at finding her gone proved it.

Anger. Lust. Want. These emotions couldn't last. A bodyguard, a man who did dirty things for the Crown, couldn't afford feelings. Emotions would ruin him. Once he started to care, deeply and personally, it would all be over.

Don't miss
CLAIMING HIS DEFIANT MISS
By Bronwyn Scott

Available May 2017
www.millsandboon.co.uk

Join Britain's BIGGEST Romance Book Club

- **EXCLUSIVE offers every month**
- **FREE delivery direc to your door**
- **NEVER MISS a title**
- **EARN Bonus Book points**

Call Customer Services
0844 844 1358*

or visit
millsandboon.co.uk/subscriptior